MY NAME IS MARY MAGDALENE

JC MILLER

JESS, MO' BOOKS LLC

JC Miller/ My Name is Mary Magdalene

Copyright © 2021 JC Miller

ISBN: 978-1-7339386-6-2

Library of Congress Control Number: 2021919181

This is a work of fiction. Any references to historical events, real people, or real places are used fictitiously. Names, characters, and places are products of the author's imagination or used in a fictitious manner.

The Holy Bible, New International Version®, NIV® Copyright © 1973, 1978, 1984, 2011 by Biblica, Inc. ™ Used by permission. All rights reserved worldwide.

The World English Bible is in the Public Domain.

"My Prayer" Ink Spots, originally written by Boulanger with the title Avant de Mourir (Before Dying) 1926. The lyrics were added by Kennedy in 1939.

"Aba Daba Honeymoon," written and published by Arthur Fields and Walter Donovan in 1914.

Book graphic design: Chanel Smith, WPD Media LLC

Editing: Tee Marshall, Marshall Editing and Consulting

Printed in New York City, NY.

First printing edition 2021.

Jess, Mo' Books LLC

P.O. Bx. 1808

Albrightsville, PA. 18210

www.jessmobooks.com

❀ Created with Vellum

CONTENTS

INTRODUCTION

Blackbird

I once was a blackbird.
I once was free.
I glistened with the splendor of midnight.
I soared with the hope of dreams.
I once was a blackbird...I once was me.
JC Miler

DEDICATION

Dedicated to those who suffer in silence.

Thou Art Loosed!

PROLOGUE - THIS MASQUERADE

"Owens...Owens!" Nurse Mulligan, a freckled face, green-eyed demon, shouted my last name as if I were in a military lineup. "It's time for your med-i-cine," she continued, mockingly singing in an irritating nasal tone, hovering over me and rousing me from sleep. She then yanked my bedding aside without care nor courtesy of exposing my frail, under-dressed exterior.

Annoyed, I slowly opened my eyes and attempted to focus, still over-stimulated by the previous day's medication. There appeared to be three fuzzy-looking Nurse Mulligans standing in the small blank room that I could not recall reentering. Then again, all my days were routine and mundane. The cafeteria. The Dayroom. Dr. Davis' office. The East Lawn. My bed. Lockdown. Drugs and more drugs. It was 1994, but even then, most of the staff at the Long Island psychiatric center where I resided showed no empathy toward an insane Black woman. An inmate doped with expensive drugs was a free ride for the state and a death sentence for me. It was all one big masquerade.

"Mary... focus!" The rational voice inside my cluttered mind sternly related, bringing me back to myself.

I shook my head so violently it cleared my vision, helping to identify the lengthy needle in Nurse Mulligan's hand.

"die, die, die," the frightening thoughts that also occupied my mind relentlessly chanted.

I wanted to respond but my mouth, dry and twisted with chapped lips, didn't cooperate with my scrambled thoughts. My speech, limited and slurred, sounded like that of a babbling fool. I wanted to hold the she-devil back, so I cringed but quickly realized my body and hands were harnessed to the bed. The overwhelming feeling of defeat crowded me...and this is why they labeled me crazy. I gritted my teeth, growling in anger. The same exasperating feelings I dealt with every day—desperate, tormented, and alone. Nurse Mulligan laughed while tapping bubbles out of the syringe. I swiftly studied my harnessed situation thinking the same thoughts I felt each day. *Maybe I can free myself? Perhaps there's a break or a tear in the fabric bonding me down? This can possibly be the day the ol' battleax grows a heart and releases me?* The definition of insanity is doing the same thing over and over again, expecting a different outcome. If I was crazy, then so were they!

Nurse Mulligan took a step closer. Her pregnant belly brushed against my arm before she touched me. I often wondered about the poor schmuck that impregnated her. Sleeping with her had to be his own personal hell. Her outward looks were a poor representation of the inward beast. A misguidance of character. Just like the fancy cross she wore.

"Nooo," I managed to mumble as she neared. "Tink, tink, tink," I continued, trying to encourage myself to come up with a plan of escape.

"Come now, Owens. Let's not fight today." Nurse Mulligan suggested but still ushered two orderlies over. "Doctor's orders, don't ya know," she added in an intolerable Irish accent, preparing an entry for the needle with an alcohol swab.

I thrust my body vigorously up and down on the paper-thin mattress where I laid. Then back and forth against the cold metal bed railings, causing the harness to grow tighter across my chest. Defenseless, I shook my head in disagreement while pleading and kicking the bedding to the floor.

"Tink, tink, tink," I continued to mutter until thinking wasn't an option. Laughing, Nurse Mulligan, in a white tent-sized uniform, appeared to quadruple in number as she documented her victory.

"Now, don't you feel better?" She asked, observing my dilated pupils with her face hanging inches above mine. If I could have mustered up the saliva, I would have spat in her face.

"Uglass, bitch," I managed to relate with the utmost contempt expressed upon my drawn face. I hated her, and she hated me, and that is how it's been for the past ten years. The sensation of the cold medication rushed through my veins, taking its effect. I closed my eyes as Nurse Mulligan, appalled by my insult, huffed, collected her troop of orderlies, and stormed away.

"Ain't nut'n good ever gon' come by ya. You too much lak ya diddy —no good fuh sho' and damn right good fuh nothing," I could hear The Grandmother saying as I drifted off. The same lies she used to speak over me, holding my spirit hostage from the very beginning.

PART I
FEAR

"Man is the cruelest animal" - *Friedrich Nietzsche*

HELLO, MY NAME IS

My name is Mary Magdalene. I know you're wondering, how did a heathen like me get stuck with such a sacred name? My mama named me—on her deathbed. I haven't thought about Mama, or me for that matter, in years. I try not to think about the past; it helps make the present more doable. Life brushes past you. Months and years seem to blend into one indistinguishable blur. It wasn't until Salmone Abrams, with his beautiful and gentle self, walked into the psychiatric ward where I was an involuntary mental patient, did I even think of such thoughts. Up until that moment, everything I knew and everything I was, was dark, hidden, and dying inside of me.

That morning, an orderly rolled me out onto the East Lawn Pavilion for breakfast. Supposedly, I was soaking up rays from the end of the summer sun. Nurse Mulligan would have never allowed such a courtesy. From the moment we met, she disliked me and handled me with mean intentions. She was, by nature, a nasty and uptight person who assaulted me every chance she got. Having no one to turn to, I was devastated and stripped down to my foundation. The first chance I got; I bit a plug out of her arm. I was placed in a Psychiatric Intensive Care Unit from that day on, and Nurse Mulligan made sure I was uncomfortable and forcibly over-medicated against my will. She kept me loopy, feeble, and isolated. But on that last sun-filled day, the evil wench had a premature delivery. An acting psych nurse, who changed the trajectory of my life, was filling in while Nurse Mulligan was on maternity leave. If I could have, I would have jumped for joy when I heard the news. As it was, I was still coming down from being drugged, and I hadn't eaten anything. My hands felt like rubber mallets; I couldn't lift a spoon, let alone bring one to my mouth. To make matters worse, my next set of meds were scheduled after breakfast; instead of numbing me, they caused me to see monkeys. If I wasn't careful of how I reacted, the meds were capable of sending me straight to lockdown in the secluded padded rooms. That was where I usually spent my afternoons—hungry and screaming at a locked door with dem damn monkeys crawling the walls.

That blessed morning, Salmone Abrams, wearing the most angelic smile I've seen in a long time, along with Nurse Lindt, the fill-in, walked across the East Lawn with a giant fluffy white teddy bear in his right hand.

"Mrs. Owens, you have a visitor," Nurse Lindt announced with a smile not quite as charming as Salmone's but kind. "It's your grandson, Mrs. Owens." She added, reiterating the information on his visitor identification badge while resting a gentle hand on my shoulder. I drew away my shoulder, rejecting her.

Next thing I know, you'll be drugging me up and locking me in too. No, ma'am. Get your hand off me, I thought, keeping my eyes on the colorful plate of food I wanted to eat but could not.

Salmone squatted down next to me and placed the gift down on the table in front of my plate. The teddy bear was holding a big red heart made of felt that read, I Love You. I didn't know how to act. I was giddy on the inside but forgot how to express myself. It had been so long since a man, smelling and looking as good as he did, brought me anything. I did get that one cracker from Eddie, a patient who frequented my room when I was incapacitated to poke his nasty drawn-up thing in me. When I say poke, that's what I mean; he thrust himself into me. We didn't have sex—it was just a thrust. I think Eddie forgot how to do the rest and he came back hoping to remember. He did give me that stinking stale cracker, though. Salmone, wearing a navy-blue open blazer over a white tee and faded jeans, inched closer to me and brushed my hair with his hand. I didn't realize I still had hair. It wasn't something you thought about often in there.

"Hey, Maw-Maw, 'memba me?" I turned toward him, and he smiled that same pleasant smile.

There was a dim flicker of recognition, but I didn't know him from Adam. I think I smiled anyway. *Why not?* He was colored, kind-looking, and called me Maw Maw—speaking the language I grew up with.

"Awww... there you go!" Nurse Lindt responded, clasping her small, white age-spotted hands together, pleased with my reaction to Salmone. "I'm going to give you two some privacy." She lightly touched him to attract his attention. He was gazing at me, and I was avoiding his eye contact. "If you need me, Mr. Abrams, I'll be in the nurse's station. Also, the orderlies in blue uniforms are here for you if needed." She added, stopping the one that I hated as he was walking by. Dino. He was one of Nurse Mulligan's flunkies. A tall, narrow, slimy piece of crap. He was strong, though. The other was a woman with a nasty facial tic. I hardly ever saw her around except when Nurse Mulligan needed her.

"Hey!" Dino responded, stopping in his tracks, and smiling wide for the new Head Nurse, with crooked, metal-wired teeth and acne scars tracing his face.

Salmone stood and shook his hand. "I do have a few questions. Is my... grandmother able to speak?" He gestured toward me, rubbing my head again. He had me curious about how I looked.

Dino glanced at Nurse Lindt first, and she nodded, giving him permission to answer. "Ahh, well no! At least not in full sentences...that I know of." He answered using facial and body expressions that implied he somehow cared. "She hasn't spoken to her treatment team...her social worker, or the unit's clinical psychologist, Dr. Davis, since her admittance."

Damn, fool! I thought, observing Salmone's immediate disheartened expression. *I talk. Just not to that raggedy-mouthed rascal.* I looked up at my teddy bear, into his big placid black glass eyes, and felt sad now myself. I wanted Salmone's company.

"Ooh," he uttered sadly, stooping down near me again. "I guess I'll sit with her for a while anyway...maybe help her eat some of this good-looking food." He picked up that heavy behind spoon, and I opened my mouth like a little bird as he scooped up some cold eggs. Lord was I happy.

Salmone didn't stay long that first day, and I wasn't sure when, or if, he would return. I didn't have any answers for him, but he did make me remember who he was. He was the preacher's kid from back home in New Orleans. Little Sal, all grown up. The little boy who used to run behind my great-niece, Rah...I claimed her as my granddaughter. He and his family lost contact with mine around the same time I did. Ten years ago. Sometime after that cursed night back in 1984 that finalized my admittance into the crazy house. Sal told me that he moved to New York City and became a cop. In his spare time, he searched for my family, mostly Rah. His childhood crush and committed friendship propelled him. He said the only public record he found on her was from high school, listing a welfare hotel in Hell's Kitchen as an address, with no forwarding information. When I left them, they were staying with me at my brownstone on Strivers' Row in Harlem. Back when I was well, and well to do.

Sal said it was like my family disappeared from the face of the earth. No listed employment, utility bills, loans, credit cards. Nothing. He looked so sad, having hit a brick wall. I wasn't much help either, and I knew he was counting on my assistance. I simply sat there while he held my hands, rubbed my arms, and looked directly into my eyes. He wasn't scared, like most people. They saw the mental unit as a locked box of angry people held against their will. It was. If the top of my head could have been unscrewed and looked into, it would have scared the hell out of most. Yet Sal looked at me with love and concern. He told me that he attempted to visit before, around three years earlier, after discovering my whereabouts. I was on lockdown, and Nurse Mulligan deliberately fed him a trough load of hogwash, deterring him from coming again. He almost didn't. Then, he figured, if Rah was gone for good, he could enjoy a piece of her in me.

I listened carefully as Sal rambled, drinking his every word. I hadn't been spoken to in so long; the words gently fell upon my ears and revived my hearing. I enjoyed Sal's youth, his zeal for life, and how his almond-shaped eyes gleamed and danced as he reminisced over old times back home in Louisiana. I didn't utter a word, and although my expression was blank, my eyes smiled in remembrance of the world I seemed to have forgotten. My thoughts were knocking around in my head, but at least they were my thoughts and not those tormenting voices. I wanted to talk to Sal. I wanted to join in his laughter, but I felt a lot of irrational shame about being there. Besides, I was afraid. I, too, didn't know where my family was. They abandoned me just as I did them. I couldn't fault them. Dr. Davis told them that I would never recover from my schizophrenic psychosis. *Was he right about me?* I wasn't sure. I definitely wasn't myself, yet I wasn't who he said I was either. I didn't know who I was anymore...but I knew that my name was Mary Magdalene.

BLACK BIRD

I t's a funny thing, but when Sal left, I felt more like myself than I had in a long time. That ol' devil does that sometimes. He leaves you alone, making you think you're normal—then he hops back on you to have his way. I could hear the muffled voices inside myself working their way up. This time the morning meds, given to me properly by Nurse Lindt herself, after witnessing me give the other nurse and attendants a hard time, worked as they were supposed to. No monkeys. I sat in the dayroom, amongst the empty white noise chatter of the other patients, with my head cocked to the right side, and a wide smile painted on my face because, for a chance, I wasn't the one screaming. I wasn't the one throwing chairs and trying to harm myself or a staff member—they all were. Then, I caught a glimpse of my reflection in Mrs. Rossellini's broken antique toaster that she carried around like a lap dog. Everything about Mrs. Rossellini was vintage, from her polyester blend orange slacks set to her synthetic auburn wig plopped on top of her head. At least they were her things. I looked down at the smelly green pattern printed hospital gowns I wore. One was turned forward and the other back- ward. When I first arrived ten years ago, Nurse Mulligan mulled through my expensive things and took them, like the thief she was.

Everything about me belonged to the state. I shuffled my feet against the cold linoleum flooring, wearing hospital socks with holes at the bottom. And wheeled my chair over to the wall where a half mirror hung above a console table adorned with a dusty plastic floral arrangement. After locking my wheelchair, I used the table to stand.

Flabbergasted, I fell back into my seat. A little old lady had occupied my body. She looked anorexic. Her once velvety black skin was leathery, dry, cracked, and ashy. Her hair. *Lord, my hair!* My hair was graying—more salt than pepper—and locking way past my shoulders. Where it wasn't locking, it was balding. *No wonder why Sal was rubbing and patting me like a pitiful dog. I probably scared the child half to death!*

I stood up again to take another look and instantly started to sob, feeling my face to make sure it was me I was looking at.

"Damn!" I said out loud. "Where you at, Mags, girl?" I whispered, ashamed and looking around to see if anyone noticed me. They hadn't; I was insignificant among the chaos and clamor.

Nurse Lindt noticed, even though she was multitasking. As it seemed, I had become her pet case. The choice patient. She sent someone over to console me.

"Hi, Miss Owens. I'm Susanna—"

"Missus!" I insisted, cutting her off. My legs were shaking under me.

"Excuse me; I don't understand?" She helped me to return to my seat properly without plopping down.

I wanted to say, *I'm Mrs. Owens, damn it! As hard as I worked for that name, that's what you fixin' to call me,* but instead, I held my hands over my face. I was hideous.

"Aww, Miss Owens," she patted my arm. "I'm Susanna. Everyone calls me Sue. I'm sort of this unit's...beautician; if you will." She held her pale face in front of mine.

Beautician? I peeked at her from between my fingers. Nurse Lindt was indeed heaven-sent. It was like she heard my every thought.

"I was wondering if you'd like Monday's beauty special...since you're up and about today. How does that sound?"

I nodded and cried into my hands. I have never been one to take no handouts, but I was desperate and clear-minded for a change. Sue wheeled me into a large bathroom area that I had never seen before. That woman undressed me and washed my body and hair, and it wasn't just the gowns that were smelly, either. She began fussing under her breath, mad about the poor care that I was given. She was an older white woman who obviously cared about her job and had some sense. Sue lotioned and powdered my body. She changed my robes and socks, then rolled me into another room that was set up like a beauty parlor. Ten years I'd been in that ward and never saw that room. I cried again, this time over the crap I was going through.

"Okay, so what are we going to do with this hair, lady?" Sue asked, sitting me in front of a well-lit wall mirror. I shrugged my shoulders and covered my face, not able to get over how I looked. It was better than before, but I still couldn't identify that woman looking back at me. I didn't care what Sue did.

Just make me into someone else—anyone else but this old lady.

Sue wet my curly hair again and cut and sprayed. She cut, pulled, and combed, working out memories of me. I sat in the chair gazing into the eyes of the woman in the mirror. *How old is she?* I couldn't remember. I had to think way back.

"MAGS!" MY SISTER YELLED, AGITATED. MAGS WAS A FAMILY NAME THAT stuck with me. "Hurry up and blow dem candles out!" I was hypnotized by the fire and feeling uncomfortable; Diddy was staring at me from over the top of his newspaper.

It was my 14th birthday. Lotti, my sister, hand-made craft paper decorations and hung them on the wall nearest the only table in the house. It was really an old wooden cable reel with a chair, and two crates pulled around it. That day should have been a joyous occasion. Lotti baked my chocolate cake herself and bought fourteen wax candles with the money she earned from helping The Grandmother. A gift was neatly wrapped in newspaper on the table along with fried something or another and buttermilk biscuits with brown butter and fig preserves. I should have been thrilled.

Growing up, The Grandmother didn't make a fuss about birthdays or holidays, for that matter. She was a simple woman. Stern and practical. She had a soft spot for Lotti, though. Lotti was her favorite, and she had made her mind up that she wanted to celebrate my birthday that year. One of the little Pritchett girls from our new school in town celebrated her birthday in class, and Lotti was taken by the idea. I couldn't care less; music and dance were all I thought about. Lotti, not much of a dancer, took to making appearances. Favoring her right foot over the left from a childhood accident when we lived in the bayou, she cared a great deal about how things looked.

I guess I could have been happier if it wasn't for him. Diddy had resurfaced after a two-year hiatus. He sat in The Grandmother's rocker staring at me over his newspaper and making me remember how he used to touch me. How he made me feel.

"You letting de candles burn down...come on, Mags! Ah wanna save 'em fuh De Grandmother's birthday too."

Stunned, The Grandmother rocked in her seat and fanned her hand out at Lotti, sort of chuckling. The inside of her lower lip was full of snuff, and she needed to spit.

"Aww, shucks...go on!" she said after spitting in a nearby Sanka can. "Do ah even got me one of dem tings?" She patted Lotti around the waist, smiling. "Hurry up, gal! Blow out my candles fuh dey burn down."

"She thankin' of sumphin good to wish fuh." Diddy proclaimed in his big gravelly voice, placing the paper down. "One bigger den her ol' diddy comin' to see her on her special day." He stood and staggered like a drunkard, walking sideways toward the table, pulling at the crotch of his overalls.

"he's gonna hurt you."

"kill ya dead."

"then take you away and bury you with ya mama."

The menacing voices were clamoring for my attention—trying to convince me of defeat before I set out.

I tightly closed my eyes. *I wish I had another diddy.* "Ah wish dis one would die," I whispered, then quickly blew out the candles before Diddy could ruin my wish.

"Yaaay!" Lotti cheered. "What you wish fuh?"

"You ain't s'posed to tell it!" I rolled my eyes.

"You ain't s'posed to tell it!" Diddy mocked, laughing and grabbing me around the waist—pretending to tickle me. He stood too close and rubbed and grabbed me in between his tickling.

"E'nuff of all dis foolishness! Ah...is...hungry!" The Grandmother stated, cutting her dagger eyes at Diddy and moving the cup of corn liquor he was drinking. She could tell he was already drunk.

"Lotti, serve ya maw-maw up some of dis here cake!" Diddy took his cup back and kissed The Grandmother dead in the eye. She hated that but loved her some Cyrus. She smiled, patting his arm. Diddy sat on my crate at the table and slid his harmonica out from his shirt pocket, licking and tucking his lips. "Black Bird, dance for ya Diddy."

"Miss Owens!" Sue was shaking my shoulder hard. I blinked, coming back from the past.

"How do you like it?" She smiled, picking up a mirror to hold to the back of my head.

I had lost myself. I blinked again to focus, then made an impressed facial expression—taking the mirror from her hand to get a better look at the back. This white woman had taken me from death's hands and brought me back to the 70s when I was young and superfine. Sue chopped off the dreading locs and cut my hair down into a curly picked-out 'fro, covering the bald spots. It was still gray, even grayer than before with the hanging black locs gone, but it was mighty fine.

"My husband is a Black man." Sue felt the need to relate, stooping down to look with me in the mirror. I made a 'hush ya mouth' face. "Yeah," she chuckled, "I cut and style Henry's 'fro all the time." She laughed again, proud of her work. I lifted my hand to lightly pat out my new afro and noticed my nails were painted RUBY RED! Chile, I jumped in my seat.

"Susanna!" I hollered, admiring them. Sue gasped, surprised to hear me speak. I was too, but the child made me feel like somebody.

"I did your toes, too!" She boasted, taking the mirror from me. I must have been zoned out for a good while.

"Nooo!" I held on to the tabletop and pushed myself back in the seat to bend over and look. "You sho' did!" I held a hand to my mouth and the other to lift my leg for a better look—then started tearing again. This time Sue did too. "Thank you, ya hear?"

"No problem." The plump-faced, pale white woman, with rosy cheeks and bushy, gray-streaked blonde hair, said. "If you promise to get better. I promise to look after you and keep you looking good." She rocked her head then hugged me around the neck.

"I promise." I wanted to add—as long as Nurse Mulligan stays away...but Sue was white too. What stopped her from helping me before?

BLUE BAYOU

It was a good month before Sal returned, and I was just as happy to see him as I was the first time. Maybe even happier. This time around, I surprised him and spoke first. A lot had happened since we last saw each other. Not only was I looking better; I felt good and was talking again. Not publicly, not yet. I didn't want word to get around to Nurse Mulligan. She might have had the notion to cut her maternity leave short out of fear of me ratting her out. Sue was the only person who heard me speak…and Eddie. That dirty behind rascal tried to sneak his butt back into my room one night to get some and boy did I let him have it. I whacked him clean in the balls, gritting my teeth, and said, "Don't you EVER come into this room again—you hear me?" He moaned, nodding his head, laying on top of his crumbled packages of stale crackers in a fetal position on the floor. "Now, get ya ass, outta here!" I demanded like I was the queen of Harlem again.

"Hey, beb, how you?" I addressed Sal after the orderly left. He almost dropped to his knees. Shocked, he froze, holding his mouth open, and instantly became teary-eyed.

"Yooo!" He said like the young folks do when they can't believe something.

"Yo to you! Come and give ya Tante Mags some sugah, boy!" I stood, flinging my arms wide.

"I can't believe it." He shook his head as we embraced in a big bear hug. "Glory," I heard him whisper. It felt good to be in someone's arms. I closed my eyes and soaked up everything about him.

I was different. My hair was growing—now more pepper than salt. I had even picked up a little weight. Sue bought me some slippers and a few lightly used outfits, and I wasn't using the wheelchair anymore. I wanted to be on my feet in case I ever had to run. But I was doing well. Nurse Lindt was watching me closely. Even though I hadn't spoken to her, she requested that my medications be decreased. Dr. Davis confirmed, but he was still concerned as to why I wasn't speaking. Nurse Lindt also assigned me a whole new care team, getting Dino off my back. Like I said, she was heaven-sent. She worked quietly in the background, watching and learning my every move; she knew I was being over-stimulated from the meds, and she also knew I could talk. I refused to give in to her—not until I knew Sal would return. He said he was a cop. I figured maybe he could help me get out of there.

My light of hope was burning dim until I saw him being escorted over by an orderly to the table where I sat near the picturesque window facing the East Lawn. The leaves were starting to change colors, and we were enjoying a beautiful Indian Summer yet not as glorious as Sal's smiling face.

"I'm happy to see you back," I said, taking a seat and pulling the sheer scarf I wore up around my mouth. I had to remain a mystery to Dino, who was nosing around. He took notice of my improvements too. Because he was a traitor, he was working on getting on my good side but couldn't figure me out.

"Truth be told, Tante Mags, I wasn't coming back," Sal confessed, taking a seat opposite of me. He pulled another stuffed animal out from a shopping bag. A brown dog this time, with sad puppy eyes and a wagging tongue. His stomach was embroidered, forgive me. I smiled and took the dog, hugging and smelling it. He had a trace of Sal's cologne. "But last night..." Sal continued. "I heard the voice of the Lord say, she has a story. Don't give up." He looked me straight in the eyes, and I started to tear because all I was thinking of were stories. "Soo, here I am...and I'm sorry for running out on you like that. I just wanted so much to find Rah..." Sal pulled out a worn bulky bible from the shopping bag and sat it in the middle of the table. "This time, I've decided to quiet my own thoughts...and check my life at the door so that I can fully be here for you." He extended his long-toned reddish-brown arms across the table with his palms laid open. I sat my dog in my lap and took Sal's hands. "How about you tell me about yourself."

I laughed and then laughed again because my own laughter sounded foreign to me. "You sure you wanna open that can of worms? I have a whole head full of stories and a lonely heart yearning to tell them."

"Oh, you ain't said nothing but a thang!" Sal joked, releasing my hands and pulling another chair over to put his feet up. He rested back in his seat. "I got the whole day off."

I snickered nervously, feeling a little intimidated.

"*don't do it. he can't help you,*" the voices echoed in my head.

I looked Sal in the eyes. He was a beautiful brown boy. So innocent and trusting, and just as much in love with the past as I was.

"*go ahead. tell him. he'll think differently of you.*" The demons teased, causing me to drop my head.

Sal was a man of integrity, and portions of my life were unsavory, to say the least. I feared losing his respect...and companionship.

Sal reached across the table, and this time placed his hands in mine. "You okay, Tante Mags. What? That ol' cat got ya tongue, again?" He laughed, treating me like I was normal and making me remember that I had a place in life. I was a sister, aunt, wife, lover, and friend.

"**You can trust him.**" I heard audibly, startling me.

I started to look around for the voice, but I knew who it was, and He knew me. I had turned my back on Him, but He never left.

"Folks think I'm fibbing when I say that I can remember my birth." I squeezed Sal's hand, and he smiled. "Now, I might be a little too crazy to explain this here to you... or you may be too sane to fully understand what I wanna say, but I remember. How can you forget a thing like taking your mother's life?"

Just like that, my mind traveled back to Baton Rouge. I remembered the red dirt roads, the pea-green swamp water crawling with tiny insects, the ghost-gray cypress trees, and images of people long forgotten.

"I remember coming out of the birth canal, already crying over Mama sparing her life and wishing the doors of her womb would have shut on me. With her last breath, she whispered, "Hush now, sweet baby, Mary Magdalene," and I quieted down. There was an eerie silence as Mama's warm embrace loosened, and I rolled into The Grandmother's hands. I can remember the sound of Diddy crying like a violent wind howling and tearing down everything in its path. The Grandmother held me in her arms, shaking her head and sucking her teeth. She knew that she would have to raise Lotti and me alone.

IF YOU LOOK AT MY LIFE...

"**I** was born on a faded and tattered quilt, spread open on the dirt floor of a sharecropper's house. It was a cursed day in May of 1931—nine months after my older sister, Charlotte. We called her Lotti. "

Sal smiled wide because he knew her well.

Mama, Adah Eucharis Auguste, was of direct African descent. Her father, Emmanuel Bebey, was from Cameroon. He was an apprentice, brought to the states by an American doctor observing the effects of holistic medicines amongst different tribes. The two met while studying in Europe. Well educated, our grandfather spoke three tribal languages and some French too. He and the doctor quickly became friends and colleagues. Back in America, they worked together until the doctor died at a ripe old age. By this time, our grandfather was married to the beautiful Charlotte Dupre' and the father of five girls. In an era saturated in bigotry and hate, the ambitious and revolutionary couple died in an alleged house fire trying to save their children. All five girls lived. Mama was the youngest. Her Grandmother and oldest sister raised her too.

Diddy, Cyrus Auguste, was proud that Lotti and I could trace our African roots. It was the only thing he ever told us about Mama. "You should be proud," he would say. The Grandmother hated it...well, The Grandmother couldn't right stand many things or people for that matter. She figured our African blood made me wild. "Untamed," in her words. She and Diddy were Louisiana Creole, Creoles of color— descendants of an ethnic gumbo of French, Spanish, Haitian, and African descent, and it showed. They were both wrapped in bleached almond skin with smooth curly brown hair and hazel eyes. Lotti and I were the opposite. We were black as coal with glistening dark silky curls, sad deep-set chestnut-shaped eyes (soul-catchers, they call them), and sharp ethnic facial features. Exotic looking, folks would later say. As kids growing up in Baton Rouge, we were just plain ugly. Where we lacked in beauty, ol' Cyrus more than made up for. Women loved Diddy, and he loved him some women.

I laughed, squeezing my stuffed animal that Sal gave me. Talking about Diddy made me feel nervous. I hoped I wasn't having one of those combustible and destabilizing conversations that Dr. Davis said I should avoid.

Diddy's heart was cold as ice. Mama was the only somebody he ever fell for. The Grandmother swore it was pure voodoo. "Straight from de Motherland," she would say. She claimed that Mama had Diddy fixed because he settled down and married her. Built us a home and everything. That is until I came around. I killed the light that was in him. Diddy went back to his doggish ways. He got him a few wives after Mama; he collected them like stamps. It was rumored Diddy had children all up and down the Mississippi River. He was a wretch of a man. Reeking in mischief and lured trouble. Every time someone's husband or family member came knocking on our door for him, we ended up moving. We were like gypsies; we moved so much. The Grandmother always found us some shack tucked away from the rest of civilization. A dirt floor here, wooden floors there, sometimes even a floor under the stars. She made it hard for the census man to keep track of us; somewhere, it is written that we belonged to that time and era.

Diddy was a sailor and the king of his suitcase; he moved with the tides. Between jail and the sea, he was hardly home. It was because his beloved wife died birthing me, and Lotti reminded him too much of her. Whenever the sea called, Cyrus answered to its waves. A 'ro-day' is what the Grandmother called him. He was a wanderer, but when he found trouble, he made his way back home. No matter where we moved, Diddy always found us. All he had to do was ask around for the local Voodoo lady, and folks would lead him straight to The Grandmother.

The Grandmother, Lucille Clementine Auguste, was a 'baby-catcher' (midwife) and Voodoo priestess. We called her The Grandmother because growing up she never gave us a proper name to call her by. Lotti and I used to hear her tell folks, mostly, Diddy, "I'm de grandmother. I'm not dey mama," and I guess it stuck. Anyhow, the passing down of her proud heritage and Voodoo traditions was customary. Lotti and I learned about 'gris-gris' bags, hexes, and charms right along with the alphabet and arithmetic. I never took to any of it, though. It scared me. Especially the abortions. I could feel the spirits of those babies scraping the floors and walls, trying to get out. The Grandmother said, "It's because you a hell-raiser, ya'self." As a child, they said I fought the devil in my sleep, and at times demons threw me to the ground in convulsions.

I looked over at Sal. I didn't want to scare him, but the demons were definitely a part of my story. I quickly changed the topic because I didn't want them thinking they were invited to sit and talk.

In every town we lived in, the townspeople felt The Grandmother's Voodoo harbored evil spirits and caused them calamity. The truth is, everything that could go wrong went wrong when she was around. Once, when we lived over in the bottom, a storm came, uprooting trees, homes, and everything. This was right after Mr. Magee, a local clergyman, insulted The Grandmother—right out front of the local grocery store. The Grandmother cussed that man out so bad I was embarrassed for him. He turned all kinds of red. We moved after that because the area had suffered tremendously. Even Mr. Magee lost his home.

Yes-sir-ee, that grandmother of ours was something else! She was a tiny, sassy, white-haired little thang too. She wasn't all mean, just stern, cold at times, and very opinionated. The Grandmother stood high on pride, and oh boy, did she have an evil streak when rubbed the wrong way. But she wasn't a troublemaker. Back then, when we grew up, Voodoo and black magic were pushed into the darkness— out in the swamps and backwoods. It didn't matter where we moved; The Grandmother never met approval, especially amongst the church. She made no apologies for herself and didn't hide her girls in the shadows of the marshland, either. We attended the local schoolhouses right with the other kids. But let somebody step on our toes, especially Lotti's; The Grandmother would fix them good. Lotti and I barely made any friends. Not only were we 'spooks,' as the kids called us, but we were lonely, sheltered, and homely. All we had was each other. It had to be that way—we were women alone in a man's world. Lotti and I were best friends.

"I sho' do miss her," I whispered, pulling the long fluffy ears of my new stuffed animal.

"I do too," Sal added, with his head laid back on the chair like he was daydreaming himself.

I decided to name the dog with the words 'forgive me' embroidered on its stomach, Lotti. Because I wished we would have forgiven each other for our wrongdoings. Life gets the best of you sometimes.

I was just about to tell Sal when I looked up, and Dino was standing behind him, grinning with his wired teeth showing.

"Excuse me. I'm just checking in. Is everything okay," Dino asked. The nurse attendants were supposed to check on patients every fifteen to twenty minutes. Yet, he wasn't assigned to me anymore. "It's great that she's talking again, huh," he added before Sal could answer the first question.

I gave Sal a swift kick from under the table.

"Ou...ahh! Talking?" he yelped, quickly catching on. "Is she speaking? Because she ain't talking to me. I'm reminiscing and reading to her...from the bible," he added, tapping his book that was still on the table.

"Mhmm." Dino vocalized, giving me a withering look as he pretended to write my status on his chart.

If he had a brain, he'd been downright dangerous. I narrowed my eyes into a slit and squared my shoulders. My face read, *Oh, I'm ready for ya now, suckah!*

Dino turned and walked away, leaving the atmosphere thick with his lousy aura.

"What's that about?" Sal asked, waiting for him to leave. "He ain't messing with you, is he?" He could tell I hated him.

I sucked my teeth, fanning Dino off, not wanting to get into that story yet. My dear sweet sister, Lotti, was on my mind. I smiled and rocked in my seat, getting comfortable again—pulling the scarf up around my mouth.

"Let me tell you about Lotti."

FOLKS USED TO THINK WE WERE TWINS BECAUSE WE WERE NINE months apart and looked just alike. The only physical difference was, Lotti was flat-chested and me, I definitely was not. What they didn't know is that we were complete opposites. Lotti, being the eldest, took on responsibilities as a cape of royalty and wore maturity as a crown. She soaked up The Grandmother's wisdom and teachings like a sponge. While I, on the other hand, was a dreamer. Instead of walking, I skipped and danced—floating around on my toes, swirling and touching rainbows with the tips of my fingers. I couldn't help that I heard music and could feel it in my soul. The Grandmother used to 'pass a switch' to my legs and bring me back to reality right fast. But she sowed too much into Lotti. Besides treating her differently, she treated her like she was my Ma instead of my sister. From as far back as I can remember, Lotti stood on a pot at the stove cooking.

"Lotti, get dinner started. Lotti sew dat rip in Mag's school dress. Lotti, run down to de sto'."

The Grandmother was always on the go. She had babies to birth into the world and some to erase. When she wasn't on the go, folks came to her for potions, remedies, and spiritual advice. You see, The Grandmother had the gift of sight. People publicly denounced her voodoo, but those same folks secretly traveled through the woods and swamp to get their fortunes told and mistakes erased. Then, they paid The Grandmother with whatever they had—coins, eggs, chickens, fruit, vegetables, pies. It wasn't much. We lived a simple life and never wanted anything. As they say, back home, The Grandmother was makin' groceries, and she paid de rent doin' lak dat dere. So, Lotti was like my Ma, but she was also my sister, and we got into some good and bad trouble together.

I laughed, remembering the time we found religion.

"Mags, stop ya lagging," Lotti yelled from walking ahead of me. She was moving those short legs of hers as fast as she could, trying to get to the revival early and secure us good seats. A girl from school was carrying on about how good Pastor John, the River Preacher, was. He made the blind see, the mute speak, and the lame walk and whatnot.

You see, the problem was The Grandmother didn't want anything to do with organized religion. She always said the lies that were told in the bible are what trapped our ancestors in slavery. But when Lotti got something in her spirit, there was no turning her back. We snuck out of the house that night and went to the tent revival, where they tossed us out on our butts quicker than beignets coming out of hot grease!

"De laks of anyone associated with witchcraft ain't welcomed in de house of de Lord," the man at the entrance stated. "Naw, scat...and don't y'all start no trouble."

Lotti and I ran down some ways into the woods; then climbed into a sturdy tree when he wasn't looking. From there, we watched all the miracles the River Preacher performed and were blown away by all the money he received. You see, other than physical, Lotti and I have one other similar trait—we love money! Maybe Lotti more than me. She worked hard and saved all her money. She said she was gonna own a house one day—with no dirt floors, broken windows, or mice and snakes coming in at night.

The girl who initially told us about the revival saw when we were turned away. The next day at school, she brought Lotti the best gift she ever received—an old pew bible she took from home. The girl, one of those folks like me who love to hear themselves talk, told us about the baptisms taking place that Sunday after service at the lake.

She said, "River Jawn says, whoever believes and is baptized will be saved, but whoever does not believe will be condemned. How ah sees it is, you can't keep nobody from being saved."

Saved from what? Both Lotti and I thought.

I didn't wanna go. Besides the money, nothing interested me. Lotti was the one who had a point to prove. She said, "What ah learned is, dem pastors is de real witch doctors. Making folk see what dey want dem to see and do what dey want dem to do, all in de name of some blue-eyed god dey peddling. We can do dat!" She said it, and she meant it, yet I could tell they hurt her feelings. I could tell there was something more. Every night she read from the old pew Bible that she hid from The Grandmother. Something from the words she read out loud was clinging to her. The Grandmother said the book oppressed our ancestors, yet Lotti...and I felt a sense of love and conviction that we couldn't deny.

That Sunday, we ventured out to get baptized by the River Preacher John. We watched for a good thirty minutes, way back yonder, hidden by a patch of shrubs. It seemed the whole town was out there in the wilderness getting saved—which was a funny word to use. *How can that man save anyone,* we wondered. The River Preacher was a tall, lanky reed of a man. He swayed back and forth against the shimmering water, dressed in a long white robe held down at the waist by a leather belt. He looked as if the wind could blow him away. I guess his faith held him down.

Lotti was getting nervous and trying to change her mind, thinking of what The Grandmother would do to us.

"We gonna get it good, fuh sho," she said, knowing she hadn't had a lickin' in years. Me, on the other hand, having just turned fourteen the day before, got licks—at least twice a week. "Besides," Lotti continued, "We got on our good dresses." Neither of us knew what baptisms were nor what they detailed when we put the dresses on that day.

I don't know what got into me; when I looked out from behind the bushes and saw the line getting down to three people waiting, I stood up.

"Mags! Whatcha doing?" Lotti whispered in surprise, yanking the tail of my new birthday dress. "Get back down here, girl."

It was too late. I had a better view of the people dancing, playing washboards and tambourines while hooting and hollering, and lost myself in the experience. Pulling from Lotti's grip, I inched out from our hiding place. Already feeling the spirit of dance in my bones as I swayed closer to the lake.

"Praise God!" I heard myself yelling. Putting on like those folks at the revival. "Praise Him!" I affirmed, moving onto the shore. If the people were hooting—I hooted louder. If they were dancing, I DANCED! "River Jawn!" I shouted. "Ah needs to be saved!" You could hear a pin drop after I said that, but I was ready to argue my point as to why. My sister wanted to be saved. I knew she did, so we were fixin' to be saved. I looked back and saw Lotti walking down, just as ready to protect me as I was to defend her.

"Child!" River John responded in a throaty voice that rose in highs and lows. "Why shall you be saved?" he asked, probably not knowing the company he was keeping. He was a guest preacher in town.

"Because ah was blind but now ah see!" I sang, strutting in a circle like a rooster with its chest poked out. One of the deacons in the lake with River John whispered something in his ear. Being animated, I shouted even louder in song, swaying my hips and clapping my hands on my knees, "Ah was a wretch, but now I's free. Save me, River Jawn!"

The preacher smiled.

"Come see, child," he said, extending his hand against the disapproval of his comrade.

I hooted and hollered even louder, checking to see if Lotti was close enough to really save me if need be. I took River John's hand, and something instantly changed. He had a different type of energy; it awakened my body and made the hairs stand straight on my arms.

"His energy was sorta like yours, Sal."

Sal was now sitting straight in his seat, engaged in the story. I smiled from under the scarf wrapped around my face.

I tell ya, my hooting turned into tears, and my hollering turned into groans. I crossed my arms over my chest, like those who had gone before me, and relaxed in River John's arms.

"Mags!" I could hear Lotti yelling, "You gon' get it good! Get o'va here, naw!"

It was peaceful there on the lake. River John whispered, as though only for me to hear, "I baptize you with water, but HE will baptize you with the Holy Spirit." Then he loudly said," I baptize you in the name of the Father, the Son, and the Holy Spirit!"

I was submerged in water for a split second, but it felt like an eternity. When I came up, I could hear with different ears; ears to be taught. I realized the hooting and the hollering were for me. I pressed my eyes with my fingers to see, panting and swaying against the murky water. Lotti was reaching for me, and I reached back for her. Before walking over, I turned and looked at River John. We had shared a moment that I can't explain, but he prepared me for the journey I didn't know I'd have to take.

As the evening sun went down behind him, River John repeatedly yelled into the crowd, "Prove by the way you live that you have repented of your sins and turned to God!"

"Praise God," I uttered for those listening and waiting to see me perform, throwing my hands in the air and waving them. Tilting my head, I looked into the heavens with a pensive expression, like the fat lady who sang at the revival did. "Praise Him!" I repeated, louder.

"You feel any different?" Lotti asked inquisitively, partly stepping into the water to catch me by the waist.

I paused for a moment and gazed wide-eyed at her as though in a trance. Lotti looked worried. At that time in my life there weren't too many things I took seriously. I made the life changing event into a joke because I couldn't explain what really happened. "Ah...ah, ah can't say ah do," I said, bursting into laughter and falling into her arms. She playfully tapped my arm then laughed too, covering her face for appearances. "You fixin' to go down, next, right, Lotti?

"Humph! Ah, 'spect not...not after dat act you put on!" We laughed again and ran all the way home, with our wet shoes tied around our necks, mimicking and joking about the people we left back by the lake.

You know, that was the last time I can remember being free like that. I mean, I've been happy but not free.

When we reached the house, The Grandmother was on her way out the door.

"Gal, wey you been?" She scorned Lotti. "Ah needs ya help! Dat lady on South Street...de one near de grocery sto', 'bout to have her baby." She cut her sharp eyes at me, then down at my wet birthday dress and rolled them in disgust. "Lotti, go grab my shawl and come on! De night air is fixin' to set in, and you both fitna be sick." She headed for her vehicle, fussing under her breath. "When ah get back ah 'spect you be ready to tell me why you wet up lak dat...in dat new dress ya sista done worked hard fuh." She shook her head and got into her old piece of truck—beeping the horn for Lotti to hurry up.

They left, and just like that, everything changed.

I WAS ABOUT TO GET INTO THE STORY WHEN I HEARD BABIES CRYING. "You hear that?" I asked Sal, getting nervous because I knew the sound was coming from the inside of my head.

"Hear what?" He asked, looking around. There was a lot to hear. The place was noisy with its usual constant drone of people talking and moving about.

"Dem babies, crying." I tightly closed my eyes, inhaling before breathing slowly out through my mouth. I was trying to slow down my racing heart. Trying to remember my grounding techniques and trying not to go there.

"You okay, Tante Mags?" Sal questioned, leaning over the table and grabbing my hands. A panic attack was coming on, and I was sweating bullets. My knees were rocking. "Tante Mags, you okay?" he repeated, before screaming, "Nurse! Nurse!"

"Somebody, please stop my babies from crying!" I whispered, ripping the scarf from around my face; it felt like it was choking me, and I was being stifled. "No, no." I pleaded with myself; I didn't want Sal to see me that way. I grabbed and hid my face.

"Mary! I'm still here... I never left you. You know that... don't you?"

FOOTPRINTS

Maybe it happened because God don't like ugly. He didn't appreciate me poking fun at the people by the lake—especially after just being baptized.

When Nurse Lindt arrived, I was lying down in my room feeling embarrassed and fearing Sal left blaming himself for what happened.

"You, okay, sweetie?" she asked. I nodded. I had refused the medication the nurse attendant tried to administer to me. Feeling defeated, she called on Nurse Lindt. "A panic attack, huh?" she assessed, taking my vitals. I nodded again. "You want a Valium?"

Hell no. I quickly shook my head.

"How 'bout I give you some more time, then I'll come back to see if you changed your mind...okay?" I agreed, but I didn't want to be sedated, and I didn't want to see anyone either. I wanted to be alone. That's the thing about treatment centers and hospitals—no privacy.

It's over, Mags. I told myself when Nurse Lindt left. *That happened years ago.* I rolled over on my back, staring up at the ceiling, trying to forget what happened at the house after Lotti and The Grandmother left. It was hard to do. My room at the institution was sparsely furnished between four white walls. It was a blank canvas for thoughts for someone like me. Trying to get comfortable, I stretched my leg, and my foot hit the bible that Sal brought in that day. I sat up, looking down at the bulky, worn leather-bound book and the two stuffed animals that sat near, and couldn't help but smile. My room wasn't so impersonal anymore. Three things belonged to me.

"It's over...and that ain't you, no more," I affirmed out loud to hear myself, hopping off the bed and walking over to the window.

The sun was going down just like the night at the lake. I could see my reflection through the glass and imagined myself wearing the beautiful yellow cotton floral dress Lotti bought for me. The sleeves were puffy. Accent lacing trimmed the collar, and the belt that tied around the waist showed off my figure. It was my first teenage dress. I could still see the fabric twirling around my legs as I slowly spun in front of the window.

The Grandmother used to say, "Dreams is a ting with wings. Dey soar with de wind and always get away from ya. Ain't nothing in life fuh sho." I was a dreamer, and I expected more.

WHEN LOTTI AND THE GRANDMOTHER LEFT, I WENT TO THE WELL AND pulled up the bottle of buttermilk that I had cooling at the bottom inside the bucket. That was my birthday gift from The Grandmother; she saved me some buttermilk after making biscuits. I was the only one, aside from Diddy, who drank it.

I had just sat down on my crate at the makeshift table to enjoy a wedge of cake, big enough to choke a horse when Diddy came stumbling in. His face was busted up from a fight, and he was barking mad. My mouth fell open, and my gaping eyes froze upon him as a hunk of cake dangled on the end of the trembling fork in my hand.

"Come help me, gal," he demanded, falling into The Grandmother's rocker. It rigidly rocked backward, hitting the wall, and scraping the paint as Diddy laid flared out.

I heard him, but I was leery. The blood staining his handsome face was running from a fresh wound over his eye. I didn't want to go near him. I turned my fork, making it into a weapon as Diddy lifted his bobbing head and looked at me with weak glazed-over eyes.

"Dat's how you gon' treat ya diddy?" He slurred; his heavy arm fell off the armrest. "Come o'va here, Bird, and give me some sugah, you ain't miss ya old man?" He laughed, obviously drunk then winced in pain. "Blackbird...make Diddy one of dem... mama's poultice rags." He sat up and held his head, cursing under his breath about how a fat son-of-abish was fixin' to get his. I got up and attempted to run past him, but he jumped and grabbed my arm. "Wey you goin'?" He laughed, stepping on my toes with his big feet and pressing his bloody clothes against my wet dress. "Ah just got here, Adah." He called me by Mama's name, biting down on his thin lip and smelling of fresh fish and corn liquor.

"Ah...ah gotta go...get de herbs to make de poultice. Ah...ah gotta go." I pointed to the door with my fork.

Diddy slyly laughed, sort of swaying to music that wasn't playing. He held me tautly, staring me in the face with piercing hazel eyes while running his calloused hand down my arm. He squeezed my wrist like he was fixing to break it, and I dropped the fork. Diddy kicked it away, stepping all over my bare feet again with his cumbersome hard boots. When he cornered me against the wall, I closed my eyes. I never knew what terror was until that day. My heart felt as if it was pounding out of my chest. My tongue swelled in my mouth and blocked the words from coming out. I could feel my body starting to twitch and my legs giving way from under me. Diddy held me up. He laid me on that godforsaken table that was really an old wooden cable reel. Stuffed a fist full of my chocolate cake into his mouth. Gulped down my buttermilk from the bottle. Wiped his dirty hand across my beautiful dress and over my breasts, around my stomach. Then, he spread my legs and took away everything innocent inside of me. It hurt so bad; I wished I was dead.

There was only a buzzing sound in my head—like I had blown a fuse. Diddy finished his business and fell against the wall panting with his overalls around his ankles and his head pushed back. I scrambled to a corner, with a fire burning between my legs, looking back at my bloody footprints—my blood or his blood—I didn't know. Blood was a symbol of sacrifice. The footprints were like prayers etched into the wooden floor. That day I shook my fist at God.

"Get me some...get me some...waa'der," Diddy slurred, "Ah need water." He was likely feeling woozy from his injury; he held his head with his large dirty hands.

The door seemed so far away—but I knew once I hit it, I could run. Scared, I mustered up the courage to inch forward, thinking Diddy would jump out at me again. This time he was caught up in crocodile tears, maybe in pain, maybe feeling remorseful, or perhaps missing mama. I don't know, but he wailed and laughed at the same time like a mad man.

Before I reached the door, it popped open. All I remember is a loud sound, a wisp of smoke, and buzzing ears. Mrs. Lackey's husband fired a single precise shot directly into Diddy's heart.

"hello," Fear introduced himself. *"we don't have to speak right now, but we'll be friends."*

MARY, DON'T YOU WEEP

After Mr. Lackey shot Diddy, he turned and walked out the door like nothing happened, with his rifle propped over his shoulder. He casually walked off and up the road, whistling Dixie. It wasn't too long after that that The Grandmother showed up with her shotgun in hand. She stood at the door for a second, taking in the room. I heard her mumbling something under her breath in creole about a 'couyon' (a foolish man). She slammed the muzzle of the gun against the floor as hard as she could in anger and hurt. Wiping the sweat from her forehead and spitting out a wad of snuff right there on the floor, she said, hardly glancing at me, "Get up, gal. Go bo'l some water and scrub ya' self with dat lye soap." That's all I got, but she watched me closely during the weeks to come. It was made clear that everything had to remain held silent within me.

Much later, I found out why The Grandmother had returned back to the house so early. Lotti said that they were waiting at the traffic light before the bridge into town when one of Diddy's friends rolled up next to them. He said Diddy had been fighting with one of his girls' husbands and was busted up real bad. The Grandmother rolled her eyes and sucked her teeth, and started to roll up the window when the man said, after he dropped Diddy off on the road back to the house, he went back to the juke joint. He overheard that the man who beat Diddy was going home for his gun. He said Diddy got the man's wife pregnant. The Grandmother made an abrupt U-turn before the light turned green and headed home.

"She had a strange look in her eyes," Lotti said, "Dey was cold and blank, lak if Mr. Lackey didn't kill Diddy, she was fixin' to do it herself."

"Hand me dat gun from back dere on de flo'," she told Lotti. "Den ah want you to stay put in dis truck, ya hear?"

Before that day, as mean as The Grandmother was to me, I thought she hated me, but in her own way, she loved me more than I knew.

Diddy's friend followed The Grandmother to the house and tried to help us get Diddy's body out to bury. Back then, the Black man's life was considered worthless, especially when that black man was a no-good piece of crap. In Diddy's case, he could die or be killed, and life would go on as usual. No questions asked. But Diddy's blood was spread everywhere, becoming as much of a nuisance as he was. Feeling overwhelmed as she stood in the middle of the room, looking around with her hands on her hips, The Grandmother finally said, "Get y'all stuff. We can't stay here no mo'." She and Diddy's friend burned our two-room shack with no indoor plumbing down to the ground. Diddy's dead body was still lying on the bloody floor, along with my birthday dress purposely left behind on that damned wooden cable reel table. We had never heard The Grandmother cry before; she always carried a stoic resignation about herself. Yet she cried that night for her no-good son as we drove up the road heading to a new town in an old rusty, dented-up pick-up truck with all our belongings tied down.

Ain't no way I could've told Sal all that, nor the rest of the story for that matter. I wasn't allowed to speak about what happened with Diddy, but I became pregnant with his baby. I've been pregnant four times. One by Diddy. The second by being curious—trying to figure out what all the fuss over sex was about. The third one was 'cause I thought I was in love. The fourth I don't talk about. The Grandmother took the first two. She's the one who got my babies scratching and crying in my head, now. With the third baby, she said, "Abortions ain't no birth control. You fixin' to get married and have you a chile." But the baby died, and my husband, who I thought I loved, ran away as fast as he could. "God saw fit to show dat baby...and man, some mercy." The Grandmother reckoned. "You ain't ready, gal...and you cursed fuh sho."

Humph, all I know is, I am, what I am, and that's all I can be. The fact is, I wasn't for everybody.

I CAME TO REALIZE THAT EVEN MORE, LYING THERE ALONE ON THAT cold linoleum floor in my room at the psych ward—wishing I had a glass of scotch on the rocks—stirred, not shaken. I needed a drink, my favorite drink; I hadn't had one in ten years. At that moment, even taking the numbing medications made sense. Anything to help kill the pain. Those thoughts scared me more than remembering about Diddy. I was not fully recovered, and I wanted to be whole again. I was tired of my body going into fight or flight mode and ending with panic attacks.

"It's okay, Mags. Diddy is gone," I told myself, rocking on the floor, trying to get him out of my head. Trying not to feel crazy. Trying to talk myself down. I could still smell the sea that was harbored in his clothes. Diddy smelled like fish all the time. I gagged; I cannot eat fish to this day.

"Lord, open a window," I cried, curled up in a fetal position and thinking of what a good friend used to tell me. "When God closes a door, He opens a window," Jo used to say. "Lord, please open one," I yelled. Trying to fight back the crazy feelings inside of me. They were pure rage.

Just then, someone knocked on the door twice. "Hi, Mary, it's Sue," I heard before the door opened and she stepped in. I hollered, crying, reaching for her from the floor. "What's wrong, sweetie, did you fall?" Sue rushed over and squatted beside me, holding me in her arms and wiping my tears as we rocked. "Can you stand; you look peaked?" she asked after a while. I nodded, trying to pull myself together as I stood to my feet along with her. We walked over to the bed.

"I can't get these damn memories out of my head," I revealed, lying down and feeling angry with myself. "I can't sleep. I can't think, eat, nothing."

"Shhh, it's okay. Don't get worked up." Sue sat on the edge of the bed, soothing my back. She knew how I felt about medication. I didn't want anything more than what I had to take, so we did breathing and focusing techniques instead. "You know, Mags, everyone makes mistakes," Sue said, exhaling with me. "But not everyone punishes themselves 24/7, 365 days a year. If you keep doing that, your life won't ever get any better. You'll stay a mess—miserable and feeling inevitable. You might even ruin the potentially great things that can come your way. We can't control memories." Sue picked up the bible lying on the bed to make room for herself. "But we can control how we react to them..." she continued, studying the book as she patted my back, inhaling and exhaling with me again. "Look..." She handed it to me. "There's a year's worth of reading right here. I bet reading will get your mind off of whatever you're thinking about."

I sniffled, remembering Lotti used to read from the bible at night and how it made me feel. I sat up straight. "Maybe you're right," I said, wiping my eyes with the back of my hand and opening the book. *God gave me a window.* Glancing over at Sue's puggy red face, I asked, "What you doing here, anyway?" Judy was my usual night nurse. I didn't know she called out, and Sue was pulling a double, taking her place.

"I'll be checking in on you every fifteen to twenty minutes. Here." She reached in her pocket and pulled out a highlighter. "Mark your favorite verses, and when I come back, I wanna hear some of them."

Lord was I happy. I was calming down already, thinking of Sue being there all night. "Where should I start?" My pounding heart was beating at a steadier pace.

"Okay, let's see..." she answered, checking her watch first. She was almost due to be in with her next patient. "The book of John is my favorite." She flipped through the pages and dog-eared the first page—

already highlighted and marked up with notes from its previous owner. I assumed they were Sal's notes, and I felt like I would be reading along with him. Noticing she wasn't needed any longer, Sue kissed me on the forehead. "Okay, sweetie. I'll see you in twenty minutes...you're okay." She stated more than she questioned.

I exhaled and nodded. "I'm feeling better, thanks." I smiled and waved as Sue left the room. God gave me a window for the remainder of that night.

Breathing deeply through my nose and slowly exhaling through my mouth, I picked up the book and held it to my face. I needed new reading glasses. "In the beginning was the Word, and the Word was with God, and the Word was God..."

The reading kept me engaged the entire night. Not one bad thought.

SOMEONE OTHER THAN ME

I was tired the next day, but I felt better. Sue was right; we cannot control the past. The problem was trying to work that through my spirit. Unfortunately, we also can't control the way that our mind thinks either. I was diagnosed with Manic Depression years ago. Over time, other disorders were collected and added on. It was because I did not take care of myself and drank heavily. I was that family member that folks warn others about. "Stay away from Tante Mags; she'll go off on you," they said...and were correct. Finally, with proper and consistent administration of my medications, things were looking up. Dr. Davis was decreasing my psychosis and schizophrenia meds, even considering a misdiagnosis based on my turnaround. I still would not talk to him. After that little episode with Sal, it crossed my mind that Dr. Davis might increase my intake again. I was feeling better...but I did hear babies crying.

That entire day I read my bible, bringing it to breakfast, lunch, and dinner, while sneaking naps in between. I swear I could hear Lotti's voice reading along, and all the notes and highlights that Sal took were dead on. Reading with such an urgency, I completed the book of John and was well into Acts. I probably could've kept reading if it wasn't for the quiet and rational voice in my head nudging me to, *"Look up and listen."*

I was in a mandatory group session—there and not there, as usual. When I was being overmedicated, the orderlies used to wheel me into the intensive group sessions to sit in and listen. After hearing the horror stories and feeling bat crazy myself, they quickly wheeled me out, screaming. Now that I was feeling better, they had me sitting in with the acute ward. I purposely ignored them. From what I knew, I was the only Black woman in the institution. *How the hell can any of them know my problems?* Haggerty had financial and family issues, which led him to a breakdown. Flannigan, she was a cutter. Banta had an eating disorder. I didn't equate myself with any of them. Even in my overmedicated state, I figured that I didn't belong. I sat in and used the time to reflect. This time a young woman was speaking. So, I stopped busying myself and listened to the child. I instantly felt a purpose other than myself. She reminded me of my niece, Poo. She was young, attractive, tall. It was her sad eyes that mostly reminded me of Poo. Don't get me wrong, my Poo was a spoiled, selfish, miserable child—but I loved her. I tried to fix myself by fixing her.

"I was raped as a child," the young woman confessed. "The man came into my bedroom, from the ground floor window where my family and I lived, and he raped me. Right there with the family asleep in the same room." She held her head down like it was her fault, and I wanted to scream, *it's not your fault,* but I wasn't speaking. No one could know my secret. Not yet.

"My parents were drug addicts," she continued, "and along with my younger siblings, we lived in the worst neighborhoods of the slum." For some reason, the young woman, Martita, made eye contact with me. Like regular people, we gazed at each other, not dodging one another's windows to the soul. "Growing up, we never had anything. I fought for everything and probably saw things I shouldn't have. So, I developed a way of separating from the bad things...you know...so that what was good in me could survive."

I sat on the edge of my seat, with a white-knuckle grip around the bible in my lap. I wanted to hug that child because I knew the desperation of living two separate lives. Folks call you crazy—but one of the separate lives has to be a fighter. That's all there is to it. One has to be a fighter for the sake of the other. The human brain works that way; it does whatever is necessary to survive. That's what Dr. Davis told me. I listened on as Martita continued while staring at me and picking the skin around her fingernails.

"Turning to drugs was my way of coping...I guess...it worked for a while, at least...but..." Her voice cracked, and she shook her head as she started to cry.

The majority of patients there were in the institution voluntarily. They admitted themselves to overcome depression, drugs, or some other issue. Some patients, like me, were detained by the Mental Health Act. We were there because we tried to commit suicide, tried to hurt others, saw and heard things that were not there. I was all the above, but this girl...it seemed like all she needed was hope, and instead, she tried to take her life.

"NO, HOPE! Shiiid!" I heard myself say out loud, about to give her the tough love I was raised on. Every mouth fell open and gawked my way as I continued. "Girl, you got more going for you than most of these folks up in here." Being that our eyes never parted, I stood and walked over, stooping in front of her. Once Nurse Lindt was over the initial shock, she smiled and busily began taking notes. "You got anyone who loves you out there?" I asked, motioning toward the window as the young girl rested a hand on my cheek.

"Yeh," she nodded, "I got a sister and a brother." She ran her fingers over the features of my face with the gentleness of a blind person constructing a visual.

"Well, damn it, that's your first defense—LOVE. You got love!" Hearing myself saying it, I realized it was the first defense for most of us sitting there. I abandoned my loved ones, and they in return left me...but things were finally turning around. Sal gave me hope. "Girl, you can beat this...and I'ma help you beat it," I continued, matter-of-factly, pointing a finger at her and nodding as I looked around at each astonished face. I had their attention. It made me feel like me again. Essential. Energetic. And impulsive. "You is a beautiful chile. What are you sitting up in here for? 'Cause life done dealt you a bad hand? Don't let that ol' devil try and steal your joy."

"who are you tryin' to help?" I heard an evil voice, laughing at me.

"SHHH! I'm speaking now!" I conveyed, then looked around, realizing I scolded the voices out loud. "That's right...I hear voices sometimes." I stood and started strutting around the group circle, about to put on a grand act. The only thing is, this time, it wasn't a show. "I know that those voices are me trying to talk myself out of living. You gotta rebuke 'em!" I turned around and pointed at Mrs. Rossellini, with the antique toaster on her lap. She heard her dead husband, Mr. Rossellini's voice. He liked his toast brown hard on both sides every morning. It was because she was lonely that she heard him. Mr. Rossellini was her everything, and now she was old and alone in a psych ward with only their beautiful memories to keep her company. "Sometimes, we just need help balancing it all out. I realize that now...and it's because of listening to this chile attempting to give up. Hell no, I say!" Martita was smiling, holding her head up high and following me with her eyes as I walked around the group circle. I was thinking about why I was the only Black woman in the ward. *Maybe I'm not, nor are my problems any different from anyone else sitting here. We all could use help. Some of us, mainly my people, are just too prideful and programmed to admit it.*

Despite my trauma with Nurse Mulligan and her crew, at that moment, I accepted that mental institutions were intended to help, not tear lives apart. People like Nurse Mulligan gave them bad names.

"While I'm here, I'ma help this baby." I pointed at Martita, "we gonna get better together." She started to cry. My speech was comforting—even if it was from a crazy old lady.

After that, I started showing up at the meetings—being present. My secret was out, but I didn't care. I needed to take back control of my life.

PART II
LUST

"The more we are filled with thoughts of lust the less we find true romantic love..."
- Douglas Horton

BLACK VELVET

"I was raped as a child too...by my father at that." I finally found the nerve to reveal. I had suppressed it for so long it didn't sound factual coming from my own mouth. However, it did feel easier sharing with someone I didn't know, with someone who didn't have any false hopes in me. Martita had become a regular tag-a-long, and it was good for the both of us. I didn't have to sit around waiting to talk to someone, mainly Sal, and she had someone to look after her. 'Pauvre ti bête', as The Grandmother would say, which meant poor little thing. Martita really did have a bad drug problem. Crack. The jury was still out on being able to come back from that one. I remembered hearing so many horrible things on the news. Then again, times had changed. It sounded like Martita had a strong support group on her side.

Growing up, Martita worked hard; she made sure her younger siblings had a proper education. They both went to college. While Martita, reminding me a lot of Lotti too (she was also a beast of burden), stayed behind and fell into the same mind trap as her addicted parents. Martita and I shared plenty of stories, but she mostly wanted to hear mine. My voice, she said, was soothing, and she didn't want to think about the past. I knew how that felt. I also knew that if anyone's life was going to help change someone's around—it would be mine.

"As far back as I can remember, Diddy touched me inappropriately —making me feel awkward and ashamed." I continued confessing to my new friend as we sat in the common area, overlooking the East Lawn. Indian Summer had come and gone, and the colors of fall were in full display. The nurses started putting out Halloween and Harvest decorations in their stations and bringing candy and chocolate snacks into work. My favorite was Mary Janes, not because of the obvious; its name, but because they reminded me of the sweets that The Grandmother used to make for us. Something nutty like Pralines, but gooier like taffy.

"I think The Grandmother knew what Diddy was doing to me. Maybe I should say—she had an idea, or one of her premonitions," I continued, popping another Mary Jane into my mouth. Martita was working on mini-Twix bars and collecting wrappers in front of her on the table. It was ridiculous, but what else was there to do? "The Grandmother didn't leave me home alone when Diddy was around...and when he drifted into town without her knowing, she always came rushing back when she found out. It would be too late... but she rushed home. He used to play with Lotti and me, giving us candy and toys. He always held me in his lap...and he always touched and rubbed on me differently from Lotti. I was the one who killed his beloved wife, so, there ya go."

"Huh?" Martita uttered, looking dumbfounded, with a mini-Twix bar hanging from her lip.

"Oh, yeah," I chuckled, with my fingers interlocking and propped up on my breast the way The Grandmother used to sit when she was telling a story. "My mama died giving birth to me." I clarified, trying to maneuver the candy stuck to the roof of my mouth with my tongue.

"Ahh, I see..." Martita responded, looking relieved to know that I wasn't a murderer. "...but that's not your fault, tho," she reasoned in a harsh Avenue C Spanish accent. I smiled because she reminded me of a lot of people.

"I know, but it felt like my fault...for a long time." I looked away from her and fixed my vision on the nurses in their stations. They were busily working with their charts in hand, collecting and inputting data into big bulky beige computers. Their movement soothed me. "Anyways," I continued. "Diddy was killed when I was fourteen, got shot for impregnating another man's wife...but not before impregnating me." I quickly glanced over at Martita and back at the nurses. Now that was a secret I was supposed to take to my grave. *But who the hell cares, now?*

"Ooh, no!" Martita removed the half-bitten candy bar from her mouth like she lost her appetite.

"Oh, yes," I answered, mentally counting everything blue in the room and trying to keep myself grounded. "I told you I got some stories, girl. Yet, I'm still here. That baby was aborted...and within the next four years, I was pregnant two more times and married once. Hmph! I was young and naive, I guess. A girl once told me that you wouldn't get pregnant if you peed right after having sex. Found out that wasn't true with my second pregnancy." Martita and I both laughed. "Fast-tailed is what The Grandmother called me. Whatever it was, those years were my freest. I didn't have any worries. Then, three things happened that changed all that...and my life forever. Life got real, real fast." I started counting purple things around the room. There wasn't much, so I went for green.

Feeling calmer, I continued, choosing to remember the people I loved over how I felt, "One, The Grandmother was murdered. Lynched." I counted down on my fingers with my vision stuck on the ugly green welcome mat at the elevator. "Two, I met the man of my dreams, Richard." I smiled. He could still make me do that. "Three...the man of my dreams was also the man of Lotti's dreams, and we stopped talking for a long time. We never regained our close relationship." I looked over at Martita and thought about her feeling sorry for herself and ruining her relationship with her siblings.

"When I tell you, I know how you feel, youngin'...I mean, I really know how you feel. Like I said, I'm still here...and being in here may not seem like a good reason for you to live. But everything is for a reason. Maybe had I gotten some help when I was as young as you—

life may have been different. I was too busy running after a man to stop and take care of myself. But God works in mysterious ways, doesn't He? Because here we are together, and I'm about to save your life. I know it!"

"I hope so. I do feel better listening to you," Martita answered, leaning back in her seat and reaching over to the empty table nearest us, using a fork from the plastic place setting to maneuver over a candy bowl.

"That's good. I'm glad to hear that." We ravished the fresh bowl of candy in search of our favorites. "Let me tell you about my old man," I said, throwing another Mary Jane into my mouth. They were like crack. Cheap and tacky.

I WAS ALWAYS PARTIAL TO YELLA' MEN WITH CURLY HAIR...AND HEAR ME when I say, Richard was one fine looking yella' fella! When we first met, he said he could see me and Lotti's butts from a mile away, knocking against each other as we walked up an old dirt road. I laughed because Diddy used to say, "Ah can spot a big butt woman comin' from de front. It's all in de hips!" He didn't lie about that. Lotti and I had hips and butt for days...and I knew how to work mine. It practically had a walk of its own. That's what caught Richard's attention that day.

Richard W. Owens casually drifted into town on a northern wind, hauling trouble and toxic pleasures. He was a saxophone player for a popular big band that toured throughout Baton Rouge and New Orleans. I remember like it was yesterday. It was a typical hot and hazy mid-summer afternoon. Lotti and I had started our own street hustle. We were selling The Grandmother's potions in town across the bridge—touting the cure to everything from leprosy to blindness. I was Lotti's guinea pig—acting like I needed healing from different ailments. Folks ate it up too! I had them eating from the palm of my hand.

Richard was visiting with an old friend between gigs. The men were driving back into town from a late breakfast in Davidsonville when they caught sight of Lotti and me. Unaware of being watched, we were giggling, bumping, and teasing one another as we walked along. I think we were heading for Mrs. Lemelle's house; her husband, Abe, needed a gout potion. Suddenly, a sleek black, well-polished classic 1946 Cadillac convertible coupe rolled slowly beside me. The man of my dreams leaned through the window and brushed his hand into mine.

"Stop the car, Joe," I heard him say before it came to a stop. "I've seen plenty of dolls throughout my days, sweetheart. But never none as beautiful as black velvet," Richard crooned in a deep, soothing, northern slang, staring me dead in the eyes as he kissed my hand. He acted like he wanted to lick the dark chocolate coating off. My heart stopped. I thought he was a movie star or something. I had never seen a man that fine in the sticks—and my Diddy was a fine man. "Delighted to make your acquaintance, Miss...?"

"What's dat, Mista? Black what? We ain't want none." Lotti jumped in front of me and pulled me away. "Come on, we gotta go! Pa will send out an army if we ain't home soon," she lied, yelling behind us.

When I tell you I was struck by Cupid's arrow—I was struck! It was pure admiration, plum love. Richard was the type of guy you dream about...tall, handsome, debonair with dimples deep enough to fall into.

The hell you say, I thought as Lotti tried to tug me away.

I stopped walking, pulled from her grasp, and went back to the car. I extended both my hands to Richard, and he gathered them into his. "Miss Mary Magdalene Auguste, sir," I purred, like a kitten, slowly and invitingly—gazing into the stranger's dark penetrating eyes. "Dis here is my sistah, Miss Charlotte Auguste," I nodded toward Lotti, who looked pissed, walking back toward the car. "Folks 'round here, call her Lotti, me Mags. You can call me Mary." I said it because it sounded more mature. That day I transformed from a free spirit into a temptress in the blink of an eye. Lotti looked at me like I had gone fool. But I felt taller, my eyes sultry. With every word, the arch in my back deepened, and my bosom grew. Richard smiled, a sly crooked smile, and a similar one crept along my face.

"Richard W. Owens," he responded, nodding in salutations. "How do you do, Miss Mary, Miss Charlotte? May I step out, ma'am?" His breath carried the refreshing scent of the peppermint candy he rolled in his mouth.

"Please do," I insisted, stepping back from the door, eating the mulatto brother up with my eyes. He was tall, lean, and fine.

"This is my old friend, Mr. Toussaint," he announced while stepping out of the car. "He's showing me around your lovely town."

"Howdy do, ladies. Howdy do?" Mr. Toussaint awkwardly snickered.

Richard extended his hand to Lotti. She stared at it for a second before choosing to give him a five. Respectfully, he smiled and nodded his head. In my spirit, I felt Lotti's heart skip a beat at the glimpse of his sparkling eyes and deep dimples; that alarmed me. He was my man. We met first.

"Ladies, I'm playing tonight at T-Ray's. I would love to be accompanied by dames as beautiful as you." Richard moved closer toward me...or did I move closer toward him? I don't remember, but he rubbed a finger across my cheek and whispered as he winked his eye, "Soft like velvet too."

I deeply exhaled and sang, "We'd love to."

"Ahhh, Mista—" Lotti began to interject, getting ready to jack up a good situation.

"Please, don't say no. It's not every day a fella entertains angels." He cupped Lotti's cheek, and she inhaled the same enticing aroma of mildly woodsy cologne that I smelled. It strayed from Richard's tailored chest and tickled our noses.

Lotti tilted her head and confined his hand between her cheek and shoulder.

"What time did you say?"

Let Lotti tell it, and I bet she would have said, that lo' life, so and so, stole her youth and robbed her of time, but I was there. Richard showed us backwoods spooks, a good ol' time. He took us to places in

Baton Rouge we ain't never been to—the Blue Room, the Brown Derby, the Green Parrot, Two Gat's Jazz Room, and the Apex Cocktail Lounge. He wined and dined us like a gentleman and worked the panties right off of us while doing so.

To be honest, even though my hemline was higher, Richard was more smitten with Lotti than me at first. I acted like the type of girl he could get any time he wanted, while Lotti, a virgin, kept her stuff sacred. She locked it up like Fort Knox while I was giving mine out like this here free candy. Shoot!

Martita and I burst into laughter at that one because we had torn that candy up. My story was getting good and better than the candy; we had stopped eating them.

Lotti made Richard work hard for her affection. He developed an interest in the things she admired and the places she liked to go. All the while, I played the third wheel. I was always invited to come along and double date with this band member or that one. There was Simon, Thomas, and Levi. It didn't matter who I was with. I wanted Richard. I cut in on him and Lotti's dances and stopped their romantic kisses and long walks under the moonlight. With me hanging around, it took Richard a few months to finally get Lotti alone to himself. He rented a motel room and sweet-talked that chastity belt from around my sister's buried treasure. Then, he turned his rusty behind self around for 'lagniappe' (something extra). He went back to the local pool hall, where he left me on a date to get what I was teasing him with all that time. Oh, yeah, my Richard was a greedy somebody. He coaxed me into the bathroom, and I tooted my fanny up in the air and let him have my jewels too. Richard was fine as wine...but greedy as hell.

I LOOKED UP AT MARTITA, FEELING MAYBE THAT WAS TOO MUCH. "Sorry, sweetie. The only way I know how to tell it is to tell it."

"I'm thirty-one years old, Mrs. Mary. You ain't sayin' nuttin' I ain't already did." She looked at me like—duh, and I chuckled.

"Well, I'm twice your age...so, we might stumble on some roads you ain't been down—youngin'!"

We laughed, saying touché and clicking our candies together.

RICHARD THOUGHT HE LEFT LOTTI SLEEPING AT THE HOTEL, BUT SHE followed him back to the pool hall. You see, Lotti had The Grandmother's premonitions. She watched as we danced. She saw me whining up on her man as he cupped my derriere in his hand. She saw him lead me into the restroom and was standing there when he came out. A good sister would have sided with her sibling when she saw the tears rolling down her face. A good sister would have helped to kick that tramp back to New York City. It was a flesh issue on my part. I had gotten a taste of that good stuff.

Richard made me feel, unlike any other guy I had ever been with. First off, he was not a boy; he was a grown man. He was thirty-five when we met, a good fifteen years older than Lotti and I. He was experienced. He didn't 'joog' his thing in me like he was taking something. He was a musician. He played his instrument—and with finesse. He wanted to hear the foreign sounds coming out of my mouth like acoustic melodies bouncing off the walls. It was my first orgasm. I tell you that. Felt so good I was ashamed and surprised at my own damn self. I hit notes I ain't know I had.

"You can sing, girl!" Richard told me afterward while taking a lengthy whiz. Sounds were like music to him. He was a creative genius. I sat up on the sink, flushed and embarrassed, fidgeting with the tail of my dress. "We leaving town tomorrow...heading for New Orleans." He shook his jimmy, zipped his fly, and turned facing me. "You should come audition for the band. We always looking for new talent!" He continued talking, checking himself out in the mirror and washing his hands while trying to convince me. But he already had me at—you should come.

Richard exited the bathroom first, giving me time to pull myself together. I saw Lotti through the crack in the door when he opened it, and she saw me too.

"You ain't gonna hold this little thing against me, now, are ya, darling?" I heard him say like the symphony we played was a backyard ho-down.

Lotti replied, "You tink you're a man? Well, you ain't! You a dawg! Dat's a tail hanging in between your legs, Mister!" She opened the door where I stood, hunched over with my eye to the keyhole. "And she ain't nothing but an ol' common bitch-dawg in heat!" she implied as I stood still hunched at the door in shock. "You both is fittin' for each other." Lotti turned and ran out of the pool hall. A woman's heart is like a vault, once you're in, you're in, but when you're out, you're out.

The music continued to play as my heart dropped into my stomach. My feet wanted to run after Lotti, but it was an impossible mending. Richard, who already had his hook in me, was left standing in the crowded room with one hand pressed against his slicked-back curls and the other on his hip. He looked as if he wanted to run after Lotti, too, but the room full of women requested his presence. He smirked and lit himself a cigarette, yelling, "Charlie! Set me up with another gin and tonic, will ya!" I ran over and planted a lingering kiss on his toxic lips, and he slid his hand down onto the shelf of my behind, then yanked me closer. The kiss reminded me of the naughty things we'd just done. Richard made me feel hot yet scared at the same time.

I whispered in his ear, "I'll see you tomorrow," then ran after Lotti. If either of us showed up at home without the other, we would both be in trouble. The Grandmother had already warned us, "Ah bet not find ya in doze juke joints ya diddy used to go to. Ah already done told ya, Mags, you cursed. De last place you need to be is in somebody's bar." She was right. I wouldn't know that for years to come, but she was right, and I've always been on the wrong side of right.

TOO MUCH, TOO LITTLE, TOO LATE

Lotti liked to take my head off when I caught up with her—calling me everything but a child of God. Talking about, "How could you?" and "We're supposed to be sisters." I couldn't make myself apologize. Although I did feel sorry for her, I wasn't sorry for being with Richard. My feelings for him were never a secret. The tension between Lotti and me grew from the moment we met him. I was acting funny toward her, and she was acting funny toward me. We both claimed to love him, and we both did in our own ways. As far as I know, Richard was the first and only man Lotti ever loved. That's just how stubborn she was...just like her grandmother. I don't even think our fighting was about him; it was more about her being made out to be a fool. If I could take it back now, I would. It wasn't worth the time we lost with each other, but at that moment, we were set on being mean and ornery.

Lotti marched the entire way home, and I ran to keep up with her. It was approximately an hour's walk across town, over the bridge, through the woods, and down an obscure clay road leading into the swamp area where the new shack we lived in was hidden. I was daydreaming, as usual, holding my water and trying to keep up because I was scared of the dark all at the same time when I bumped right into Lotti.

"You smell dat?" she asked, sniffing around. It was just about daybreak. We were supposedly spending the night at a pretend friend's house and hadn't made up any excuses for being home so early. I just knew Lotti was fixing to tell everything and make me out to be the bad guy. But her nose caught wind of smoke, and she took off like lightning. I ran behind her, smelling it myself. When we reached the house, we paused in disbelief. The police and fire department were there.

"Mama!" Lotti screeched, running to the place where our house once stood. It was burnt to the ground. All I could do was make water. I stood right there, out in the open, and peed myself.

The authorities explained that our closest neighbors reported smoke. They assured us that no bodies were found before proceeding to question our whereabouts. No one knew where The Grandmother had gone.

Her body was reported later that evening, forty miles out from our small town. She had been lynched—beaten then hung from a tree. Her body, wrapped in burlap, laid a few feet away from the site. The remains of a soot-covered wooden cross accompanied her like a blazing symbol of the assailant's faith.

"LET'S STOP FOR A MINUTE," I EXPRESSED TO MARTITA, WHO WAS CRYING as hard as I was. Her tears incited me to cry more. I must have grabbed at least twenty napkins from the center of the table, wiping my eyes and runny nose.

Martita rushed over and sat near me, practically in my lap, wrapping both of her arms around me. We sat in silence for a few moments, looking out of the picture window. The wind was picking up and whisking colorful swirling leaves around the lawn like tumbleweed.

"Give me some of 'em napkins..." Martita insisted, taking a few from my hand when she was done using my shoulder. "Damn...you took all of 'em!" she said, sorting through the used ones. We laughed and cried, enjoying the warmth of each other's company.

Martita had fallen in love with my family, like characters from a favorite movie. The Grandmother was no saint, but even she didn't deserve such a cruel death. I guess that's why I didn't make a fuss about being locked away all those years. I kind of figured it was my lot. Life was rough for colored folks back when I was growing up, especially in the southern states. Martita missed that era, but she knew all too well about getting the short end of the stick. She was half Mexican, half Cuban. A beautiful combination of both ethnicities. She said she was tall and olive-complexioned like her Cuban father and had straight deep black hair like her mother—which she kept shoulder-length with an annoying bang that hid her face. She hated her looks and beat herself up as most women do. I found her very attractive.

"Did they ever find out who did that to The Grandmother?" She asked, laying her head back on my shoulder. I drew her nearer and slightly turned, twisting my lips to kiss her forehead.

"Yeah, Lotti and I had a good idea."

THE GRANDMOTHER DIDN'T HAVE MANY FRIENDS. SHE KEPT IN TOUCH with Mama's elder sister, Tante Bae, and she sometimes frequented Madame Queen—but she didn't like her too much. She said she was a hateful busy woman. The Grandmother visited her occasionally when she couldn't sort out her visions. Madame Queen was a voodoo priestess of darkness. She practiced black magic, and The Grandmother didn't want anything to do with that. She said she had enough bad luck on her own. That didn't stop Lotti from hunting Madame Queen down that night. You see, it's safe to say that we grew up steeped in voodoo traditions. For Lotti, it made sense to seek revenge. Blood for blood.

News spreads fast in a small town. Richard found out about The Grandmother before he left town and got a ride from his old friend Mr. Toussaint to come out and check on us. I knew he cared because he missed his bus ride with the band to New Orleans. He and Mr. Toussaint drove us out to where The Grandmother was found. They sat laughing and talking in the front of the car while Lotti and I sat in the back on either side, pouting, with our arms folded and legs crossed, mad at each other. Richard's appearance made us remember that we were supposed to be angry. As we got closer to the site, we both could feel The Grandmother's spirit calling. We hurried up and grabbed each other in an embrace. The Grandmother would have said, "Y'all is all ya got."

The area was taped off, her body had been removed. Lotti and I clung to one another, attempting to piece the mystery together. Ten minutes into our mourning, we noticed an older Black man nearby. He was gazing at the oak tree but didn't make a sound.

"Can we help you?" Lotti asked, pushing me behind her.

He turned and stated, "Ah seen what done happened to ya maw-maw." He went on to tell us about a parked pickup truck and the three men in white sheets; he even overheard their names. They were in the process of moving The Grandmother's body when he stepped on a branch, alerting them to his presence. They chased after him. The older man, familiar with the area, lost them by hiding in an aban-doned, camouflaged duck blind. "Dey searched for me near 'bout an hour. Ah sat o'va in dat blind praying and de Lord heard me. A police car drove by. Dey spoke. Den er'rybody went dere separate ways. Ah waited a while longer den hot-footed back home. Ah wasn't fixin' to call de police, den ah figured ya maw-maw done been through enough. So, ah called, but ah ain't say who ah was tho. No, ma'am."

Lotti and I knew the men. They frequently harassed The Grand-mother about moving away from their small God-fearing town, and The Grandmother adamantly refused.

RICHARD PUT ME UP IN A MOTEL THAT NIGHT, THEN LEFT TO MAKE HIS gig in New Orleans. Lotti refused to take anything from him. She used money from her savings that she salvaged from a lockbox hidden under a loose floorboard at the house to pay for her lodging. We had agreed to go our separate ways. Lotti was heading for Gonzales to resume hustling The Grandmother's potions and elixirs while I was determined to audition for Richard's band. He left an open bus ticket to New Orleans and was expecting me in a day or so. That night, while I attempted to sleep alone for the first time, Lotti, still set on avenging The Grandmother's death, went and found Madame Queen. I don't know what happened out there in the swamp, but all three men were found dead over the next three days.

I HAD TO STOP MY STORY BECAUSE MARTITA WAS SLACK JAWED, BANGING the table about to snatch my arm from its socket, shaking it in excitement.

"Mhmm." I nodded with a dimpled grin. "If I'm lying, grits ain't grocery."

ON THE FIRST DAY, I STARTED COUNTING THEM DOWN. KLAN LEADER and local pastor, Reverend White, or Sweaty Pig, as The Grandmother called him, was found dead in his home. He choked to death on a bone while eating supper. Deacon Breaux, the Reverend's flunky, ran his car off of the road on day two. He hit a tree and died upon impact. On night three, Walter Hebert, an ex-con known to like his liquor and women, was called in dead by a prostitute. Heart attack.

Now, I'm not saying I believe in voodoo cause I ain't never agreed with it; but if you think on something well enough, you can 'will' that thing into existence. Lotti was stubborn and angry enough to do that. We parted ways, promising to send a telegram to the local post office when we each reached our destinations safely. After that, we didn't speak or see one another for five years.

MISS MARY MAGS

"**W**hat men say and what they do are two different things. Just because he wants to make love doesn't mean he loves you." I warned Martita, teaching her lessons I'd learned the hard way. It had been a few days later, and we were participating in crafts during a relaxation session. It was evident to us that we were each other's tranquility. Martita wasn't tired of my stories yet, and I wasn't done telling them. It's funny; I often wonder if memories are real...or are they stories we tell ourselves. *Did those people feel the way I felt? Did they see things the way I did?* My loved ones were gone. Now, I was telling their stories, and I hoped I wasn't making myself more than I was.

"Richard was true to his promise. He got me an audition with his band, and it went better than we both imagined." I continued reflecting, tracing my hand onto black craft paper. We were making hand turkeys. The next holiday was Thanksgiving. "Anyway, I was hoping to join Richard's band, get married, and have babies with him, in that order. He was thinking more like, she sings, we need a singer...and I can get a little 'sumpin, sumpin' on the side whenever I want. Why buy the cow when you can get the milk for free, is what The Grandmother used to say."

"Punk-azz," Martita mumbled, sucking her teeth, already gluing feathers onto her brown hand turkey.

"What did you say?" I heard her but was stunned. I needed to hear it again. There was a time when I would have gone off on anyone talking about my man.

"I said...Richard was a punk-azz!" She reiterated, rolling her neck like she meant it.

I started laughing. Probably harder than I should have. Tears and everything. Hearing Martita say that humored me. Richard was indeed obnoxious at times. I wanted to shoot him in the head on many occasions.

"Anything you ladies wanna to share with the group?" The art teacher asked sarcastically. Martita waved her hands no, laughing as hard as I was.

WHEN I GOT OFF THE BUS IN NEW ORLEANS, I WENT STRAIGHT TO THE Claude Motel as Richard instructed. The city was just as I remembered. Once, when Lotti and I were younger, Diddy took us to Mardi Gras. The Grandmother didn't do stuff like that; she barely left 'The Bottom' (southern Baton Rouge). Richard left a message with the desk clerk saying he'd be at practice at the Star Gaze in Tremé until four o'clock. The desk clerk said it was about a five-minute walk. After checking me into Richard's room, he drew a map of how to get there. When I reached the club, it was a quarter after two. I used a little time to freshen up. All of my belongings burned in the fire. The only formal dress I had was the one I was wearing that night. Lotti surprised me and bought me a casual day dress with five dollars in the pocket, a nightgown, and a toothbrush. She left them all lying at the door to my room before she left. I would never forget my sister and swore to pay back her kindness, somehow. Lotti was a giver, but she didn't receive gifts well... unless it was money.

When I walked into the Star Gaze, the guys were playing their signature tune. A little melody Richard composed. He arranged a lot of their music. I straightened myself, hoping my formal attire didn't reek of smoke, and walked stiffly through the club, praying my rear wasn't doing its own thing as usual. There were a few white men scattered around, making me nervous as they quietly conversed, staring. The click of my heels ricocheted off the hard floors throughout the room, distracting the bandleader. When I reached the stage, he stopped the music, smiled, and took my hand.

"Are you the young lady auditioning for us today...umm, Miss Auguste?"

"Yes, sir—."

"Yeah, Slick..." Richard interrupted, stepping out of the line-up. He was a tenor and played front and center. "This is Miss Mary Mags... she can really blow. Get ready, 'cause you ain't ready." He teased, amping everyone up as he jumped off the stage, polishing his ax with the hand towel around his neck. "You ready, baby?" he whispered in my ear, greeting me with a soft kiss on the cheekbone. I nodded, inhaling his confidence. "Don't make no fool of me. I ain't never wrong about music."

"Well, alright!" Slick shouted, slapping his hands and taking a seat. "Sounds like we got us a new singer, guys." The band whooped and followed Slick in getting comfortable. Everyone called him Slick because his hair was conked and slicked back with pomade real nice. Slick was about as yella' as Richard. He was the front man, the bandleader; he had to be yella' for appearances. He wasn't as handsome as Richard, though. Slick wore dark shadows beneath his eyes from lack of sleep. He was short, a little heavy around the waist, and smiled too much for my taste.

Richard led me up some stairs leading to the stage and planted me dead center. Standing above my petite frame, he positioned his sax and licked his lips like Diddy used to do when he was preparing to blow his harmonica. It threw me off for a second. All I could see was Diddy.

"You hear me...Mary?" Richard repeated, situating his back to the band. "You ain't getting nervous, are you?" He pressed his hand against the small of my back, drawing me in. "I'ma give you an intro...like this," he blew a little tune, "then you sing." I started to interject. The scattered white men were watching.

I was a backwoods spook, as the kids used to tease, standing on somebody's stage about to sing. I had never sung out loud in my life. Maybe when I danced and twirled with Lotti; when we were free, roaming through the bayou. Maybe I hummed to Diddy's harmonica when he issued, "Dance for Diddy, Blackbird." But who was I, as black as I was, to be standing on somebody's stage thinking I was gonna sing?

"Give 'em a taste of what it feels like to be in between your thighs, suguh," Richard whispered, crooning in my ear as his hand slid down my hip. My heart raced, and my breathing changed. "Give 'em a lil' piece of heaven, Miss Mary Mags." Then he blew his sax.

"Ooo-wee!" I slammed the table, remembering how Richard made me feel. I could still feel the heat on my flesh. "He was speaking my language." Martita had stopped decorating her turkey and was mesmerized. That punk-azz was working on her too.

"Shhh, ladies. Let's watch our tone." The teacher insisted.

"I'm sorry." I made sure to apologize. The nurses were entering notes into their charts. "I'm sorry," I repeated, snickering with Martita. We both wanted to get the heck up out of there; we didn't need any bad reports.

Anyway, remembering how the fat woman sang at the revival all those years ago. I whined my waist in that smoky-smelling dress, planted my feet into the stage, claiming it as mine, then opened my mouth. I surprised myself when a deep savory voice that sent shivers up my spine came out. Giving my audience the Sunday morning Jesus they needed and the Saturday night devil they longed for, I sang to everything that I had lost.

"MY PRAYER, IS-RAPTURED-IN-BLUUUE," I STOOD, SINGING OUT LOUD into a glue stick that Eddie the perv was fixing to eat. Martita slid her chair back and crossed her arms, readying for a show. "In-a-world-far-awaay, and your lips are close to minnne." I continued to the end and received a standing ovation from the floor. Nurses included. "Thank you, thank you very much. That was The Ink Spots, 1939." I took a bow.

I WAS AN INSTANT SUCCESS. WHEN I WAS ON STAGE, FOLKS SAW something different than what I saw when I looked into the mirror. What they actually got was a dark-skinned, exotic-looking, curvy woman who could sing and dance. They loved me. "Miss Mary Mags, Miss Mary Mags!" I became what Richard named me. I was the band's lead singer and eventually their showgirl too. Richard didn't see that one coming, but I could dance better than I could sing. I've always been one to pick up on things quickly. The years of hustling The Grandmother's potions and capturing attention prepared me for the spotlight. I quickly gained recognition, headlining a few shows, and even gaining the attention of a larger New York City band. They specifically asked for me to accompany them on a live album. So, if you ever hear "Raindrops" by the Davey Willis band, that's me singing the chorus.

Miss Mary Mags swung her hips, whined her waist, and teased her way into the hearts of longing men and the envy of women. Richard continued to accompany me everywhere, only because I was the head-liner. I have no doubt that he would have sent this swamp girl packing if I didn't make it. Because I did, he introduced me to a world different from the one I knew, and I instantly became its lover.

TRAMP

I f I had to drop a beat behind the next five years of my life, it would be titled "Lusty Trails." Richard and I, young and horny, blazed a trail, dancing and jiving our way through that time, high on life. If there was trouble, we were likely to find it—and laugh in its face. We had a good ol' time. The only problem was, I had to share the good times with all his women. My charming ways allotted me the possession of all I desired except him. I loved Richard, but Richard loved all women. He kept me around because I was making money, and men were screaming my name. He would have been a fool to let me go.

I was the only woman amongst a motley crew of scoundrels. Each band member of The Slick Miller Quartet, which wasn't a quartet at all, was in pursuit of his big break. They would lie, cheat, and steal to make it. We grew close, despite their tarnished reputations. I especially admired the rhythm section. Simon, Thomas, Levi, and Slick were thick as thieves. Thank goodness I never slept with any of them when Richard had his boys distract me while he was playing games back in Baton Rouge pursuing Lotti. Simon, we called him Fatso, was my favorite; he was like the brother I never had. He wasn't actually heavy; he was super thin, so they called him Fatso, and boy, did he have an appetite. Fatso played the drums. He could pick up a beat and lay that thing down like nobody's business. You want a juke jumpin'—let Fatso play. All of the guys could have had individual careers; instead, they were friends looking for their big break together.

Then there was Thomas the Tomcat; what can I say about this brother that his name doesn't already imply. He was a sly somebody. Tomcat was married with children. He was the only one in the band with a wife; the kids' part is another story. I think they all had children spread around. Tomcat was like an encyclopedia. Whenever you needed to know something, he was the man. The reason being is that he didn't believe anything he heard until he researched it himself. Tomcat was a fatso, but he was a big barrel-chested man, and the women loved him. He played the bass guitar. He never really broke a sweat just played it cool with shades on sitting in the corner on a stool. When it was his time to play—he shined. Then again, the bass player is always the coolest.

Levi, never seen without his black Pork Pie hat with the goose feather tucked in on the side, was the pianist. He was also the band's secretary and accountant. He was a quiet and painfully shy man, but he jumped on dem keys—tickling the ivory. Watching Levi play was like watching a young Chuck Berry. He was animated and electric. Levi gave good, sound advice. He was the only one who flat-out told me to leave Richard.

Slick...well, Slick was slick. He was silver-tongued and debonair. Every gig we got was because Slick talked his way into the establishment. He managed the band and kept us booked year-round. He and Richard founded the quartet when it really was a quartet. They ran the streets of New York City together as teenagers, playing the jazz circuit. Slick was older than Richard, so the band was named after him. He was also a vocalist, and a multi-instrumentalist, playing the piano, guitar, and sax. He and Tomcat sang backup vocals for me sometimes. Doo-wop, doo-wop. Slick was okay. If it wasn't for him and Richard's relationship, I probably wouldn't have had anything to do with him. One, he slept with his eyes open, and I've always been leery of folks who do that. Two, he was a tramp...and he encouraged

Richard to be a tramp as well. All the men loved women, some more than the others, but it was the way that Slick treated women that bothered me. He gassed them up, talking about the lion roaring in his pocket, then treated them pretty much like underwear. Changed them every day. And there was the freaky stuff that he was into. I could imagine all the things they did before I came along, which is the point I'm getting to. I'll love Richard always, but I lost my respect for him within those first five years.

The Slick Miller Quartet was touring throughout the United States. I had cut a song on a Billboard chart-climbing album, so we were headliners. Besides New Orleans and Baton Rouge, as the band was accustomed to, we toured other major cities and stayed in fabulous hotels. As long as we took the servant's elevators, we got royal treatment. This one particular time in New York City, we played the Savoy Ballroom, which was a big deal. I didn't like New York City at first, and it was because of Richard and Slick. They knew too much about the ends and outs of the city and did just about everything there. Too many empty nights, I found myself sitting up waiting for Richard to return to the hotel when we performed there. Back then, the clubs weren't like they are now; there were no VIP sections, everyone was combined. Jazz brought out the groovy people. There was a lot of interracial mingling. The pimps and the hustlers socialized, and the entertainers sat, drank, and danced with the fans. New York City was especially a melting pot. When the white women blatantly eyed my man, it hit me differently. I hadn't heard any voices in years, but that night they told me, *"richard is with a white woman, and they're in this hotel."* Sometimes the voices pretended we were friends and helped me out only to hurt me in the end.

I hurried and got up, slipping into a black silk kimono. I had planned a memorable evening and was smelling and looking good all by my damn self. I ran through the hotel hallway, listening to the doors. When I remembered what room Slick was in—422, I pressed the elevator going up.

Before I got there, I could hear laughter. It was one big ol' party, and I wasn't invited. I knocked, "Room service," I said, standing to the side. Someone opened the door, and I forced my way in, marching through the suite to the bedroom. Richard was there with Slick and not one but three white women. Startled, I stepped out, closing the door to catch my composure and breath. That's when I heard those menacing voices again.

"open the door and go back. show them who you are."

I looked back at the person who let me in; it was Tomcat, barely dressed, holding in his stomach, ashamed. "Come here," I motioned him over as though I was his mother, and he shuffled his big ass across the floor, looking everywhere but at me. "So, you all up in here being nasty-nasty, huh," I said, pulling his ear then reopening the bedroom door. They were all getting dressed and scrambling for their clothes. To their surprise, I let my silk kimono robe slide off my glistening dark body and said, "Where ya going? De party just started." I popped Tomcat on his rump as hard as I could, then stepped into hell, throwing back someone's drink from the bureau table. I laughed and moved as slinky as the naked white women crawling into the king-size bed. Richard sat in a high-back chair, watching and waiting for me to snap. He lit a stogie. Slick grinned, with his freaky self, exposing a mirror that was lined with coke.

Now, I've done some wretched things in the past, but none like that. They all were calling my name by morning light, and I was satisfied with proving myself as indispensable. I quietly slid back into my expensive silk kimono robe, picking up Richard's jacket off the floor and draping it across my shoulders. I walked out as they slept peacefully, dreaming of the blackbird.

"WHAT!" MARTITA WAS IN COMPLETE SHOCK. THAT WAS THE QUIETEST I had ever seen her.

"If I'm lying, I'm flying," I responded.

"You...are like my freaking hero right now," she expressed, enunciating every word with hand and head motions. "What! I can't believe it."

We were the only ones left in the cafeteria after dinner.

"Yeah, I did it, but I'm not proud of it." I started wiping crumbs off the table into a napkin—helping to tidy up. "At that time in my life, it was all about how things made me feel. Mentally, that didn't feel right. It felt like I was doing something I really didn't care to do just to keep Richard. To make him want me. That didn't feel good, and it shifted my feelings toward him. I still wanted him. I wanted to be confirmed by him, he was a fine-looking brother, but he was no longer the air that I breathed. I don't know how to explain, but we lost something and never regained it."

AFTER THAT, WE TRAVELED TO MEMPHIS, AND NOBODY, AND I MEAN nobody, mentioned what happened in New York City. Richard was all up on me, following me around, opening doors, and treating me like royalty. Every time he pegged me to be one way, I proved to be another. I finally had his nose open, but his longing for other women was still there, and now he expected me to be involved with that crap. He said I was his queen, but he treated me like a damn fool.

I remember singing on stage that night in Memphis, watching as Richard flirted with a group of women in the audience. Every night, I did this thing where I zeroed in on one guy and sang to him in all my acts. That usually caused a big commotion with the fans. This time, I purposely poured my heart out, tearfully singing "Sincerely" by The Moonglows, directly to Richard as the crowd cheered. He was uncomfortable and knew I was leaving him. All I could see were red dirt roads, 'fais-do-dos', and gumbo dinners cooked by saggy armed, happy, Black women with names like Pearl. I wanted Baton Rouge. I wanted to go home and 'pass a good time'. It's where ah know, ya know?

PART III
ENTITLEMENT

"For success, attitude is equally important as ability." – Walter Scott

COUNTRY FRIED CHICKEN

I had been secretly worrying that I might have scared Sal off, even though he called a few times to check in on me. He also left his number. I could have called him anytime I wanted, but I was old-fashioned about calling men's houses. I knew Sal was working and would visit when he could, but I missed my link to family and the outside world. In the meantime, he had flowers delivered, and them sumbitches confiscated them. It was a beautiful, thoughtful arrangement of Louisiana natives—Swamp azaleas, Phlox, Iris, and Spicebush. The receiving orderly, Dino, said flowers were not allowed. I started to go off on him; he had it coming anyway. What really pissed me off is how he coyly smiled while writing notes down on his chart. I wanted to snatch it from him and bash his head in. Martita had to calm me down. I wasn't acting crazy. I was mad, you messin' with my baby's flowers, angry.

"You're doing so good!" Martita yelled, grabbing me by my arms. I was mad as hell. "Don't let them get to you. It's in the rule book...no flowers or electrical devices. Sal didn't know." She turned my face toward her. "Look at me," she said more calmly. "You promised to be here for me...this is nothing." She was right, and I was calming down. "Look, see, Nurse Lindt, put them where you can see them." I guess she thought that would make me feel better, but I would rather them thrown away than be tortured to look and not touch or smell. My nose flared in anger. I wanted to hit someone. Thank goodness, this time, my better judgment told me otherwise, and I listened. There was a time where I would have torn that joint apart.

I was in a funk for the rest of the day until Nurse Lindt walked over with a Kentucky Fried Chicken bag in hand.

"Hi, ladies," she said, stooping to me and Martita's level. We were sitting at the table playing cards. "I'm really sorry about what happened this morning. If it were up to me, Mrs. Owens, you would have those flowers." She sat the aromatic bag on the table and took my hand, slipping me a sprig of the Spicebush. "I called your grandson and explained our rules. He apologized and—"

"Pfft!" I cut her off, about to get mad again. *Sal didn't have to apologize to anyone.*

"I know...I know." She quickly patted and soothed my hand. "He had this dinner delivered for you and Martita." Martita grabbed and opened the bag before Nurse Lindt could get her sentence out well. She had been salivating since the food was placed on the table. It did smell good, but the sprig of Spicebush I had clenched to my nose smelled better. It smelled like memories from my past. The more you crushed the leaves, the stronger the aroma of Allspice.

"Thank you," I forced myself to say, forgetting my complaints and changing my expression to a smile. "I appreciate that."

"No, problem." Nurse Lindt winked and stood. "Us Marys have to stick together." I took notice of her name tag. M. Lindt. "Enjoy your dinner," she patted my arm, and this time I let her. "It smells delicious."

"You want a piece?" I offered, about to share my three-piece, dark meat meal box. Martita was already devouring hers.

"No, no... please enjoy. I know it's a change from the cafeteria food." She smiled and walked away before I could debate the issue. I bit into the juicy hot, flavorful leg that I would have given her, then smelled the flower in my hand again.

Yup, I miss home. Baton Rouge.

LOVE POTION NO.9

Eventually, I grew tired of Richard's unfaithfulness and reached out to Lotti for help. She knew all The Grandmother's tricks and remedies. There had to be one to force Richard into loving me. Lotti was doing domestic work in Gonzales, Louisiana, where she was a live-in nanny on a plantation. That's where I met her and Richard's five-year-old daughter, Puah Marie Auguste.

Over the years, Lotti and I kept in touch via mail. Just to check in with one another. I sent her postcards from the many cities and places I sang in, along with a piece of money, as The Grandmother used to say. Lotti never mentioned in her short, impersonal letters sent directly to the band's post office box in Tremé that she and Richard had a baby together.

 I'm doing fine. I'm a nanny for these three bad-ass kids here at the Fontaine Plantation. I still sells The Grandmother's potions, and I does terminations, healing, and spiritual advice once a week on my day off.
Charlotte

That's all I knew about Lotti, and it broke my heart. I guess I broke hers too, but even though I did, she never mentioned nor rubbed in my face the fact that she gave Richard the one thing I couldn't, a baby. Trust me, I tried to have one, especially when Richard wasn't paying me any attention. Like most naive young girls, I thought having a baby would change things. Unfortunately, I never conceived with him. My two abortions and the stillbirth were my only chances of becoming a mother. Then, just like that, I found out my big sister had one for me.

I GLANCED OVER AT MARTITA. SHE WAS THOROUGHLY ENJOYING MY story, along with the Colonel's chocolate Little Bucket Parfait. "You fixin' to be sick," I warned, sliding my strawberry one her way. I wasn't a big dessert eater anymore. When I started drinking heavily, I lost the taste for that.

Martita paused and grumbled, "Thanks." She looked at me like —*well, what happened next—finish the story.*

"I'm getting to it!"

LOTTI WAS STILL ACTING BITTER OVER WHAT HAPPENED BETWEEN US with Richard; she didn't give me any leeway. I was going to pay for that. When Lotti was mad, she was mad. She'd been that way since childhood. She could hold a grudge for years, never talking about it, just treating you differently. The Grandmother used to say, "It's a long road dat never turns." Lotti had to get off sooner or later. However, the last time she detoured from her usual, she stole my Richard, and we were never the same. Yet, Lotti found unexpected pleasure assisting me with fixing him. I could only pray that she wasn't fixing the both of us.

Getting straight to business, she danced and chanted back in the woods near The Fontaine's plantation, calling on the spirits of the ancestors like The Grandmother used to do. I didn't believe in voodoo growing up, and I can't say I believed in it then. I was desperate, and desperate times called for desperate measures. That would become my calling card—Miss Desperate Measures.

After a few days, one of The Grandmother's mojos was concocted to capture Richard's heart. Lotti handed it to me in a small brown tinted bottle with a cork top.

"Only one drop is needed," she cautioned with a sly smile on her face. She even looked like The Grandmother. "A drop fuh him, and a drop fuh you—"

"But ah—" I tried to interrupt. I didn't want to take any potions from Lotti.

"De partaker will seek its host. He'll feel your energy. And whenever de potion wears off, give him another drop. O'va time, you'll become his destiny. He'll always love you, and you'll love what your heart desires."

At that, I slyly smiled too. *His destiny*, I thought, longing to be loved by Richard.

The remainder of our visit was short, polite, and centered around the beautiful caramel-colored five-year-old that Lotti shared with my man. Poo was the prettiest red baby I have ever seen. I pretended she was mine and Richard's together, spoiling her rotten. It was a long time before I told Richard about her. Somehow keeping Poo a secret made her mine and his. Telling him took that feeling away and made him into a deadbeat father—like Diddy. Richard didn't have any interest in meeting Poo. Instead, he confessed about a son in California he only met once. I welcomed Poo from the beginning. Yeah, it was hard at first, but I had a niece, and my love for both Lotti and Richard exceeded all the useless drama. Even though Lotti carried a grudge, she and I never discussed Richard or how I stole him from her. I was glad about that. I don't have time for folks who visit my past more than I do. We spent the rest of that week together, drunk and reminiscing on the good times.

WE'RE IN THIS LOVE TOGETHER

I caught up with the band back in Tremé to finish out the year.
Our touring season was coming to an end, and the fellas were
anxious to see their families for the holidays. Richard, Slick, and
I usually followed Tomcat home to celebrate with his large, boisterous
family back in Georgia. We always showed up with armloads of gifts
for the kids and fresh beignets and bottles of booze for the adults.
Tomcat's wife, Trudy, a pleasant, tolerable woman, was an excellent
cook and hostess. The weary Victorian they lived in wasn't the neat-
est; there were too many kids for that, but the southern hospitality
was unequivocally bar none to any luxury hotel. I would miss them
that year because Richard and I stayed back in Tremé. He knew I was
growing tired of the road and living out of suitcases. Mainly, I grew
tired of competing with his appetite for the opposite sex.

We rented a small, fully decorated apartment overlooking Congo
Square on North Rampart Street. We shacked up like lovers do—
playing house. I was trying to give Richard a chance to naturally show
me that he loved me. So, I showed him that I knew how to keep a
man. I cooked large Creole meals, cleaned the house, and wore his
butt out every time he looked sideways. It worked for a minute. I kept

him so tired, he couldn't run the streets. After all my efforts, Richard was looking to get his itch scratched by someone else by the third day.

"You wanna share dis here cold drink?" I asked, pulling out a Coke and my brown tinted bottle with the cork top.

"I'd rather my cold beer from the back of the fridge," he answered, sitting on the edge of the sofa. He was partly listening to a game on the radio and vigorously polishing his best shoes, readying himself to hit the town.

I poured myself half a glass. *Now, Lotti knows I'm too greedy for a drop of anything.* That was the problem; Richard suited my relentless greed. His flawless attractiveness was fit for the big screen. He had an outgoing character that drew crowds. His musical talent was gifted from God, and most of all—he could work that thang. There's slang for that—but I'm not gonna get into it. Let's just say...I've slept with other men, and Richard was reigning king. I didn't want to risk giving that up, so I poured half the love potion in his beer bottle and the rest into my glass. *Why wait around for someone to fall out of love with you when you're their destiny?* We tapped our drinks, clicking the glass together, and guzzled them down.

"Being in love is full of suffering!" I slurred, plopping down next to Richard and making him spill the end of his beer on his clean white tee. I felt light-headed and woozy.

"Say that again, sugah," he slurred back. His eyes were slanted, and his face was all up in mine. "Look at them dancing eyes you got, gal. You sure are a pretty woman." He could talk sweet like that, you know.

"What you want me to say, Lovah?" I swung my heavy feeling legs across his lap and fell back into the sofa cushions—giggling.

"Hell! Say anything." He laid on my chest, playing with my bottom lip. "I like to see ya mouth make words." He laughed. "Your tongue does this cute little thing with the s's. Anything you say sounds pretty." We attempted to kiss, but our lips were numb. "Why don't you haul off and love me," Richard issued, referring to an old Bull 'Moose' Jackson song. I sat up, looking at him wide-eyed, realizing something was happening. Something other than the drool rolling from the corner of my mouth. "Mary Magdalene Auguste, I need you. If you don't give me ya sweet lovin', I'm likely to die."

My heart melted because the negro was fine, but my mouth said, "Love you! You don't amount to a hill of beans. Tell me de truth about how ya feel about me and shame de devil."

"Gawdamn, Mary!" He slammed the coffee table and rattled our drinks. "I'm tryin', to be honest. My nose is wide open for ya, can't you tell? I love you." He sat up, staring me straight in the eyes. I returned his gaze. He looked sincere, even though he was intoxicated on love potion number nine.

My heart burst with joy but at the same time, I felt like I wanted more. I wanted more than an 'I love you.' I wanted more than Richard's good looks, personality, and special talents. I wanted it all; I was Miss Mary Mags, the gifted dancer and singer he lived off. I was headlining; folks loved me. They screamed my name. I tell ya the truth, the ego is a hell of a drug. I opened my legs and made Richard show me how much he cared. He didn't go out that night. What happened was—we got married.

"So, YOUR SISTER CURSED YOU?" MARTITA INTERRUPTED.

"What you mean?"

"Lotti said, you'll love whatever your heart desires. When Richard finally told you he loved you, you didn't say it back." I looked at Martita dumbfounded. I had never seen it that way. Sometimes the ears test words, and they hear what they want. Lotti knew precisely what I loved the most; she loved it too. Over the next course of years, everything I did was for the love of money, power, and respect.

"Then again," I finally answered, considering everything, because the potion did taste like corn liquor and flat coke. "Like I said once before when you really want something—you can WILL that thing into existence. I know because things got really turned around after that."

FOR THE NEXT FIVE YEARS, RICHARD AND I WERE HAPPY. HE TREATED ME with the love and affection I longed for, but he still had roaming eyes. He said it was because he appreciated women's beauty, but his whole heart was devoted to me. Whether he liked it or not. My heart, on the other hand, grew cold. I wasn't a bayou lassie anymore. I was a grown woman who knew what she wanted. When I wasn't singing, I sat around with my legs crossed, sipping on scotch and ice, smoking cigarettes, and being catered to. I was good at making money and spending money. Richard and Lotti were the ones who saved. Lotti wanted a house, and Richard wanted his own jazz club. They'd starve to death before they spent any of their savings. I indulged in the luxury of expensive living. Everything my heart desired I obtained. I spent money like water and allowed Richard to spoil me with his kisses and praise. I even went and got Poo every summer and spent more money traveling with her across the country. I gave her all the things that I never received as a child. Fancy clothes, shoes, toys; she had it all. Besides, I didn't like how Lotti tugged her along on her days off. Teaching Poo about abortions, potions, and crap. Lotti claimed she wanted her to be a nurse.

"Well, teach de chile about appreciating life!" I argued.

Lotti didn't like me nosing around and getting in her business. "You here to see Poo, right? Well, dey she go. Don't pay me no mind." I laughed. My sister was a mess.

We still wrote letters to each other—me claiming to write to Poo, while Lotti claimed to be responding on her behalf. The letters were notes between the both of us. That's how we corresponded. I saw Lotti twice a year when I retrieved Poo from Gonzales for our annual summer trip and again when we returned, and I called her every Christmas. After Slick died, the trips and monthly money that I sent them slowed down.

THAT MILKY WHITE WAY

"**M**ake Jesus the Lord of your life!"

That's what the preacher said at the funeral, eyeballing each and every band member—especially me. His mission was to reach into our hearts and touch our souls, and he delivered. We were in Mississippi for Slick's homecoming service, his birthplace. Before then, it was fast living—music, booze, money, and sex. Losing Slick gave us a reality check. It was only the week before that we were all laughing and joking around, waiting in the dressing room to go on stage in Jacksonville. Slick slipped away into the bathroom for his usual fix, and that's where we found him. He was dead, sitting on the toilet with a needle stuck in his arm and his head between his legs.

"Dis here world is God's house," the preacher continued, coming down into the aisle. "And in my Father's house!" he said with a roaring voice that echoed off the wooden rafters of the old church. "There are many rooms. Death!" His cadence carried a melody. "Merely pushes aside de doors..." He mimicked, pushing doors open as he worked his way back to the pulpit. "So dat we might! Pass from one room to de other." The amen-corner of the church started chiming in, saying, "hallelujah, preach preacher, well," letting him know that he was hitting a home run. "And before it comes time for you to travel along de King's highway...please, brothers and sisters, what-so-in-evers you do..." He groaned, bouncing on the ball of his feet, "do it for de Lord. Because on dat great gettin' up morning, you gon' wanna hear Him say...very well...let us pray."

Before the service ended, half the band was baptized, including Fatso, Tomcat, Levi, and Richard. The word trifling doesn't begin to epitomize their behavior over the years. Slick's death made them aware of their own totality.

When the preacher said to me, "Miss Mary, I'm interested in your soul's status...has it been saved, chile?" I figured it was.

"Why, yes, sir. Ah was baptized in de river long ago."

"Have you backslidden? Do you tithe? Do you do any good works?" I must've looked clueless because he went on and said, "Sista prepare. De day of de Lord will come lak a thief in de night. And when you meet Him, He will surely ask you why have you forsaken Me." My heart was persuaded, but my feet remained. I opened my purse and ended that conversation.

After the baptisms, we took a boat out on the river with Slick's brother and caught catfish for dinner. We sat out there in the dark; fishing, drinking, laughing, and remembering Slick. Mainly, we discussed the changes that we all knew were coming. Tomcat, who by nature was skeptical about anything he didn't have a good answer or proof for, went deep into his newly found religion. Shortly after that, he left the band and went back home to Trudy and their six kids. Fatso fell into his faith hard too, but besides me, he was the only one to remain loyal to Richard and his vision. Levi met himself a pretty little bible-thumping farm girl named Helen at the funeral. We were all holding our breath waiting for him to ask for her hand in marriage. Besides Slick, Levi held our band together; he managed the books, knew all the contacts, and did our scheduling. My Richard, poor thing, was a little Judas. He went into the water a sinner and came up a wet one. Nothing changed, except we all learned that he couldn't manage a band. Richard was a sax player and a damn good one. He was no Slick. Although he accompanied him booking gigs, he didn't obtain any of Slick's savoir-faire. Richard was bull-headed and flipped his top too quickly.

We toured for a while after the funeral, fulfilling prior engagements and picking up a few juke joints. The band wasn't the same. Besides Tomcat, we lost some of the horn section and had replacements that weren't worthy of The Slick Miller Quartet name. Then, as they say in show business, the phone stopped ringing. It got quieter and quieter until one day, we all realized we'd better do something different. Richard sold the raggedy old band bus that held more memories than a little to pay the remaining band their final checks. He then convinced me to sell my brand new 1960 Cadillac Coupe de Ville, so we could start over in New York City.

The band's final hurrah together was Levi and Helen's wedding. For us, it marked a sad occasion. It meant the end of our whirlwind journey. Everyone was settling down, finding jobs and blending in as civilians. Richard, Fatso, and I were the only ones holding on to a dream. What else could I do? I didn't know I would be a singer until I opened up my mouth and sang. For me, it was a matter of identity. I sang the lyrics that the band played.

During our last performance at the wedding, I cried, performing an overly emotional rendition of the band's signature song, barely making it to the end. Someone asked, "Are you okay?"

"Yeah," I answered, wiping my eyes and sipping from the glass they handed me. "I'd be better if you could turn this water to wine."

We laughed, hugged necks, kissed cheeks, then loaded into Fatso's car and headed off to New York City.

PART IV
GREED

"He who cannot give anything away cannot feel anything either" - Friedrich Nietzsche "

A DINNER GUEST

"Hey, Tante Mags!" Sal's tight hugs felt like a bright smile with long wrapping arms. I never wanted them to end. "You look good! Turn around, let me see you, beb!" I felt giddy when he was around. I wasn't being fresh, nor was he being fresh with me. It was an old friendly language or custom dance. He took the lead, and I curtsied right into the routine.

"Boy, I just love seeing your face." I slowly spun around, holding his hand, admiring the large baby blue teddy bear with extended arms he gave me.

"I know, and I'm sorry it took me so long to get back." He pulled out a chair for me to take a seat. We were at our usual table. This time Sal bought Church's fried chicken, enough for him to stay and have dinner with Martita and me.

"No, apologies. I've been keeping busy." I sat down at my plate. Nurse Lindt had the table set for us.

"Yes, I hear..." Sal loosened his suit jacket and joined me. He was a gentleman and always wore nice jackets in the presence of my company, even though he paired them with jeans. His parents did an excellent job at teaching him how to entertain a lady. "Where is this,

Mar-rita? I've been dying to meet her. I hear you two have become a regular Lucy and Ethel routine around here. I'm a little jealous."

I laughed, correcting him, "Martita. Yeah, we're besties nowadays. She'll be with us in a bit." I unfolded my napkin just as Sal was doing and placed it on my lap. My table manners were left behind somewhere in the eighties with my silverware and china.

"She actually has a visitor today. See, that's her right over there." I pointed across the room to Martita, who was wrapping up a visitation with her sister. They waved toward us before deciding to walk over. Sal stood as they approached, clearing his throat.

"Hello." He extended his hand, flashing a smile that showed his boyish insecurities.

"Hi, I'm Maria, Tita's sister." They briefly shook hands.

"Hi," Martita shyly responded, lowering her head and eyes and allowing the long bang she wore to fall and cover her face. I knew Sal was fine, but, *damn girl, don't make it so obvious!*

"Ahh, so you're the one trying to steal my Tante Mags from me." Sal joked, shaking a finger at her, and we all laughed.

"Mrs. Owens—"

"Uh-uh, no, ma'am," I cut Maria off, "none of that—we family now. It's Tante Mags to you."

Maria nervously laughed, correcting herself. "Ahh, yes, thank you...Tan-te Mags." She had a thicker accent than Martita. "I just wanted to come by before I left and thank you again for all the time you've spent with my sister." She held Martita's hand, and Martita had the biggest smile. It was obvious she was proud of her sibling. "It's been rough adjusting for her, but you make it all a lot better...thank you." Maria extended her hand to me, and I shook it, standing. Everybody else was standing.

"Nonsense! It's been my pleasure. We've been helping each other...why don't you join us for dinner." I turned to pull up the chair my teddy bear was occupying for her. Sal helped.

"No, no, no, I'm leaving." Maria insisted, waving her hands.

"You sure...there's more than enough." Sal offered. "I don't necessarily have to eat like a bear tonight." Martita laughed, snorting at his joke. She knew she would be eating like one.

"That's kind of you, but I have to get back into the city. I hear traffic gets crazy around here." Sal nodded, taking his seat. I followed suit. "Bye, Tita...nos vemos." She hugged Martita tightly around the neck. She was equally tall and slim.

"Adios...te veo, Maria," Martita answered affectionately, squeezing Maria's hand before she left.

"Aww, that was nice." I noticed Martita's sudden wet eyes and instantly started rubbing her arm as she took her seat.

"Yeah, she's a great kid. I didn't do too bad, huh?" She joked, tucking a napkin in her shirt. She intended to get busy on that chicken.

"Oh...okay!" Sal responded, tucking a napkin into his shirt too. "Pfft...I like your style." He took his fork and followed Martita's lead, stabbing a piece of chicken from the bucket instead of making a plate.

"Dis is how we do it in da hood." She ripped into a chicken thigh. I knew she would show that bucket no mercy, so I removed my three pieces and loaded the rest of my plate with fried okra.

"Naw dats how we do it in my hood!" I said, knowing Sal chose okra instead of fries for me.

"Mmm, I never had this; what is it?" Martita filled her plate with the crispy golden okra nuggets too.

"Oh, you ain't never had fried okra...you in for a treat..." Sal poured more on her plate. "I have another box. This is like popcorn back home. You like hot sauce?" he asked, tearing a package with his teeth. "You like hot sauce? Wow, this feels like a date. I got me two ladies." He drizzled a little over her plate.

Martita nodded, stuffing her face, "Yeah, I do...I like him, Tante Mags!" she said with a mouth full. We laughed.

"Shoot! Fried okra is all Richard, and I could afford when we moved to Harlem." I poured more on my plate too. I could see that etiquette was out the window. Sal removed his jacket and rolled up his sleeves with us. "That...and a cold can of beer. Brings back memories."

"Where in Harlem did you live?" Martita asked; I knew she wanted to get back into my stories, but I wasn't sure if Sal wanted to go there with me after the last time.

"You lived in Harlem, Tante Mags? I lived there too when I first moved here for a while. Washington Heights." Sal mentioned, already on his second piece of chicken and trying to keep up with Martita.

"Oh, yeah...we lived there...and 110th Street, Lenox Ave, Graham Court, and finally, Strivers' Row."

"How did a bayou girl like you get to Harlem, anyway?"

Martita and I laughed. There was so much that Sal had missed, but I had more. A whole lot more.

"You don't wanna hear my crazy old stories." I fanned him off. Martita stopped eating and looked at me sadly.

"No, no, I love your stories...that's if you're up to it." He didn't want me flipping out.

"Yeh, he loves your stories! Please." Martita begged like a five-year-old. I laughed.

"Well, I'm always up for a good story."

That's all I needed was an invitation. I popped two or three pieces of okra in my mouth and chased them down with some sweet tea. The meal combination that Sal chose took me right back across 110th Street in Harlem.

DROP ME OFF IN HARLEM

New York City! Well, they say if you can make it there, you can make it anywhere. I didn't believe it until I saw the busted apartment that Richard sold my beautiful new car for. Don't get me wrong, I'm from the sticks; growing up, we stayed in some of the shabbiest looking spots you'd ever want to see, but The Grandmother never paid an arm and a leg to live in one. Then, there I was, the eminent, Miss Mary Mags, living in the most expensive hole-in-the-wall in Harlem. Richard was used to taking care of only himself; he was orphaned at eight years old. As long as he had his sax and a corner to rest his head, he was okay. Whatever else he needed, he stole or used his looks and charm to obtain. At this point, he was a married man. I needed more than the four corners, four walls, hard cold bare floors, and one and a half windows facing a brick wall that sunlight had to fight its way through, he was offering. I was boxed in with no room to grow.

"YOU SEE, SAL, BEFORE MOVING TO HARLEM, THIS SIMPLE BAYOU GIRL was a famous jazz singer and showgirl. Richard, that's my husband, he played the sax. We traveled the States with The Slick Miller Quartet...I know, it's before your time, but we were sort of a big deal."

"Wow, that's impressive. I didn't know that," he said, picking his teeth.

"Mhmm. I can see Lotti not telling anyone. She hated anything that had to do with Richard."

WHEN THE BAND FOLDED, RICHARD AND I, ALONG WITH ANOTHER BAND member, Fatso, whose real name was Simon-Peter Thornton, packed and moved to New York City to open a jazz club. What a sad reception, is all I can say about that. Fatso and I followed Richard, who could find trouble in a Sunday school class, all the way to New York City without a clue or a friggin' dime to buy one. That was our Richard. He was a product of the slum; always trying to get over.

I was twenty-nine-years-old when we arrived in Harlem. A dark and exotic-looking bayou flower. According to the standards of Blacks in showbiz, none of my features were soft or workable. I wasn't tall and slim; I was short and curvy, with boobs and butt for days. I wasn't high-yella or brown; I was dark-skinned with sharp sub-Saharan features that demanded attention before their time. Because of Richard, I saw myself differently. There were no issues. That was one good thing about him; he made me feel beautiful. I took care of myself and didn't wear muumuus, hiding the bulge of fat around my waist like Lotti.

"WATCH IT NOW!" SAL INTERRUPTED. "DON'T BE TALKIN' 'BOUT MY Mama Lotti. Me and Rah had us some good naps on that big belly." He laughed, defending his childhood memories of Lotti.

"I know that's right...and ain't nothing wrong with a little fluff around the waist!" I squeezed my growing belly, and we all chuckled. In the horrible state I was previously in, it was good to finally see one.

AT THAT TIME, THE MUSIC INDUSTRY WAS CHANGING. A WOMAN WITH my unique looks could sing with a group of musicians but putting her center stage and shining a spotlight down on her wasn't well received. Unless she was Nina Simone, Sarah Vaughn, Pearl Bailey, or somebody like that. I heard the same 'NO' every time we went into a club for work. Richard ended up searching for gigs alone; he could pass for white if it wasn't for his rhythm. Once he started to play, it was a rap. They signed him up, expecting the equally talented band he spoke of. Fatso and I joined him on performance nights. I hid in the wings until I was called. I'd start by singing loudly from the sideline, allowing the audience to hear a sultry voice before seeing me walk gracefully in full ball gowns across the stage.

Once on stage, I became whoever they needed me to be. My long, smooth, curly black hair was pinned up neatly, and my face powdered to look as light as possible. I actually looked gray. Once I got to singing, dancing, and interacting with upbeat humor and a sense of well-roundedness, the audience forgot what they were seeing. New Yorkers found the accent that I worked hard to rid myself of warm and inviting. So, while on stage, I'd soup it up, speaking creole and talking about all the other cats we played with and the fancy spots we visited. I had them eating out of my Black hands. Richard and Fatso could play anything, and I had a gift of imitating anyone I heard once. My tone sounded like chanting—a spiritual mix of zydeco along with hope and mourning. What I couldn't do, I danced it out. We inadvertently found success with smaller nightclubs that couldn't afford the real deal for a few years. Richard was happy with the fame. He saved every penny he earned for his big investment. But I grew depressed.

Mondays through Thursdays were the problem. You see, we got kicked out of the hole-in-the-wall apartment because we couldn't keep up with our lifestyle and pay rent with only Friday through Saturday night gigs. So, we all ended up taking day jobs. Richard worked in nightclubs, restaurants, and bars, learning the ends and outs of the hospitality business. I had never worked a day in my life besides helping Lotti with the laundry jobs she took and helping her sell potions. I was more of a hype man than anything, but because of that, I talked my way into getting any job I found. I was a seamstress for a hot minute; 'til they found out I couldn't sew. A secretary 'til they found out I couldn't type. I was even a cashier at the supermarket until I gave out more than I brought in.

Fatso slept on his brother Andrew's couch, who lived in Mount Vernon, until he found his own pad. He took a job working in the Bronx as a barber at a beauty salon, where he quickly befriended the owner, Joanna. Fatso was a handsome fella. He wasn't big until he met Jo; then, the nickname suited him. Lord, that woman could cook, you hear me! Jo was your typical gossiping hairdresser. She launched into wild stories within seconds of meeting a person—often before customary greetings were exchanged. Jo loved to talk and drop the 411. In the beginning, I felt she talked too much and was too loud of a woman for Fatso. Besides, I had heard she was newly divorced and took all her husband's money—they said that's how she opened the salon. I was wrong; Jo had a heart of gold. We grew to be the best of friends. She always told me the truth no matter how much it hurt, and we both loved plants. We snipped sprigs from wherever we went to re-root at home. The stolen ones grew the prettiest. Our plant babies were the kids neither of us had.

The day I met Joanna, Fatso had me come into the parlor for an interview. Jo was cursing this woman out the door, and when I say, out the door—they were literally in the streets.

"You gon' rue the day you ever set foot in this shop!" she screeched, being held back from the woman. Jo had caught her stealing. Now, I love money, but Jo was all business. You steal from her, and she'd cut you. Fatso, who was still skinny at the time, picked her up by the waist to keep her from killing that lady. I think that's when Jo fell in love with him; she said, "Any man who can lift my thick butt off the ground like that is a keeper." The next day she made Fatso one of her home-wrecking peach cobblers, and she's been Mrs. Simon-Peter Thornton ever since.

"Come right on in here, baby girl, with ya pretty self." Jo was much older than me. "When God closes a door, He sho'nuff opens a window." She mumbled to herself out loud, throwing an apron around my waist. No interview was needed. She took a seat, still panting from acting a fool in the streets. "Pour me a cup of that coffee, will ya, ahh... what's ya name again, beautiful?"

"Mary Magdalene Auguste, but folks call me Mags," I answered, about good and tired of the compliments. I was extremely adverse toward them and didn't trust anyone with my looks but Richard. "How do you like your coffee, Ms. Joanna?"

"Hmm," she crossed her thick legs and scooted to the side. "Like I like my men—hot, black, and strong." She eyeballed Fatso. "Yup, I just know you, godsent, Mags. I got a good feeling." But she never stopped looking at Fatso.

It's a good thing I knew how to do hair. As much hair as The Grandmother, Lotti, and I had, it was a necessity. I never thought about it, but I was good at it. I did my own hair and makeup on the road and always got complimented. Jo said I had hair-growing hands. I could work an inch of hair and make it into a mile. Everyone who came into the shop asked for Jo and me. I liked my new job and loved Jo. It felt like a small family again, working amongst her and the other technicians. Crazy me; I wanted something more.

Richard and I barely made enough money to pay the rent for the next hole-in-the-wall we lived in. Every month, early in the morning, our superintendent, Pepi, yelled throughout the halls, knocking once on everybody's door, "Ahh rent!" And every month Richard and I didn't have it. Even though our kitchen sink dripped all night long, the walls needed painting, and a fierce draft was coming in through the window over our bed that put a hurting on my voice—we still owed rent. Things got so bad that I stopped sending Lotti and Poo money, and then she started sending me some. I'll admit it; life could have been better if I knew how to manage my finances. I overspent, making myself look nice. It made me feel good. I bought nice outfits, purses, and shoes, then Richard and I took in the scene, drinking and smoking cigarettes. It was 1962, New York City; just like I pictured it —bright lights and everything!

As much money as I spent, Richard kept his wallet closed tight. He refused to come off his savings.

"Stop bugging me, woman!" He insisted when I asked for money to pay the bills. "I love music...this is my dream! You ain't taking that away from me." Like I stole something of his.

"But, Richard, we can't eat dreams!"

"Then, I don't wanna eat." And he meant that.

We were already living off the stale bagels with cream cheese and lox he bought home from the Jewish deli where he worked on Wednesdays. And I didn't even eat fish. The owner's son was a jazz fanatic, and he and Richard became close. They frolicked throughout the city, taking in music and culture. Besides our singing engagements, Richard and I barely spent time together. He claimed 'making it' was all about the people you knew. Well, Richard knew a lot of people. He was hot-headed but a smooth cat.

That night I was so pissed with him that I took our last two dollars and walked out of the apartment to the corner bar. I passed a church, smelling of country fried chicken dinners with all the trimmings, and started to change my mind about the drink. Remembering what the preacher in Mississippi said, saved folks are givers, I decided to walk over. I guess I didn't look the part because the sanctified heifers standing around in front gathered around the doors and wouldn't let me into their building. Had they let me in that night, things might have gone differently for me. Instead, for the next four years of my life, I skirted between legal and criminal activity.

"What!" Martita yelled, shocking both Sal and me from the trance I had us in. Remorseful, I nodded my head, remembering all I had done.

"Yeah, a numbers and prostitution racket." Martita sighed heavily, falling back against the back of her seat. I knew she had sold her body for drugs in the past. It sounds horrible, but it's an easy thing to fall into when you're desperate, uneducated, and sold out to sin.

"Auntie, should I be hearing this? "Sal asked with a boyish grin on his face. I felt he already knew. He was a cop, and if he did his job as well as he took notice of the small details that brightened my days—he knew about my past. He was being considerate.

"Yeah, I can talk about it...now. I did my time."

"You were in jail!" Martita yelled, causing everyone in the dayroom to turn around and look at us.

"Damn!" I issued, then whispered, "you wanna send a telegram? President Clinton didn't hear you."

"I'm sorry." She laughed, digging ice from the bottom of her cup of iced tea and chomping on it. "I just love your stories!" She patted her cold hand on mine. "You make me feel like I can do anything when I get out of here, yo. I think I love you more than I did five seconds ago."

I looked her square in the eyes. "I hope you don't plan on following my lead. I've done things I don't even wanna know about. Now, look where I am." I lowered my eyes, embarrassed because of Sal. He had sat up from his reclined position when Martita blew up my spot and was looking concerned.

Martita rested her cup on the table and took both my hands, "Because you took chances and never gave up on life, I feel like I can do anything. Yeah, you made mistakes, but I'm talking about your courageousness. Whoever you were when you got here, that woman doesn't exist anymore." Sal leaned into the table, nodding his head in agreement. "And you...Tante Mags don't belong here. You're notorious." I smiled.

My name was a byword for notorious once upon a time.

STRANGE FRUIT

Well, if I couldn't eat, I would drink to forget that I was hungry. So, I sat at a barstool hidden in the corner of a smoky, crowded bar on 7th Avenue and 125th Street and asked the bartender for a shot of vodka. It was cheap and effective.

"Ooh, che bella! You wanna take a spin with Vinny?" A random Italian fella, overdressed in multiple patterns with a handlebar mustache that consumed his face, asked from nowhere.

"Hell no!" I responded, shocked and agitated. Did he take me for a joke? All I wanted was a drink; I didn't want any trouble. He moved on, giving the next woman he met the same tired line. This woman in her size eight dress, hugging her size ten body, left with him. *What a sleaze.* I initially condemned her without knowing her circumstances. "Bartender, I'll have another."

After the second shot kicked in, things started to make sense. If Richard and I didn't come up with the rent by noon the next day, we would be in the streets again. Our gigs were growing far and few between, and I felt it was my fault. Folks didn't want to see an ashy, hard-kneed dark-skinned girl, shaking her shimmies on stage anymore. They wanted the girls that looked white—mulattos and

Latinas. Then, I remembered what The Grandmother used to say, "What folks say in public and what dey do in de dark, is two different tings." I opened my eyes and looked around the crowded bar again. *What are all these Italian cats doing here in Harlem?*

As the scales fell off my eyes, I realized I was sitting in the middle of mingling hours. The men weren't looking at me with disgust; they were curious. I arched my back and allowed the shimmering gold colored shawl I was wearing to fall off my shoulders as I licked my lips. *Yup, the darker the berry, the sweeter the juice, babee.* The next man who asked how much, I repeated what I heard the sleaze say, and we left the bar together.

I told you that my calling card was Miss Desperate Measures.

I knew it wasn't for me right away, but I followed through because we owed rent. Standing in a dark alley, with my cheeks pressed into the cold brick wall behind me, a word came to mind.

"make him pay. make him pay for every woman he's ever degraded."

I gave Mr. Ba-da-bing bada-boom more than he expected, gassing him about how good he was, as I stole his wallet from up under him. Silly me, I didn't ask for cash in advance. That mothersucker got his jollies off and thought he was gonna stiff me.

"Sorry, doll, that's the way the cookies crumble," he said, zipping his fly.

I laughed heartily, "Yeah, well, tell that crap to Linda." I removed his wife's picture from his wallet and tucked it deep into my bosom, along with all his cash and his driver's license.

He stuttered, "What the hell," amongst some other belittling obscenities that made me laugh even harder. I repeated his wife's name along with the address that I committed to memory.

After that, all I can remember is him going for his pant leg, seeing a police badge, and him pulling out a gun. I ran regardless, feeling it wasn't my time to die or go to jail. As I approached the vacant side-walk, I twisted an ankle in the 3-inch heels I wore then he hit me on the back of the head with his gun. I remember falling, hearing a loud siren, and seeing flashing lights.

"Freeze," I heard, and he ran away.

When I came to, I was lying on a beat-up camel-colored sofa in someone's dim apartment.

"Why is a good-looking chick like you working the streets? You ain't got no man to take care of you, mama?" I tried to sit up, but the lump on the back of my head laid me out flat. I was still somewhat disorientated.

"Jive turkey tried to beat me outta my money," I recalled, drawing my focus on the fine dark-skinned brother sitting wide legged on a coffee table in front of me with an ice pack in his hand. I winced and held my head. There was a cool rag already placed on my forehead. I thought to thank him, but I was confused. *What am I doing here?*

"Who you work for? I ain't never seen you around." His inquisitions made me nervous.

"You sure do ask a lot of questions...you da fuzz?" I took another look around the sparsely decorated studio apartment with the only light coming in from a wide undressed window facing the 138th Street bridge.

"Far from that." The brother loosened his tie, staring me in the eyes like he knew me. "You should've asked that cop you were messing with that same question. What made him run like that...besides my DT siren." He grinned devilishly, gently repositioning my head to place the ice pack.

I felt that I was in good company, so I dug into my bosom and pulled out the cop's ID along with his wife's picture and handed it to him. Boy, did we laugh; him more than me. He had a big burly laugh to go along with his big beefy body.

"Girl you just made my night," he said wiping tears away from laughter. "My name is William Jeremy Daughtry. People call me Tiny." He extended a huge, rough hand, and I shook it, feeling intrigued.

"I'm Miss Mary Mags, and I'm not a hooker." I removed the cool compress from my forehead and sat up. "I'm a jazz singer, on hard times...who happens to be posing as a beautician right now."

Tiny smiled, shaking his finger. "I could tell you sang by that little tune you was humming in the car on the way over here."

"Where da hell is here, anyway?" I asked, but for some reason, I was totally at ease. Tiny had big brown bedroom eyes and a certain home-spun deposition. Besides, I wasn't dead, and I should have been. He stood up, and it took him a really long time to get up there. I tilted my head way back. He was a giant! "Damn, how tall are you?" I asked, choking on my words. He was a big guy! Tiny only smiled and bent over to scoop me into his massive arms. I didn't resist him. This brother could have smashed me into the ground like a nail with his bare hammer-like fist, and for some reason, I wasn't scared. The Grandmother used to say that I was naive. Blind intrigue was a problem of mine. I let life lead the way.

"You at one of my spots in the Bronx," he finally answered, carrying me into a steamy bathroom where he had run a tub of hot water. "Get ya'self a bath, so you can feel like somebody again." He placed me on my feet, and I remembered I twisted my ankle and fell back into his arms. "Whoa, you okay?"

I stood a foot above Tiny's navel, pressed against his solid body and inhaling the intoxicating scent of an immaculately dressed man. "I'm sorry..." I stuttered. "I think I twisted my ankle."

"You need my help." His voice was rough, like his vocal cords were scratched by sandpaper, yet deep and smooth at the same time.

"I think I can manage," I answered, a little nervous because no other man but Richard had ever got me...woozy like that.

I looked over at Sal, who had his chin resting on the palms of his hands in interest. This wasn't a conversation between two women anymore. I cleared my throat, remembering Tiny. The thought of him did unspeakable things to me.

Tiny turned his back as I undressed in his bathroom. Leaning against the doorframe, he continued to tell me about himself. He wasn't a cop; I don't know where he got the beacon light with the siren from. He said he was a bodyguard. Once I stepped into the tub of hot water, he shut the lights and turned around. A small candle burned by the sink. In the back of my mind, I wondered just what the brother had planned, but his kindness made me look the other way. Besides the apartment that Richard and I rented only had a shower, and I missed taking long baths.

"Ahhh," I sighed, seeping into the hot water.

Tiny walked over and sat on the toilet near the tub, rolling up his sleeves before lathering a washcloth. I was hesitant at first, but I could tell he was used to tending to some woman, so I sat up and drew my knees in, resting my head on them.

"What got you out here?" He started washing my back with strong pressing hands, and I literally moaned, letting my shoulders fall forward.

"Rent," I released in an exhale.

"I thought you said you have an old man." I sort of laughed, having not mentioned anything about Richard.

"What I got is a musician living in the past and holding on to old dreams."

"Hmm," he responded, working his way around to the front. "You mind?" He asked with a serious face. I slid my legs down and raised my arms so this stranger could get under the girls. He was good trouble and just the distraction I needed.

"If we don't pay our rent by noon tomorrow, we're on the streets again, and I'm tired of taking handouts and sending my sister change of address postcards every few months. I know she's thinking the worst of me by now." That sort of made me sad, but Tiny had my leg up in the air by the ankle washing up and down my thigh. "I used to be somebody long ago," I added, thinking of how Richard used to care for me like that.

"You done gave up?" He let my relaxed leg fall into the water, making a splash. "Cause I don't mess with folks who give up." His eyes darted across my face. "Let me hear you sing something."

Now, I've always been partial to yella' men with nice curly hair. William Daugherty had neither. This was strictly a grown-folk attraction. Tiny was a dark-Gable with a distinguished-looking nose that flared in attention across his face. My favorite part was his supple pouty lips that peeked from a thin, neatly trimmed mustache. He put me in mind of someone familiar, like the kid you grew up with from school who picked his boogers but turned out to be super fine. I started singing "Strange Fruit" by Billie Holiday. The moment was dim, silent and eerie, and I deemed Tiny the type of brother that would definitely be found hanging from a poplar tree in the southern breeze. He was Goliath, feared because he was too big and too strong. I sang directly into his eyes, and he reached out and touched my face with a tear running along his cheek. Strange Fruit. There was nothing left for us to do but embrace. Suddenly, I found myself wondering about the bed of another man. Longing to feel the heat of his body against my flesh.

That night, all Tiny did was drive me home after a wonderful evening of engaging conversation regarding just ordinary things. He walked me to my door even though I told him I was married.

He sucked his teeth and said, "That's why I found you about to get ya ass beat in an alley, right? Because you married? You gotta be jivin'! I ain't studdin' him."

Thank goodness Richard wasn't home. He was still somewhere blowing his horn.

The next day, I awoke to Pepi banging on our front door, yelling, "Ahh rent!"

I shuffled across the floor, opened the door, threw the money out at him, and slammed the door in his face.

"And fix this got-damn leaky pipe too!" I yelled before returning to the mattress on the floor. Richard was there, laying on his back, smiling smugly.

"Where'd you get the money?" He asked, looking at me with the devil in his eyes and rubbing his hand up my thigh. He was the most stubborn, never-ending impossible man I knew.

"I sold my body. Got knocked over the head by a cop and rescued by a giant named Tiny," I responded, flopping heavily on my back and sighing. Richard snickered, working his magic fingers underneath my nightgown. I closed my eyes and thought of Tiny. He kissed me, and I kissed him back, but my feelings weren't all there. I endowed them to someone else and hoped Richard couldn't feel the separation; he was now a spare.

CHANCES ARE

Jo and I were standing outside of her beauty shop on another cigarette break when a slow-driving, sky blue 1963 Caddy with fishtails and crisp whitewall tires pulled up. Tiny stepped out of the vehicle, looking dignified and as fine as the ride he drove. Immediately the neighborhood kids playing in the streets surrounded him. Because of his height, they probably mistook him for a basketball player. We shared a smile from across the top of the car as he engaged with his young admirers, patting them on their heads, letting them swing from his muscular arms, and handing out pocket change.

"Look but don't touch," he warned as they stepped back, allowing the giant to glide around to the passenger side. "Get in; I want you to meet somebody," he issued to me, holding the car door open.

I stood there for a second slack-jawed with forbidden intrigue. All the women in the salon and a few guys had come out to see the fancy ride and the tall fine bear of a brother in neat threads driving. I knew the word would get back to Richard if I left with him. Jo elbowed me. I had already filled her in on the 411 of my Saturday night.

"I think he's talking to you, Betty Boop," she whispered from the side of her mouth, blowing smoke with her arms folded in front of her in a blasé attitude. She wasn't impressed. Jo was from Harlem, she was used to it all, but a silly grin crept alongside my face because Tiny was near, and it was me he was after.

"I'll be back in a minute, Jo." I quickly stamped out my cigarette and ran, throwing my apron back to her.

"No, she won't, Jo," Tiny added, shutting my door.

"So, you bathe me, and now you automatically think that you can boss me around?" I joked, admiring and touching all the shiny chrome knobs and finishes of the car like a kid at Christmas. Tiny adjusted himself, getting back inside with an air of confidence that border-lined arrogance.

"I want a car like this," I announced, mostly speaking my goals into existence. Tiny, who wasn't acting as alluring as he was with the kids, honked the horn and waved at them before speeding off—giving them a little gas.

"I need to know something right now," he spoke after driving a few blocks from the salon. I stopped daydreaming and gave him my full attention. He looked agitated.

"Where's your heart, Miss Mary Mags? Are you into this prostitu-tion thing, or do you wanna do something big with your life? What are you into?" He pulled the car over before crossing the bridge and repositioned himself to face me. I felt slightly intimidated as he extended his arm across my headrest with his eyes glued to mine. He looked so stern in the black fedora hat.

"I'm into money!" I answered without a doubt. "But I ain't no hooker. I done told you that before."

"Well, who was that red-looking dude, kissing all over you in front of the beauty shop?" I threw my head back in surprise; Tiny had been stalking me. Richard and Fatso had just left together. Richard came by the salon to tell us that he and his Jewish friend, Albert, finally pooled together and bought a jazz supper club on Lenox Ave. He was excited and treated me like he used to, kissing and rubbing on me in public. He slapped my rear before leaving and told me he named the place Bayou House of Blues because I drove him crazy.

"That's my husband, fool!" I barked. I may have complained about

Richard to Tiny, but until the do was done, he was still reigning king. I didn't have to answer to no one but him. Tiny smiled, that same crooked smile that initially made me feel at home with him.

"Aiight, cool down, mama, don't blow your top." He pulled back into traffic, laughing. "I just really need to know that you're the one; you know what I'm sayin'."

"The one for what?" I bit my lip and ran my hand along the slab of meat called his thigh, deeming he was jealous. Tiny glanced at my hand and then at me, issuing a warning that read, *you don't want none of this.* His wide eyes read cautiously enough to make me draw my hand back.

"When I saw you running from that cop, I figured you're the type of woman I'm looking for. I was actually there casing him out. He's a dirty mofo...been cheating The Madame out of money for years." I didn't know what Tiny was talking about besides "Chances Are" by my favorite artist, the dreamboat Johnny Mathis, was playing on the radio. Tiny focused more on his driving than holding me near, and I could feel the chemistry between us even though he wouldn't act the part.

He continued, smiling coyly at me, "When you gave me that picture of his wife...and his damn driver's license too—that crap was like hitting the jackpot!" He laughed and bounced in his seat, rocking the car.

"Now, we got that mofo right where we want him!" He hopped off the FDR at the 96th Street exit. Black folks didn't have many reasons to take the 96th Street exit. "Letting those types load off on you, over and over again ain't no kind of life for no lady. That crap will make you old real fast. The trick is, you get 'em before you get got." He glanced my way and pinched my cheek with his knuckles.

"That's what I see in you...a fighter, doll face." I smiled; he was right about that; I was a fighter, and there were a lot of titles under my belt.

I didn't know what we were doing on the Upper East Side, but Tiny had a magnetic charm that made me want to follow him wherever he went. "Well, damn it," I said, fixing to light a cigarette. "I enjoy sex way too much for it to ever become a task, anyway!" I laughed, lighting up. Tiny snatched the cigarette from my lips and tossed it out the window. "What de hell" I yelled, watching my last cig float down the street. "Got damn-it...don't you know smokes cost thirty-six cents a pack, niggro!"

"And don't you know whose car you sitting in? She don't like no smoke ruining her interior." He pointed to the ML monogrammed into the leather seats. I guess I looked dumbfounded because Tiny went on saying, "This is the Queen of Harlem's car, The Madame...Madame LaRue?"

"Never heard of her." I crossed my arms, sulking. That was my last cigarette. I'd have to wait for Richard to get home and bum one off of him. Tiny could tell I was mad and softened his speech.

"If you follow me and do everything I tell ya, you'll be able to afford ten packs of dem cancer sticks a day by next week, if that's what you want." He parked the car in front of a tall luxury building. "And then you'll be able to keep that fine-azz of yours to ya'self." He leaned in like he wanted to tell me a secret and instantly my composure slipped. I froze stiffly in my seat. The enticing fragrance he wore hit my nose before our cheeks touched. His breath laid heavy on my neck momentarily as he hesitated before gently pecking my jawbone. He tilted my head and pressed his full, supple lips against mine. I literally melted.

"That's if you wanna keep it to yourself?" He whispered, rolling his tongue under his bottom lip and straightening his tie because he knew he had me. I gave him a smile and a playful tap on the arm.

Tiny proceeded to tell me a bit about Madame LaRue before the valet came. He told me some more about her in the elevator and in the hall. Before he rang her bell, I knew she was the one responsible for how he treated a lady, and I would be forever in her debt. My Tiny was a good man.

A butler took Tiny's hat and said, "Walk this way." Tiny used an extra second to fix himself in the hall mirror. He was nothing but an overgrown 'Bama boy, living out city dreams. His anxiousness made me feel self-conscious of the work dress and shoes I had on. Thank goodness, my makeup was done, and my hair was neatly tamed into a bun. The butler escorted us into a large sitting room. A beautiful older woman, wearing a colorful silk house dress, sat tall by a bay window. Her legs were crossed as she continuously stroked an overweight Persian cat sitting comfortably in her lap.

"Madame." Tiny addressed her, abandoning me at the doorway. He kissed her outstretched hand. "Madame, this is the one I done told you about, Miss Mary Mags. She green, like you was. Creole. Straight from Baton Rouge, but she's a fighter. She knows what she wants and how to get it." The Madame smiled delicately the entire time Tiny spoke, rubbing her cat.

"You neglected to mention how lovely she was," she remarked with a hint of jealousy, slightly turning her face but not taking her eyes off me.

"Yes, ma'am, but she got spunk."

The Madame ignored him and stretched both hands toward me.

"'Komen ça va', 'cher' Mari? Come here so I can see you better."

"'Bonswa', madame," I answered, startling her. "'Çé bon, mo byin'." I walked further into the room like a tourist, unable to keep myself from admiring all the beautiful pieces of furniture she collected. I had never owned furniture and up until that point, I never saw the need for any. With The Grandmother and then Richard, we packed light. "'Bèl kay'!" I said, taking her cold frail hands and squeezing them firmly. I was already a better woman because of her.

"'Mo byin'," she responded. "Although I'm afraid I'm not the decorator. Please, dear, take a seat." Tiny had already pulled up a chair for me. He was on top of her every whim.

"'Li santi bon pou pale kreyòl'," I said, happy to have someone to speak Creole with.

"Oh, my," she laughed, "you got me there. My Creole is... 'comme ci, comme ca'. I was born in Baton Rouge, but we didn't stay for long. My mother spoke some around the house, but my father disapproved of it."

"Ahh, I see...what I said was, 'it feels good to have someone to speak Creole with'." I took the cigarette that Tiny offered and followed

The Madame placing it between my lips for him to light, although hers was a cigar.

"Yes, yes, maybe you can help me brush up. That'll be something fun to do in my retirement."

"I'd love to... 'piti á piti'," I made my hands go back and forth. "Little by little—it'll come back to you."

"I'm sure...Tiny, darling." She lifted a finger. He was standing near, at her beck and call. "Be a doll and pour our guest a drink. Do you prefer wine or whiskey?"

"Wine is fine, but liquor's quicker," I answered, getting comfortable with my surroundings and imagining myself living that lifestyle. Tiny snickered, picking out a bottle of scotch for me. "Neat," I requested, and he nodded.

"One must keep a sober mind in this business, 'mon cher', Mari," she stated, taking a glass of white wine from Tiny.

I spread my legs and rested my elbows on them. "I thought you said you were from Baton Rouge?" I threw back the liquor Tiny handed me and held out the glass for another. "'Laissez les bons temps rouler'...let the good times roll!"

The Madame laughed. "I like this woman."

We spent the rest of the evening drinking, sharing laughs, and shop talk. The Madame filled me in on tricks of the trade and said whatever she forgot, Tiny would remember. Madame LaRue ran an independent numbers racket for over twenty years. Being a numbers woman, she said she knew when her time was up. The Madame was retiring and selling her businesses in shares. The mob had been after her policy banks for years. So, before she retired, she cut a deal selling them a few locations to keep them off Tiny's back. She wanted him in charge of the portion that made the most money. Tiny knew all the ins and outs. As a young man, he ran numbers for her and worked his way up to lieutenant. Madame LaRue could trust him with her life, but the people were used to him breaking legs and roughing them around. Harlem needed a fresh face, a new Queen Pin to trust. People were looking for someone familiar. It was a rash decision, but Richard and I needed the bread, so I did it. I didn't know anything about playing numbers, just like I didn't think I could sing.

Tiny treated Madame LaRue like she was royalty and me equally. It was customary, but it made The Madame a little jealous. She noticed how he looked at me, so she took his hand and stroked his strong arm in a manner that suggested she already had him. I didn't care because I was taught never to leave money on the table, and I was about to get paid.

The Madame took me under her wings, then she slid into the background where I should have been. I could have kept on cleaning houses and doing hair; instead, I took on running a numbers racket and call-girls. Tiny pretended to be my flunky and bodyguard, but I didn't make a move without him. So, for the next four and a half years, Tiny and I ran Harlem.

I remember my first assignment like it was yesterday. Before we left Madame LaRue's house, she told Tiny to pick up Lew, another henchman, and take me on a trip to Long Island to break me in. The trip was to Officer Rossi's house, the John I had from the other night.

We sat in a car, parked at the end of Rossi's driveway. He lived on a dark tree-lined street in the middle of Nowhere-Ville. It was so quiet and strangely still there that not even a dog barked.

Tiny hunched over me, wearing brass knuckles and that black Fedora hat, tilted over his eyes, and said, "Now, here's what I want you to do, kid. Just sit here and look as pretty as The Madame looked earlier. Don't cry. Don't bat an eye. Don't say shit...just sit here and smoke ya cigarettes."

He and Lew exited the car, leisurely walked up the driveway to the house, and rang the bell. When Officer Rossi answered, they stepped in and beat the crap out of him. I heard Lew tell his wife, "If you scream, Linda, I'ma break his freakin' neck and yours too."

Tiny dragged Officer Rossi out of his house and down to the car. He motioned for me to roll down the window, and I hurriedly obeyed.

"You see this face?" He yelled in the officer's ear, holding his face close to the window. Rossi and I both nodded, instantly recognizing each other.

"This is the new face of Harlem, Madame Mary Mags. You got something you wanna say to her?" Tiny pulled him by the hair so hard his eyeballs rolled back.

"Yes, yes!" he stuttered, coughing. "I'm sorry, Madame. I really am...I'm, I'm at your service."

I didn't move. I didn't cry. Instead, I locked my jaw and didn't utter a word, as I was told. My face was solemn. Somehow Officer Rossi reminded me of Diddy, so I hacked up a wad of spit and spat in his face.

Tiny grinned, groaning, "Yeaah!" Crap like that turned him on.

That was my initiation into the business. I was handed a sleek pearl-handled Saturday night special and told it would get me through closed doors. I was the new Queen of Harlem, Madame Mary Mags. I got in to make a quick buck and instead made a small empire for myself and Richard.

MISTER MAGIC

After Tiny broke me in, he set me up with my own headquarters. A numbers bank. That was where we tallied all the money. My favorite spot. A small two-bedroom apartment over an old bar, fallen vacant to vandalism and crime. Drugs were becoming a big issue in the city that the government could no longer ignore; it was eating away at the numbers game too. A lot of policy bank owners turned to selling dope, but Tiny and I stuck it out. Tiny loaned me the money and convinced me to buy the building with the neighborhood bar attached in Richard's name. It was best not to acquire property in your own name without legal records of earnings. The deal was to make money look respectable, so it could be openly used. Since Richard owned a business and he and I were never legally married, his name was on everything I bought until I acquired the laundered money. Now, I know I told you we got married in New Orleans. We did. We were married by a drunken Rabbi at a speakeasy in the French Quarters. Witnesses and everything! We just didn't obtain the license, but to us, we were married—at least by common law, that is. I didn't go by Mary Owens on paper until I was committed to the mental facility, and that was Poo's doing. She filled out all the paperwork.

Anyway, not only did Tiny protect me; he taught me everything he knew. He showed me how to make smart investments to accrue legit funds. You'd never know from his lifestyle, but Tiny sat on a small fortune. He secured everything in his sister, Val's name, who lived in New Jersey. Tiny lived modestly. He purposely chose not to call too much attention to himself. His height was already an attraction on its own. So, he drove a modest car, had several small apartments throughout the city, and didn't flaunt jewelry, money, or women. His clothes were custom made, only because they had to be. Tiny wanted to retire to a comfortable life in a big house with lots of land in the sun-baked south and happily sit rocking on a porch watching grand-children play. That's where we differed and often bumped heads; I spent BIG money! Needless to say, I got me one of those Hogs with fishtails and fat whitewall tires—1964, Matador Red Metallic. Tiny hated driving me around in that thing. I can laugh about it now...boy, did I give him a hard time. It kept him on his toes.

When I told Richard about my new business venture, he laughed, saying, "Woman, you been hitting the Kool-Aid too hard, ain't ya!" He thought I was kidding, but I've always been straight up with him. He didn't really believe me until his grand opening night.

Richard and his Jewish friend and business partner, Albert, had renovated the quaint and savvy supper club on Lenox Ave and were ready for business. I didn't like Albert, he was too nosy, and his port-hole was always open. Ain't nothing less attractive than a chrome dome sloppy man who walks around with his fly open. He and Richard signed a crazy contract stating if one owner died, the other received full ownership. Not only was Richard a Black man, which raised his stakes, he was also much older. If anything happened to him, I would be left high and dry. That's another reason I did what I had to do; Richard didn't think for the both of us.

Bayou House of Blues wasn't a large establishment, but it wasn't small either. It was perfect for small parties and intimate dinner shows. Richard hired Jo to manage the kitchen, and after her trial month, she leased her beauty parlor out to her sister. Jo's food was so good, Richard expanded the kitchen to incorporate catering. Her food actually kept the club running years after live jazz bands died down. Fatso was in charge of the house. He and Richard booked entertainment. Albert mostly sat back in his seersucker suit—ate, took in the music, and counted every penny. He was good at his craft, and he did teach Richard how to run a well-polished business.

On opening night, I walked into Bayou House of Blues, dressed to the nines, sparkling in diamonds, and laid back in white fur. Madame LaRue, dressed equally as elegant, was by my side with Tiny and Lew walking close behind us. It was sort of my debut. The Madame wanted Harlem to know I was taking her place, so she sold out Richard's spot that night, and he didn't ask me any more questions. We kept business, business, and our marriage estranged.

"Richard," I called out, and he headed over to escort us to our table.

"Oh-ooo-oo-o!" he sang when he saw me. "Who's the vixen with all the fixins?" he teased, kissing me like no one else was standing there. "Baby, you is fyne!" he shouted, making me blush in front of Tiny, who pretended to be observing the room.

"Stop playing; you're crushing my dress," I whispered, worming from his embrace. His breath smelled like he started the party early. "I'd like you to meet, Madame LaRue...the Queen of Harlem—"

"Eh-eh, dear, the ex-queen." She extended her hand for Richard to kiss like he did mine. Being a lady's man, he knew what to do. He had The Madame blushing and gushing too before the night was over.

"And this is Lew and Tiny," I added to distract him from The Madame. She looked as if she had plans for my man that didn't include any of us.

We took our seats in the front of the house.

"Wuzhappnin?" Richard offered Lew a homeboy handshake.

"Nothin' to it," Lew responded, engaging him in the routine. Lew was a big ol' Latin brother; folks called him and Tiny 'double trouble'. I called them Baby Huey and Spike—that dog from Tom and Jerry. If you played numbers, you knew who they were, and if you saw them coming, you better have had your act straight. Because they were breaking legs and taking numbers.

"Solid," Richard continued, readying to enter the same routine with Tiny, who was now seated next to me. Richard extended his hand, "What's happenin', bro?" he repeated with less enthusiasm.

"I got enough friends," Tiny responded, ignoring his hand. "I'm here strictly for work...bro." He added, still observing his surroundings.

Richard sort of laughed, held the back of my seat, leaned in between us, and spoke loudly over the horn solo playing. "Well, we're short on help in the kitchen. You bus bubbles? How does five dollars for the night sound?" He took Tiny for just a bodyguard.

"Sounds like a drop in a bucket," Tiny answered loudly but still ignoring his presence.

"Saay, blood, it feels like you gotta problem with me?" Richard stood erect and unbuttoned his crisp white hosting tuxedo jacket, sort of spreading his arms. Too cool for words. I hadn't seen him act in that manner in a long time.

"If I had a problem, you'd know about it." Tiny slowly turned in his seat, about to stand. The Madame reached across me and grabbed his hand.

"I hear what you saying, but I see you coming...and I promise you if you cross the line," Richard looked at me, "you gonna limp back, ya dig?"

Tiny stood, all 6 feet 10 inches of him.

"Gentlemen, please!" The Madame stood also. "Let's not make a scene." I was rather enjoying the display. "It's Madame Mary's debut...and Mr. Owens." She caressed Richard's side, taking his arm like the sawed-off wench I later found out she was. "This is your grand opening. Tiny is simply doing his job. He protects us. Now...do show me around your establishment." She ran her fingers up his black buttoned chest. "I want to see every part." Richard was too hot to acknowledge her advances then, but later that night, he would.

"Yeah, well, as long as TINY knows...I got my wife's back when she's with me!" He grabbed my arm, refusing to leave me alone with Tiny. "Come on, Mary, I got some people I want to introduce you to." The Madame motioned for Lew to follow us.

Richard was full of it. Once we began making money, he started chasing skirts like before, leaving me no choice but to pursue Tiny. One monkey don't stop the show. I know I told you before that my Richard was a fine, mello' fello'! It's true. He was cooler than the other side of the pillow...sleek, charming, and savvy too. City fine is what I call it, dazzling and oozing with confidence. His head rocked in arrogance when he strutted into a room. With Richard, I felt validated, worthy, maybe even beautiful. But Tiny demanded a different kind of attention. He was a big, burly Black man. His face was grimaced and stern. His presence brought about fear. With Tiny, I felt safe...and Lord, chile, HOT in the seat!

"Tante Mags!" Sal shouted, laughing.

"I can only tell it how it T-I-is!" I laughed, falling on Martita's shoulder. She was laughing so hard she had tears in her eyes. My stories and humor brought joy to those young folks.

Tiny was a straightforward type of brother who liked to get to the quick of things. He pulled them up from the roots, straight from the start. He told me he had a woman and kid in Brooklyn, with another on the way. He said he didn't love her, but their relationship was convenient, and she was the mother of his kids, so that was that. Yet, there was a physical attraction between us. It's funny how a man can treat one woman differently from the next. The Grandmother used to say, "A man only loves de woman he's with." I was everything Tiny wanted, and his girl, Yvonne...she was what he had. When I first met her, I noticed the black and blue marks hidden under the makeup on her face. I knew I drove Tiny crazy, and Yvonne probably paid for my waywardness. I wasn't into breaking up families, but Tiny laid something down on me mightier than anything I've ever felt before. He was the air I breathed. My earth, moon, sun, and stars. For years, I flirted around him, and he never touched me. My protection meant more than his desires. He made his intentions clear from the beginning, "We can't tie romance with business. It gets too messy." But I was used to getting my way.

In hindsight, I guess I was something like Diddy. The Grandmother was right. I didn't make it by playing by the rules, either. I loved those times, though, not because they were good but because they were raw. There was always music playing that expressed exactly how you were feeling and what you were going through. The pace of life was slower, people respected one another, and most importantly, I was young, vibrant, and loaded! If you had a dime in your pocket and were ready to hit the jackpot, you were looking for Madame Mary Mags.

Richard and I moved into a penthouse apartment in Graham Court on 7th Avenue between West 116th and 117th Street—and boy, was it grand. The lobbies had crystal chandeliers and elevators with sliding metal gate doors. An operator turned a big golden wheel to open and close them. Our apartment had several windows facing Central Park, a claw-foot bathtub, and two working fireplaces. We owned sleek modern furniture and collected art and antiques, as The Madame taught me. We were like George and Weezy, baby; we were movin' on up. I had everything I wanted but Tiny. So, being the new Madame, I realized I had to order him to make love to me; otherwise, he wouldn't. He was committed to my safety.

I remember we were coming back from a spring break in Florida. I had started traveling with Poo again. She was maturing into a beautiful young lady with legs that went on for days. She definitely got her height from her trifling father, who was too busy to accommodate us on our annual trips. On that particular trip, Richard said he had business in Memphis. He was recruiting an up-and-coming band for the supper club. So, once again, Tiny escorted Poo and me to and fro. He was always such a pleasure on the trips. It was like we were one big happy family. Mister Magic, that's what I called him because whatever I wanted, he made it happen—except for touching me. I was growing tired of looking at that fine man and not being able to have him. So, when we arrived back at my apartment and Richard was still away on his trip, I wrapped my arms around Tiny's waist and demanded he do his duty.

"Do your duty, Mr. Magic!" I purred.

Tiny lifted me off my feet and laid me on the couch, teasing, kissing, and rubbing me over—like we were about to do the business. He whispered something in my ear, turning me on just to turn me off.

"Not fo nuttin', but you know The Madame started ordering me to have sex with her when I was way too young." He sat up and brought me into his arms. My hair fell loose, and he played with the curls, continuing his point. "She made me do things I didn't want to do because I was simple, young, and depending on her. I was a runner at the time; too tall and big to be thirteen but just right for lovin'. The Madame introduced me to a lot of things." I released Tiny from my embrace because I knew what it felt like to be forced out of your youth. My eyes fell in embarrassment and shame.

Tiny lifted my chin and cupped my face between his enormous hands. "Madame Mary Mags, I'ma make love to you in the right place, at the right time, and when I'm damn well ready." With that, he scooted me aside and stood. "When does that husband of yours get back? You need someone to stay with you?" I didn't know what to say. I was ashamed, but I wanted him even more than before.

I cleared my throat. "Ahh, he's back Friday." It was Wednesday evening, and I knew Tiny was tired from the long drive.

"How 'bout I go, ahh…" He scratched his head and straightened his clothes. "How 'bout I go over to Sylvia's and grab us two fried chicken dinners… I'll call Lew and see if he can sit with you tonight." He looked at me with empathy, and that made me feel worse. "I'll be back in the morning." I nodded, regretting treating him like a hunk of meat. He probably wanted to see his kids. He and Yvonne had split, but Tiny was utterly in love with his children, especially the boy. Jeremy was a four-year-old mini replica of him, and he tried his best to do everything just like his dear old dad.

That night, Tiny and I ate potato salad and sucked on bones while watching Peyton Place on ABC. Tiny zonked out on the sofa with his mouth wide open. He never did call Lew. I kissed him on his forehead and retired to my bedroom, crushing on him like a teenager.

Our passion for each other smoldered through the night. Our hungry bodies tossed and turned in misery and discomfort. By morning, we were blazing like a flaming fire. Hot as an oven. Tiny barged into my bedroom and ripped off his shirt.

"Damn-it, woman! What kinda hold you got over me?"

It was over; Richard lost his crown. I could go on and on about how great of a lover Tiny was. That brother made all the pit stops. But it wasn't the sex that did it. You see, sex was another part of my erratic lifestyle. I don't know how to explain, but be it pleasure or pain, I mostly did things to feel something...anything other than dead and dying. I needed to know that I truly existed in this world. I found validation in Tiny's love. Someone loved me first, and I gave him my heart because he actually admired mine. That type of love doesn't come knocking every day.

———

"As old as I am, I've come to know one thing for sure, all good things come to an end. Just like this story." I smiled and motioned over to Nurse Sue who was approaching us. Sue was always a pleasure to see.

"Oh, wow!" Sal said, looking down at his watch. "Our time is up already?"

"Hi, guys!" Sue said, resting her hand on my shoulder. I squeezed it, letting her know that I was okay. "I'm sorry, visiting hours are over."

"Ahh, man!" Martita moaned, surprisingly hugging Sal before he could stand up good.

"Aww," he expressed. "It was good meeting you too." He awkwardly hugged her back.

"You guys looked like you were having a really good conversation. I'm sorry I had to break it up," Sue said, pulling out her chart. "How are you feeling, Ms. Lady?" She smiled at me. "You look cheery." She checked my pulse.

"Yeah, seeing this ol' boy does that for me." I took Sal's hand with my free one. He looked like he needed help escaping Martita's embrace.

"Hey, listen, Nurse Sue...," he removed Martita's tightly gripped hands from around his waist. My story must have gotten her into her feelings. "Can I have a moment alone with my grandmother...please?" He walked behind my chair and held my shoulders like I belonged to him.

Sue looked at us and then, her watch and moaned in surrender. "Well, okay...but just a moment. Come on, Martita." She flipped the pages on her chart. "And how are you feeling?" she asked as they stepped off to the side.

"Tante Mags, listen..." Sal whispered, stooping in front of me. "So, I've been on this important case for a few years now, and it seems it's coming to an end." He lowered his head. "I don't know when I'll be able to get back here now that they changed the visiting hours. I may be able to come on a Saturday in the afternoon. I'm not really sure, though."

I patted his hand, resting on my knee. "Please, beb, don't worry, none. I'll be here...then again, I'm hoping to be gone."

"Yeah!" His downcast eyes perked up. "I was speaking with your caseworker the other day...ahh, Ms. Simmons. I wanted to be added to your records as a point of contact. She said you may be needing a release provider soon...that is, if you continue to improve. She said you're not communicating with your therapist yet. Why?"

I lowered my eyes. "I don't know... scared of what I'll say, I guess. I don't wanna say the wrong things. Some people are funny, you know? They may not like what I gotta say about this place." I looked back up at him. His kind eyes looked worried. "I have some things I wanna tell ya about what's been going on in here. Maybe we can set up a phone call?"

"Yeah, sure, but are you okay? Ain't nobody hurt you, did they? I didn't like how that Dino fella was acting last time I was here." Sal stood, looking around and getting agitated, ready to protect me.

"No, no...not anymore. I hear the hospital got rid of that rascal." I took Sal's hand to ease his nerves.

"Mr. Abrams...the time." Sue reminded us. "I'm truly sorry."

"Okay, okay." Sal stooped back down in front of me and grabbed both of my hands firmly. "Listen, Tante Mags, talk to your therapist...and call me every day until you reach me, okay. I don't wanna hear that 'I don't call a man's house' business...I live alone."

"Will do, precious." I kissed his hands.

"Hey," he looked me square in the eyes, "don't take your purpose to the grave sitting up in here. You're blessed on purpose...for a purpose. You don't belong here, Tante Mags. Talk to him." A shiver ran up my spine as he kissed my cheek. "Love you."

"Love you too, beb."

PART V
MISERY

"Hell is empty and all the devils are here." – *William Shakespeare*

THE REVOLUTION WILL NOT BE TELEVISED

D r. Davis was a short plain-looking fella. He only wore gray suits with navy blue ties and a pair of black-framed, round-shaped glasses that took over his face. The flashiest thing he ever wore was his socks. Because of his socks, I could tell that somewhere underneath his dull exterior was a fascinating guy. When we first met ten years ago, he had a pair of black socks on with orange flames tiled around them. I knew then that Dr. Davis was undercover fabulous. During our sessions, he usually did all the talking while I listened. His voice was dry and tame. It had no hills and valleys, only plains and plateaus. When I was over-medicated, I used to sit and fall asleep listening to him. When I was alert, I heard every word. He often went on about his own troubles. I guess he thought no one was really listening.

"Hello, Mrs. Owens. How are you today?" he asked, not expecting an answer, just going through the motions as he looked through my weekly charts. I visited Dr. Davis' small corner office so often that I had memorized all the quotes from the pictures hanging on the wall. My favorite was a man climbing a mountain. Believe you can, and you're halfway there, Theodore Roosevelt. "It looks like you had a rather full week..." he went on, recapping my days. "Ahh, fried chicken...I had to give that up." He was rambling to himself.

"Why?" I asked, reassuring myself that a therapist was like any other person; *he's simply a human being.* Dr. Davis lowered his head and looked over his glasses at me. His facial expression remained blank.

"My LDL levels were escalating. I had to remove all saturated fats from my diet." He released the paperwork he was thumbing through and gave me his attention.

"Everything in moderation..." I continued, looking into my lap for courage. "That's what The Grandmother used to tell us." Speaking to doctors always made me feel examined and undressed. I thought of Sal and what he said about taking purpose to the grave. Both The Grandmother and Lotti were dead. "Too much of anything ain't good for ya, huh, Doc?" I looked up at Dr. Davis, feeling a little more determined to get back what was mine. I had to head for the mountain top.

"R-right." he stuttered, surprised by my direct eye contact. He cleared his throat. "So, how do you do, Mrs. Owens?" he asked, as though meeting me for the first time. "I'm Dr. Paul Davis." He smiled and slightly stood, extending his right hand across the desk, knocking over a cup of markers. He nervously laughed. The moment was awkward.

"I'm good, Dr. Davis," I answered with an assertion. My name is Mary Magdalene Owens."

"I'm glad to meet you...I truly am." He sat back down. "I was starting to feel chided; you've been communicating with everyone but me; why?"

I crossed my legs and got comfortable. "Well... cause I was saving all the juicy stuff just for you."

"Oh, really?" He smiled again; he had a charming smile. "I guess I should feel honored, then, huh?" He tilted back in his office chair, rolling a pen between his fingers. "Do tell."

"Well, what I haven't been telling others is about my disorder. This manic depression."

"I see; tell me about it, Mrs. Owens."

"Okay...well, you see, I've been telling everyone my life story, and I feel like I'm reliving it myself through their eyes. But what I've been excluding...well, not fully disclosing is about the mental hell I was going through." I got up and walked to the window; Dr. Davis had a street view. There were snow flurries. I spread my fingers and placed my hand against the glass, wanting to know how cold it was outdoors and longing to feel like a part of the outside world again. Everyone was bundled up in their winter gear. I could see life moving forward and people living. It helped to distract any anxieties I was feeling about going down that dark road of depression.

"I think it all started in my early twenties, on the road with the band. Oh!" I glanced at him. "I used to sing with a jazz band."

"I've heard." He raised his eyebrows like he was impressed.

THE GUYS USED TO CALL ME GRASSHOPPER BECAUSE I WAS ALWAYS hopping around doing something. During my manic episodes, there were clear changes in my behavior; besides my increased energy, I couldn't sleep properly. I used to go on for days, just talking their ears off. I used to make myself into more than what I really was, ordering them around like servants one minute, then snapping at folks like an angry, snapping turtle the next. The guys being guys kept me drunk when I was like that. They thought it was funny seeing me pass out but drinking heavily led to my depressive episodes. I would cry, moping around, missing home, Poo, and Lotti. The guys dismissed me as acting foolish, just being a woman. Richard, that's my husband; he handled me pretty well. When he grew tired of my mess, he threw me over his shoulder, carried me off somewhere, plopped me down, and shook the demon out.

"Stop it! Stop it this instant," he'd say in an authoritative tone. "I'm about good and sicca you! If you don't quit, I'm leaving. I swear for God." That usually sobered me up until the next episode. Back then, they were less frequent and appeared more emotional than anything.

Tiny, that's my man...I know, just follow along, Doc. From the very beginning, Tiny called me out.

"You know you can get help for that shit nowadays, right?" He said when I was acting a fool, treating everyone like peons and drinking heavily. I was laughing and living it up, one minute, then crying the next. Then there were my anger issues. Let's just say I had everyone walking on eggshells. Tiny pretty much handled me like Richard, grabbed me sternly, shook me up a little, and said, "If you don't stop, you gonna find ya ass right back in that alley." I'd cry, falling into his arms. Tiny was patient with me for the most part. He held me on many nights, just talking. He told me he lost his mother to depression and mental illness. She was admitted when he was ten years old. It was just him and his older sister, Val. They moved to New York City, and it's been them ever since. "You just say the word, and we'll go visit one of them fancy doctors downtown." Tiny would say to me. For some reason, him mentioning doctors used to scare me straight. I didn't want to be carried away nor labeled crazy. I would stop drinking for a while and act like I had some sense, even though inside, I constantly felt like I was standing on a ledge.

Being bipolar is a nightmare. You get tired of people telling you to have a positive attitude when depression is saying it's forever. It says darkness is your closest friend. I had many years of ups and downs before I was diagnosed. That's pretty much why I stuck with Richard. He could have kicked my crazy behind to the curb a long time ago, but in his way, he loved me. And it wasn't a bottle of love-potion type love either. Richard put up with some real crap.

You know how folks say they can remember where they were when the lights went out in the city or when Kennedy or Martin Luther King died? Well, when King died, I was waking up, lying naked in the arms of my lover. Tiny and I had stayed in bed an entire day, making up for lost time and enjoying each other's bodies. The room was dark. I remember calling 1212 for the time because Richard kept our bedroom so dark you couldn't tell the time of day. He couldn't stand the light coming in from anywhere when he was sleeping. That's the life of an entertainer; you sleep when you can sleep.

"Good evening," the recording said. "At the tone, the time will be 8:55 and 50 seconds." As soon as I hung up, the phone rang. It was Jo, and she was crying.

"Girl, you heard?" She asked, sniffling.

"Heard what?" I sat up and shook Tiny awake. The man was sleeping like a log next to me, but he woke up fighting. "It's Jo!" I told him. "Jo, what's wrong?" She was frantic, and I could hear wailing in the background.

"Turn on the news." She hung up, and for some reason, I froze.

"What is it, baby?" Tiny was already up with a leg in his pants.

"I don't know." He turned on the lights, and we both squinted. "She said...turn on the news." I jumped out of bed, wrapping a sheet around me, and ran into the living room to turn on the tube. Tiny followed, putting on his shirt.

"This is Dan Rather, reporting for CBS News from New York City...The Reverend Martin Luther King, Jr. was shot to death by an assassin late today..."

That, and Tiny shouting obscenities and violently banging the wall with his fist, was all I heard. The pain was so deep it churned and burned inside my stomach. I ran into the bathroom and threw up all the takeout that Tiny and I had binged on. Losing Dr. King was like losing hope.

The streets of Harlem were like a battle zone, not as it had been the year prior in the wave of race riots titled 'The long, hot summer of 1967'. This time, only some people were setting fires and looting. Tiny and I got to the headquarters as soon as we heard. A few of our betting parlors were hit that night but not as much damage as we expected.

———

"I'M SORRY, DOC, THIS IS THE PERIOD IN MY LIFE WHERE I WAS RUNNING a numbers racket. You know, something like the lottery, but with people betting with bookies at bars, barbershops, bodegas—betting parlors. Runners ran the money and betting slips between the parlors and the headquarters or the numbers bank. Tiny and I ran that operation in Harlem; we were Harlem elites...and yes, it was illegal.

"I see." Dr. Davis nodded his head and scribbled something down without looking.

So, WHILE THOUSANDS OF YOUNG PEOPLE WERE MARCHING THROUGH Times Square the next day, bound for City Hall, gambling folks were placing their bets throughout the boroughs. Of course, there were tears and many sad stories. We lost a great civil rights leader. Between the tears, I discovered that people healed by playing numbers. On top of the usual number, 769, the dream book number for death, everybody and their mama played April 4th, 404. Also, the address of the Lorraine Motel where King died—450 Mulberry Street—handle, straight, or combo. While the hearts of Americans grieved for a leader of his people, Tiny and I made our best, and sadly, our last two weeks of earnings. Those two weeks were also the last I spent with my beloved. If I had to pick a moment of regret in my life, I'd say it was those last two weeks. I wish we'd chosen love over money.

The day after King's death, Richard arrived home early from his business trip in Memphis. Tiny had just dropped me off. He wanted to stay but needed to check in on his kids in Brooklyn. We kissed, sharing a long goodnight at the door. He left, promising to be back later or early in the morning. I had just stepped away from the door when the bell rang. I smiled, did a little dance, and ran back, excited about Tiny returning.

"So, you changed your mind," I said, pulling the door open. It was Richard. He had left his keys at home again. He looked startled but not as startled as I was. Seeing him made what I was doing with Tiny feel tainted.

"You were expecting...someone else?" He looked at me suspiciously but leaned in and kissed me anyway. "I was worried about you, so I took an earlier flight." He slipped his arm around my waist and walked into the house.

I don't know why I felt so uneasy. Richard cheated all the time, but I did it right there in our home. Thank goodness for our cleaning lady; she had the place looking spic and span after me and Tiny's escapade. Richard put a damper on my time alone with Tiny. He felt the need to be near me during the weeks after King's death. Between Richard and the chaos of collecting and dishing out all that money, Tiny and I maybe had one other moment alone before the romance was over.

I remember it like yesterday; we were at his spot in the Bronx, right over the 138th Street Bridge. We were lying across the pull-out sofa, watching traffic build-up from the window and talking of getting away from all the madness. Maybe retiring from it all.

"If anything ever happens to me, I want you to pack up and head for Canada or Mexico to lay low for a bit. Lew can help you do that."

I always cut him off when he talked like that. I was a day-to-day type of person. My past was too depressing to recall, and the future wasn't promised. I put out my cigarette and kissed Tiny's words away. He wasn't a crying man. When he was scared, he worried. When he was sad, he fought. But he always took his time with me. For such a big guy, he was a gentle lover. He intentionally roamed my body, looking for ways to please me. I could cry just thinking about how special he was. At the time, I was unaware of the treasure I had in him. Tiny told me he loved me that night and asked if I would share his front porch with him one day. That porch was Tiny's dream, and although I preferred diamonds, I said yes, because I knew he would turn mountains to bring me diamonds if he had to. A woman is lucky to get one good romance in her lifetime. Mine was with William 'Tiny' Daughtry.

After our tryst, we dressed and battled the traffic heading back to the headquarters. Once there, Tiny and I, along with Peaches (the new lieutenant, a ruthless gangster from Brooklyn), and a few other big wigs were counting out money—piled high to our necks. We were making payments when nosey-azz Albert, Richard's business partner, barged in using a key he said Richard gave him. He claimed he was picking up some cases of liquor. We used to stock the overflow of inventory from the bar and club up there. But we hadn't done that in years.

"Oh, yeah!" I glanced over at Dr. Davis again. "My husband ran a bar as well as a jazz supper club back then."

Anyway, all guns were drawn on Albert, and he was full of apologies. Unfortunately, he saw too much. There was smack laying on the table and everything. Some dudes from the Bronx were trying to convince us to sell it, but I didn't want anything to do with that junk. Tiny and another fella followed Albert out.

"Just talk to him, okay, Tiny." I knew it was a stupid request.

"Yeah...I'll just talk to him," he smirked, winked at me, and left. That was the last I saw of him.

The next day the papers read, 'Bagel boy turned jazz club owner murdered in Central Park East.' I hadn't heard from Tiny and didn't know what to think or do. When I confided in Richard, he said he never gave Albert a key. He also mentioned that Albert had been questioning about the apartment over the bar.

It doesn't take Jack Frost to recognize a snow job. Back then, we were called the Black Mafia, and a white syndicate took over, using cops to maneuver the change in control by raiding Negro racketeers. We ran the area in Harlem with the heaviest cluster of number players, and we killed it in those few weeks. Everyone was looking for a cut. At the time, Tiny and I had a big payroll, including bookies, runners, controllers, accountants, security, bail bondsmen, lawyers, and even cops. When Tiny went undercover, that left me in control of everything, and I was a nervous wreck. I had never made a move without him. With Peaches' help, I was able to finish the payouts.

Tiny and I had spoken of what to do if he ever went missing. Yet, I was unsure of taking the drastic measure of closing the business down and getting out of the country. I got rid of all the new money as quickly as possible. I took some to Yvonne, Tiny's babies' mama; she was happy as hell. I met his sister off the New Jersey Turnpike and gave her the rest of his cut to secure as usual. Richard took my half. He put some away in the safety deposit at the bank. With the rest, he and Fatso made their customary investments and casino runs, laundering the money. I went to Madame LaRue for help, but she was getting old and senile. She said, "Sell to Mookie the Mouth," some old-time gangster, "then get out."

Tiny and I were set up, but I couldn't figure out how or why Albert got involved. I became sick as a dog, waiting for the other shoe to drop. Tiny said never to look for him if he went missing. If I wanted to, I didn't know where to begin. Outside of my company, Tiny was a mystery to me. All I knew was that we both agreed that Peaches would be next in line for the business if we had to sell. It wasn't something that I was prepared to do because I felt we still had good years ahead of us. However, I folded and did as Tiny advised and sold to Peaches.

I was packing for a long trip to Canada when I heard Richard yell my name from the living room. He had planted himself in front of the television, waiting anxiously to hear any news. There, I saw my beloved being hauled away in handcuffs from an unfamiliar apartment building.

The reporter said, "The second suspect in the murder of Bagel Boy was apprehended this afternoon in the Van Pelt Avenue Corridor section of Staten Island." Apparently, there were eyewitnesses.

Once Tiny was arrested, Officer Rossi felt liberated enough to sing like a canary. He told all of our sordid affairs, piling up the charges against us. Tiny ignored our lawyer's advice and confessed to running the Harlem numbers racket. He turned over fake ledgers that he kept at his Bronx apartment to keep me from being involved in an investigation and trial. On top of the racketeering admission, he was charged as an accomplice to second-degree murder. Being a two-time offender, Tiny received a life sentence, with a minimum of fifteen to twenty-five years. When he really only stood accused of loving me too much.

The feds didn't let me off as easily as Tiny would have liked. I, too, got the royal shaft. I was picked up along with Peaches at the headquarters the next day during a raid. My name was mentioned by Rossi, but Tiny insisted I was only a cover-up. He was King Pin. The fake ledgers made it hard for the DA to make indictments. The police force was thoroughly corrupted by bribes from the numbers bosses. Federal names and politicians were listed throughout. I was arrested and charged as a runner and madame. A white woman running a brothel in Manhattan was arrested the month before on similar charges and slapped with a penalty and community service. I got two years in a state pen. The DA needed legitimacy, so they indicted me, Tiny, Peaches, and a few other bookies to make it look suitable for the newspapers. 'Your number is up,' the Daily News read. 'A Harlem numbers racket busted by the NYPD'. Harlem knew the truth, and the numbers racket continued without us fully controlled by the Mafia.

Officer Rossi was later found dead. Not too long afterward, Richard received a letter postmarked from Puerto Rico addressed to MMM. It simply stated 'I handled that for you and my brother, Spike. Signed, Baby Huey.'

BEELZEBUL, THE LORD OF DUNG

Without warning or reasoning for my sudden action, I quickly turned from the window that I was gazing out of and erratically marched towards Dr. Davis. I plopped my hands onto his desk and leaned heavily over them. I wanted him to hear me clearly and do everything within his power to help. "Okay, Doc, this is the part I've been afraid to tell." I sat down, needing to feel grounded, and gripped the edge of his desk, needing something to hold to. I had been feeling anxious about speaking of my demons. I was doing so well and didn't want to slip back into darkness. I didn't want to go there because that place within me was too scary. That place within me was dark and oozing with loneliness and pain. It was too much hurt to recover from. There were too many memories to escape. So, I allowed them to fester. I let them become more prominent than the space containing them. Until one day...I snapped. The dam broke, and the levees lifted.

Dr. Davis sat erect, leaning into his desk in full attention. "Doc, all my life, I've heard small voices telling me what to do...some good, some bad. As a child, The Grandmother used to lay hands on me, casting the demons out. She said I was cursed, like my diddy, evil to the core. When they put me in prison..." I shook and lowered my head. "...them voices became louder—more tormenting than anything else."

I WAS PLACED IN SOLITARY CONFINEMENT ON THE VERY FIRST DAY OF MY sentence. They thought I was being defiant, but I was going crazy. I was riddled with demons with only death and darkness as a companion. Going to prison not only strips you of your freedom, your pride, and your livelihood—you can actually lose your mind there. Those first two months, I spent most of my time in confinement, fighting myself and fighting the voices. It was there that I had my first visual hallucination. I was lying on the cell floor, in solitary again, when suddenly vibrant colors painted the walls and started to dance around me. They were tangible textures of green, yellow, red, and orange, all swirled together. I felt like I was locked inside of a kaleidoscope, and at the end of this parade of colors, way up past the ceiling, was a baby and The Grandmother dressed in glistening white taking it away. I hauled over screaming and crying in pain, my stomach cramped with spasms. When the guards came the next day, they said there was blood everywhere. I woke up in the prison infirmary, strapped to a bed. The doctor tried to explain that I suffered a miscarriage, but I was inconsolable and had to be sedated. I lost Tiny's baby in prison; I never told him that. I never told anybody.

A sadness grew inside of me that still holds my spirit hostage. I was a part of my everyday surroundings but only a speck of existence. Everything seemed to be in mid-blur. Contrasted. Glitched. I began talking to myself and pulling out my beautiful hair. They placed me in a different ward where I was sedated and confined twenty-four hours a day. After six months of being heavily medicated, I was somewhat better and able to start receiving guests. Richard, Fatso, and Jo alternated weekends for the remainder of my sentence. Richard was pleasant and surprisingly remorseful.

He said, "As your husband, I should have insisted that you never participate in all that. I got caught up!" he expressed, holding his head.

"I let money rule over better judgment...now you're in here, and Albert..." He couldn't speak about Albert without water coming to his eyes. He swore that if Albert somehow became involved, it was because he was a scapegoat and in the wrong place, at the wrong time. Richard acquired full ownership of Bayou House of Blues. He withdrew Albert's initial investment, plus the interest over the years, and sent it to his widow.

Fatso, who really was a hefty man by then, visited in between Richard and Jo. The scandal had grounded him further into his religion. The thing about Fatso was that he wasn't godless. He, too, got caught up in what I was slinging, but he was grateful that all that money that crossed his hands didn't lead him to jail. He told me that he started playing drums at a local church on the Grand Concourse that he and Jo joined. They married a long time ago, but both committed themselves to the Lord together and got rebaptized. I was happy for him. We were a long way off from traveling in a busted bus across the country to play good jazz music.

"Smarten up, Meatball," he told me. "It's time to start living right. God ain't gonna give us but so many more chances. As a friend and big bro, I'm telling you—ya slip is hanging." He took my hand. "Humble yourself, Mags, baby, under God's mighty hand. Cast all those anxieties on Him because he cares for you. Stay alert and sober-minded. The enemy...the devil, he prowls around like a roaring lion looking for someone to devour." Fatso was a man of few words, and that was the most I'd ever heard him say in one sitting. In my head, I made plans to abide by his wisdom. It was my feet that led me another way.

I was happiest to see Jo. Once she assured me that she adopted all my plant babies and had my furs packed away in storage, we commenced into fulfilling conversations. Jo and I were in some ways alike. Our grandmothers raised us (Jo's mom ran off after a no-good man when she was just a girl). Jo suffered a nervous breakdown before getting rid of her first husband. And we both were wealthy and married to musicians. In our visitation time together, Jo did two things for me: she read from the bible, which soothed me more than you could imagine. The words she placed in my head kept me from week to week. More importantly, she wrote to Tiny on my behalf. Prisoners were prohibited from communicating with prisoners in other facilities.

Tiny's first message to me read,

> MMM:
>   Don't worry about me. I always land on my feet. I love you and be strong.
>   Mister Magic

Tiny was the type of man born with a boot on his neck. He expected trouble and counted it as his lot in life. "We'll make it through," he used to say. Even though his messages sent through Jo were impersonal, knowing he still loved me and was okay helped to complete my sentence.

The next fourteen months flew by, and the antidepressants they had me on helped me function in basic ways, like getting out of bed. Mentally, I felt like I was coming out of a dark cave. But that old devil likes to prowl. The month of my release, during a visit, Richard came smelling like a woman's perfume.

"Save the riff, McGriff, ya spot is blown up!" I yelled, and he was full of excuses, but I lost it anyway.

I spent an extra month in solitary for that, but I never forgot that scent. I could smell it the entire time. It lingered in my cell, standing out over the rank odor of piss. Have you ever been so mad that it made you sick? All that remorse Richard was feeling at the beginning of my sentence fell off like shackles. He was living on the outside like a playboy. At least that's what the voices told me. I started worrying about what he was doing, who he was with, and if them trollops were wearing my stuff. I was in love with Tiny, but Richard was all I had. On top of being depressed, I grew angry and paranoid. There was no middle ground anymore.

I spent one year, eight months, three weeks, seven hours, fifteen minutes, and twenty seconds in an incredibly dark and painful place without a bottom. Then, I was finally released. We celebrated at Swamp Water, the bar Richard and I owned. The old crew was back together—even Lew returned from Puerto Rico. He had turned over a new leaf in life and was bartending. He said that rubbing pennies together, trying to make them into dimes, was better than spreading his cheeks in a prison cell. Lord, I hoped that wasn't true for Tiny's sake. Anyway, there was a new barmaid at Swamp Water. She was a pretty young thang with a mouth full of pearly white teeth, bright eyes, smooth skin, and a stacked frock. She was everything I wasn't. I had turned into a fighter. I was scarred on the inside and out from being a hellraiser, just as The Grandmother had said. The new barmaid filled the orders Lew took and came over with our drinks after he finished his hellos. I saw how she looked at Richard and smelled that same scent that I smelled on him during our visitation.

Doc, something snapped in me that I've never been able to recover. It's like I literally crossed over to the dark side. What I experienced after losing Tiny's baby was fear, sadness, and hysteria. This was more like fulfilling an overdue extended invitation from an old friend, saying, 'Come on over—It's never too late.' I broke that girl's arm in two places. I still don't know how Richard 'n' 'em got her not to press charges. But that was my acceptance to the Lord of Dung's invitation he extended long ago, and he's been running my life into shit ever since.

STRAIGHT, NO CHASER

Getting back into a civilian livelihood was tough, Doc. I had done it before when we moved to Harlem; then, I replaced my lifestyle as an entertainer with criminal activity. This time, I replaced it all with alcohol. Drinking was the worst old habit I ever had. I drank because I felt out of place and out of touch. My scotch neat was familiar. Richard moved us from the beautiful penthouse apartment in Graham Court to a brownstone on Strivers' Row. It was a beautiful home, and I had three floors of rooms to decorate but no inspiration. I left all of our expensive things just lying around. When you've owned and bought as much crap as I have, sooner or later, that's what it becomes. I learned in prison that wealth does not endure.

What was really bothering me was that I couldn't reach my sister, Lotti, and niece, Poo. The lady at the Fontaine Plantation where they lived said Lotti no longer worked there. I didn't know why they hadn't tried to reach me. On top of that, Tiny had written me a goodbye letter.

> *Dearest Mags,*
> *This will be my last letter. Please don't write to me*

anymore. You should be finished with your sentence by now. I pray that you were able to keep your sanity. It can be rough here, and although you pretend to be tough, I know that you're fragile—not like a flower but like a sensitive time bomb. I'm trying to keep my own sanity. Knowing that you're on the outside, and not dying in some cell will help me make it through. Yvonne wrote to me, our baby girl passed away. Pneumonia. Poor thing, she was never fully right in the head. I want you, Yvonne, and the boy to forget me. My sentence is too long to have folks waiting around. The Lord giveth and the Lord has taken away. I can't deal with death anymore. I need you to live...even if it means losing you to that husband of yours. I've sinned against everything I know is right. This is my burden to bear. You were an innocent bystander. Stay clean and enjoy all that money on life and love. You'll always be in my heart.

Tiny

I went into a deep depression, drinking morning, noon, and night. The only time I straightened up was for my parole appointments. They referred me to a doctor, but I had seen enough brain-benders in prison; I refused to go. They all had a monopoly of wisdom but no actual answers. My perception of life was at the bottom of a bottle. My drinking got so bad that Richard confessed that he was withholding information about Lotti. He was afraid to tell me in prison. The news wasn't good. He thought maybe if I knew she called, I'd stop trying to kill myself.

After nineteen years, he and Lotti had finally spoken. Although I wished I was there to hear the conversation they had, more importantly, she called to inform me that Poo had some trouble with one of the spoiled Fontaine kids she worked for. After years of employment with them, Lotti was fired. She didn't know where she and Poo were going to live but would be in touch when they settled.

After Richard's confession, he gave me the number where Lotti could be reached. Rolling my eyes at him, I called my sister while pouring myself another glass of scotch. I thought it would help do the talking for me, but as soon as I heard Lotti's voice, I fell apart.

"Hell-o," she answered, sounding like The Grandmother.

"Hi, hi, Lotti." I stuttered.

"Beb! Where y'at!" she yelled cheerfully, acknowledging me with local sentiment upon hearing my voice.

"Awright, how you?" I sniffled, trying to sober up and be an adult.

"Ooh, fair-to-middling. We been waiting for you to call...Poo and me. Dat niguh of yourns said you got ya'self in some trouble. Is erry'ting okay?" I sure didn't want Lotti and Poo to know about my jail sentence. I rolled my eyes at Richard again, who was sitting nervously in the parlor watching me. He didn't know what to do anymore. If he was right, he was wrong. If only he could have been silent. That would've been the wisest thing to do.

"No, no, I'm okay. Had me some trouble...but I'm back now." I took a drink. "So, what's this I hear about my girl?" The alcohol reached my stomach and flopped.

"Ooh, don't worry none; ah done handled it." She sounded far away...in her spirit.

"Handled what, Lotti?" I straightened up because I knew something wasn't right. "Where's Poo?"

"She...she out with friends," she lied. The truth was Poo wasn't speaking at all. My baby was traumatized. Lotti didn't want me traveling down there to make matters worse.

"What friends?" Lotti didn't let Poo breathe, let alone entertain friends without her.

"She, dey..." Lotti deeply sighed. "Look, Mags, Poo done went and got herself raped." My stomach flopped again, along with my heart this time.

"What?" I whispered. The word raped meandered about and crisscrossed in the empty and dark space at the back of my head.

"We stayin' out in New Awlins right naw with one of Poo's childhood friends, Minton. Ah don't know if you memba him. But ah found us a place. We fixin' to move soon." Lotti continued, starting another conversation like the one she shared didn't happen. I couldn't help but cry when I knew she wanted me to be strong. She needed me to play along.

"Lotti, I—"

"Ah know, ah know...but ain't no need in crying," she said, sadly like I should have been around to cry then. "Ah told ya, ah done fixed it," she insisted, trying to encourage herself and me. "Ah had Tee-John cursed," she revealed. "Ah know it ain't as satisfying as blood, but he's cursed for life. Erry time dat bastard get a yearnin' to be with a woman and can't, he'll tink of Mama Lotti. Hot damn!"

I didn't want to laugh, but I did with my sister because both of our hearts were broken. She continued, blowing smoke in my eyes every time I called, saying that Poo was unavailable to speak. The silence opened an opportunity for my demons to speak lies to me. They issued deceptions of abandonment. No one wanted anything to do with me, I told myself. So, I continued drinking.

PART VI
DEPENDENCY

"Life is a balance of holding on and letting go" - Rumi

WONDERFUL, WONDERFUL

I didn't know why I was seemingly endlessly confused, angry, lost, and tortured. When I wasn't, I was tired, unmotivated, and numb. I was living dormant while demons ran my life. I knew I was tanking, but I couldn't get my mind wrapped around a solution. There wasn't a day that passed that I didn't curse someone out and make them cry. I hid from love and tried to make it hate me by pushing away the people who loved me most. Richard attempted to help, but he was always on the go. He said he was the sole bread-winner of the household and was needed at his businesses. We weren't short on cash. He worked to avoid me. I attempted helping at the supper club for a minute, but I couldn't find a place where I fit in, and folks were getting on my nerves. Everything about socializing reminded me of Tiny and being alone reminded me of Poo and Lotti. The alone time was fine but being lonely is a different kind of hell. Scotch and Mathis were the antidotes.

When I was younger, Lotti used to read aloud stories from her bible. One about a king named Saul comes to mind. He required a harpist to soothe him from his angry rants. Well, all I needed was Mister Wonderful, Wonderful, Johnny Mathis. I loved me some Johnny—still do. Next to Richard, I thought he was the finest man alive. Whenever I heard him sing, I melted. Needless to say, my rants had gotten so bad that Richard started keeping me inebriated to shut me up. When I started cutting up, he threw on a Mathis album, piled my collection up near me, made me a drink, then, he hit the road. He did that nearly every day after Lotti's call. I had lost my grip on reality and developed an elbow problem...I bent it too much. It was scotch, straight, no chaser for me.

Once, I laid into Richard so hard he almost hit me. My tongue was like a razor sometimes; insanity was telling it what to say, and I became damned by my own comments. Richard gnashed his teeth, standing and staring over me with veins protruding from his neck, his hands clenched into balls, and his body stiff. He huffed and stormed out of the room before he hit me. I had been laying across the bed for three days in a silk house dress, cursing him out and drowning in my own funk and sorrows. Even showering was a hassle. Everything felt like an endless drain. My mood was—I'm already tired tomorrow.

Richard could be heard from downstairs banging and slamming things around. He returned with a bottle of scotch, an ice tray, and a heavy bottom lowball glass, he threw it all on the bed. He rolled my record player over and started a Johnny Mathis album. Before leaving, he stood over me again and sighed, exasperated. I was frozen in place. Richard had never lost his temper with me; he was usually nonchalant. He moved, and I flinched nervously, but all he did was collect the items he threw on the bed and made a drink. After handing me the glass, he kissed my forehead instead of pouring it in my face as he should have and turned to leave.

"I know what you're trying to do for me, and I'm sorry for acting a fool," I said before he left the room. He'd been so strong that I never saw what my illness was costing him. Seeing Richard upset broke my heart.

He stopped at the door, and choosing not to look at me directly, said, "You know you're my world, right? I love you, Mary..." He ran his finger along the grooves of the wooden door frame. There was a nick where I threw the fire iron at him and missed. "I don't know how much more of this I can take." His head was lowered. "You're an evil sumpin' when you wanna be…but sumpins gotta give."

That night, I left home. I ran away. I felt too different, misunderstood, and so very far off from everyone else. When I was younger, not fitting in felt like a flaw in me; not fitting in as an adult…well, that felt like me against the world. I ignored the many differences in everyone else's circumstances and only saw my faults. So, I packed a suitcase and two bottles of scotch and got into my hardly driven 1968 candy apple red Caddy wanting to barrel down the highway with the wind in my hair. Scotch and I drove two hours and ten minutes to Sag Harbor. Richard and I had bought a house there some years back. In its heyday, Sag Harbor was the Black elite's answer to Martha's Vineyard. We had to own property. After all, The Madame vacationed there all the time.

When I reached the beach, I couldn't even recall how I got there. I was high as a kite and blazing down the highway in a trance. It was two in the morning, and with only one mile left from the house, I crashed, wrapping the car around a tree. The car burst into flames, yet I managed to walk away without a scratch. Unscathed, I fell to my knees. That's when God spoke to me, in no uncertain terms.

"If you continue to do this, you will die."

I got up, sobered and scared straight, grabbed my purse off the road, and walked an hour to the house. I locked myself in and cried and prayed the rest of the night.

The insurance company called Richard and told him that his car was abandoned and totaled in Sag Harbor. Richard lied and said the vehicle was stolen. If it was found in Sag Harbor, that meant I was there too. There was an intervention that week. Fatso, Jo, and Richard tried to convince me to enter rehab at Bellevue Hospital. Of course, I rebuked them. I was doing fine at distancing myself from mean fair-weather friends and cruel family members. They were the ones who told me that I was sick and crazy and needed to get help, so I stopped speaking to them. All I needed was myself, scotch, and Johnny. Needless to say, I was non-compliant. That's when Richard handed me a letter from Lotti.

"This came yesterday, looks like you got a new reason to live."

There was a black and white picture of a cute pale yella' baby, barely lifting her head, and a note that read,

> *Look what the stork brought us. Meet Rahab Auguste. We'll talk soon.*
> *Lotti*

I left the room and went and laid down for three days, looking back and forth at that picture. On the third day, I got up, showered, and had Richard drive me home to pack for the hospital. My intervention team was having too much fun lounging on the beach, anyway.

I can't explain it. It felt like new life coming from dried bones. I looked forward to having a baby in the family, nuzzling her neck and pinching her cheeks. I needed to get myself together to travel home to Louisiana. Feeling the urge to sing, I convinced Richard to stop by Swamp Water for my last hurrah—which wasn't hard to do. You see, I'm an alcoholic, but so was Richard; the only difference was he was functional. We both needed nightcaps to sleep and a drink other than coffee to wake us up in the morning. Mine was scotch neat, and Richards was gin and tonic. We stopped by the bar, and I put a dime in the jukebox, climbed up on a table, and sang a song for my great-niece, Rahab Auguste. I hadn't sung in years. Everyone cheered. Richard helped me down, and I was admitted into Bellevue. I did it for Poo, Lotti, and Rah. That's where I was diagnosed as manic depressive or bipolar. Whichever you choose to call it. A few weeks later, Puah Marie showed up on my doorstep. I never made it to Louisiana.

"MY TIME IS 'BOUT UP, AIN'T IT, DOC?" I WAS CURIOUS TO HEAR WHAT Dr. Davis had to say about my bare-naked acknowledgment of the torment I'd been through.

"Huh? Oh yes, it is." He cleared his throat and kinda shook his head, coming from the place where I took him. He stood and walked it off, pacing from one wall to the next. When he stopped pacing, he sat on the edge of his desk, placing his hands neatly in his lap, facing me. "First off, let me start by saying I'm very impressed by you, Mrs. Owens." He was looking into my eyes, and I was fixed on his every word. "Not only have you led a fascinating life, but it's almost as if you're awakening from a coma." I snickered.

"I feel like I'm coming from a coma...in more ways than one! It's like a light switch has been turned on. I'm living for the first time."

"That's remarkable." He stood and walked back behind his desk, taking a seat and rummaging through my file. "Nurse Lindt has informed me that you filed a formal complaint against one Nurse Mulligan." I nodded. It was true. Martita convinced me to approach Nurse Lindt about it, and it seemed like she was waiting on me to make the call.

"I'm extremely proud of you, Mrs. Owens," Nurse Lindt said. "And please know that I do not take this lightly. I will make sure your voice is heard." We both had tears in our eyes. From the moment we met, I knew Nurse Lindt was heaven-sent. She already knew my story.

Dr. Davis went on, "You are not the only one who has recently filed against Nurse Mulligan," he said. "We're calling you 'the sleepers' because we haven't heard a peep from any of you in years. You, however, seem to be the most vocal." My eyes started to well, thinking about all those years of darkness and silence—and then others having suffered through that pain. "People think because of that piece of paper on the wall..." He pointed to his license. "...that I'm only educated. They think I'm not empathetic. I am." I knew he was because I heard all of his rambling when he thought I wasn't listening. I didn't want to cause him any embarrassment, so I said nothing. "Hearing your story, and frankly, believing all that you've been through, I'd like to reassure you that we are taking your complaint very seriously. And I would like to apologize on behalf of myself, the staff, and this facility as a whole. This should have never happened in this day and age. You entrusted us...and we failed you. I'm ashamed, personally." I inhaled deeply and then, exhaled, feeling the breath of life returning into my lungs.

Dr. Davis stood, looking a bit emotional himself. He cleared his throat. "Now, I don't want to be hasty in determining your release. Even considering the accusations brought up against Nurse Mulligan, your recovery as a schizophrenic patient is incredible. Only perhaps ten percent of affected persons return to normal health. I'm considering a misdiagnosis based on your physical state these past years and our inability to compose sufficient data. But let's schedule a few more sessions and then work with your case manager on a release treatment plan."

Overwhelmed with emotion, I stood and hugged him. It took him by surprise, and he was initially hesitant but gave in and patted my back before grabbing my arms sternly.

"You are an incredibly resilient woman, Mrs. Owens. Please continue your therapy. I cannot express that enough." Dr. Davis put his arm around my shoulders and directed me toward my seat. "I heard you mention your grandmother and father...please take a seat." I nodded, sitting down. "I would like you to consider digging deeper into those relationships." He sat on his desk nearest to me. "You see, as a doctor, I usually base my decisions on a series of questions, statistics, numbers, clauses, and effects. Well, it's a proven fact that past issues, relationships, and or trauma can throw one off balance. I feel you just need to know that you're normal; you are." I choked up. No one had ever called me normal before.

"Don't worry, Doc, I ain't suing you." I tried to laugh. "I know I'm far from normal; that's okay." He laughed too.

"No, you are normal, Mrs. Owens. Your brain is functioning differently. And you know what else...and I'm not excusing any of your past behaviors..." He reached out a hand and touched my shoulder. "A large percentage of prisoners...and or jail inmates have serious psychological distress. It's not an easy experience to endure; the mind feels the need to escape. When a violent event occurs, the human brain and heart can never make sense of the event, like a train that goes off the tracks. What medication does is assist the train back onto the track. In your case, you do require medication to maintain a proper chemical balance. Everyone is different. Your brain functions differently than mine, but so what. No one person is alike. But you can live a normal life again, and that's whatever normal means to you."

"I mean, I understand that I'm bipolar, Doc. I just don't want that title holding me down. I don't want to use my illness as a dodge from life...having people feel sorry for me. I want to claim my errors and...I want to live and enjoy life again, unmedicated." He picked up his notepad and a pen and began scribbling something down.

"Anything is possible. Your ability to bounce back is proof of that. I don't want to sound discouraging, but there is no real cure for depression...it's kinda like a shadow—some days you see it, and others you can't. The real goal should be some form of remission. Here's the thing, consider how you're feeling today, compared to how you felt unmedicated in the past. I wouldn't suggest coming off of meds nor ending therapy without a proper plan or medical advice from a CBT...your cognitive behavior therapist. Let me ask you a question. Are you still hallucinating and hearing voices?"

Shoot! I didn't want him to ask me that question. "I haven't had any hallucinations since prison...and the voices...well maybe a month or so...but don't even pay that no never mind, Doc. That thing goes way back. And I feel it's more of an inner voice trying to discourage me."

"It's possible." He was fervently writing. "Welp!" He looked at the time, placed his notepad down, and slid it away. "Like I said, let's have a few more sessions." I held my head down. "Don't be discouraged." Dr. Davis took my hand and squeezed it firmly. "Remain faithful. Did you know that when your grandson walked in here several months ago that he gave you hope? Hope is a saving grace. Your mindset changes when you get serious about finding purpose and walking in it. Don't give up."

ONE FOR DADDY-O

Martita had done her time as an involuntary inpatient and was preparing to be released. We were both sad about her leaving, but I was excited for her to test her wings. It was Thanksgiving, and the cafeteria was serving a three-course meal with all the trimmings. I knew it would be tasteless, but I was grateful, nonetheless. Martita and I gave thanks, holding hands, sitting at a fully set, linen-covered table.

"I'm really going to miss you." She pushed her plate aside.

In the time I had come to know her, she had never refused food. I knew she was worried about relapsing.

"Well, starving yourself isn't going to solve anything." She had barely eaten breakfast. I poured extra gravy over my turkey and mashed potatoes, then pushed the cranberry sauce off my plate into a napkin. "Have I told you about Poo yet?" I asked, remembering when Poo was in a fix.

"No," she answered, sort of sulking as she picked up my napkin and dumped the cranberry sauce onto her plate. My stories recharged her. We would have to talk often.

IT WAS DECEMBER 1970 WHEN POO SHOWED UP ON OUR STOOP IN Harlem. I was just coming home from Bellevue and planning to travel to Louisiana when suddenly the doorbell rang. Not expecting a guest, we ignored it at first until after the third gong. I swung the door open, aggravated because Richard was sitting nearby and wouldn't move. There stood my dear sweet baby girl screaming, "Surprise, Tante Ma!" That's what she called me, being that I'm her aunt and stepmother at the same time. I stood in the doorway, shocked as Poo threw her long slender arms around my neck. Her brilliant smile was full of the youth and innocence of her age. I hugged her back, but all the while, I was wondering, *where's the baby?* A tall, good-looking, Hershey chocolate-colored brother stood behind her, smiling and freezing in the cold. Neither one had on a proper coat, and the snap of winter was in the air. Although the brother's smile was charming and full of white teeth, I felt a nudge in my spirit when he walked through the door. Minton was young, educated, and, again, very handsome, but that was the first time I ever had a premonition about someone. He was bad news. Poo had just given birth three months prior, yet somehow this young man convinced her to abandon her baby with her mother and leave with him to start over. Their lives were packed into the back of his brand-new Ford pickup and transported to New York City.

Clearly, Lotti was livid, and Minton wasn't even worth a mother's tears. Poo stowed away in the middle of the night, leaving a note and taking Lotti's savings account booklet containing the money she saved for Poo's nursing education.

Poo said, "I could never love Rah as mama does."

She didn't feel she could raise a baby conceived through rape. She said she didn't ask for her in the first place. I knew how it felt to be pregnant with a child that wasn't supposed to be. The Grandmother got rid of mine. They were carried straight from the womb to the grave. Well! My girl was home, and that was going to be put behind us.

Richard had never met his daughter. They spoke on the phone when Poo and I vacationed together. Poo was always full of questions about her dad, and although Richard's curiosity grew too, I still couldn't get him to join us during our trips. Lotti refused to allow Poo to visit us at home; she said, "If dat sorry-azz niggro of yourns wasn't der, maybe." Maybe, meant never.

For a split second, I noticed something different in Richard when he saw Poo for the first time. He must have recognized himself in her. They were both tall, lean, and wrapped in lightly creamed caramel coatings. Poo had deep-set eyes like mine and Lotti's and her full lips curled into the brightest smile. She and Richard hugged for a while, then he looked at her again. This time different—*like damn, this girl is fine!* The knee-jerk emotion he initially felt quickly reversed into perverse desires.

"Good googly moogly, I ain't do bad, huh, Mary." He spun Poo around, checking her out. "Not bad at all," he murmured as Poo laughed nervously.

Minton cleared his throat and came to her rescue, holding her firmly in his arms.

"We looking for a place to stay for a while. I'm interested in buying some real estate in the Bronx," he expressed with a slightly hostile tone in his voice.

"The burnt down Bronx!" Richard yelled. Only jazz and talking business could get his mind off of women.

It was good to have company again; besides Jo, I didn't have any friends, and she wasn't good company anymore. She and Fatso were dedicated to their church. If they weren't in the church, they were helping the church or at Bayou House of Blues, cooking and playing music. As for me, I had finally found work for myself. I worked Richard's credit cards out. Poo and I shopped until we dropped, then came home and fixed up the place—cleaning and decorating each floor in hopes of one day entertaining guests.

Poo and I acted the same toward each other, although we both had changed. Prison had changed me, whereas Poo matured; she carried too much luggage for a young woman to bear. She wore the same smile, but the sparkle in her eyes was gone. Her disappointment with herself hung on her face. That piece of crap she was with humped fake smiles on her face but didn't do anything to recover her heart. He was, however, good company for Richard. Richard showed Minton the ropes and introduced him to some business associates. Minton was an entrepreneur as well. He had owned a dry-cleaning business in New Orleans. He became interested in starting over in the Bronx because he read in some fancy business magazine that there were cheap investments there. It was good having them both around, even though Richard and I were used to living in our own private hell. We complemented each other's demons. When Poo and Minton came, it felt like they were peeking in on our madness. Unfortunately, it would soon spill over into their own lives.

Richard's lust for Poo permeated through the house, leaving everyone feeling uncomfortable in its sinful nature. I hated that part of him, his longing for women—not sex because I never withheld sex from him. It was our private parts he was after, even that of his own daughter—like her cooch was somehow different. That part of Richard I loathed. He hugged and rubbed on Poo longer than a father should. And believe me, I got on him over it. Of course, he denied everything, but I wasn't the only one who noticed this time. It got to the point where Minton couldn't take his lustful gawking any longer. I was sure that he and Richard were going to bump heads, and Minton was a big strapping bayou boy. So, they left. I was saddened, but Poo was safe from her father's gaze.

STRAIGHTEN UP, AND FLY RIGHT

When Poo and Minton moved to New York City, I was an old thirty-nine, and Richard a young fifty-five. The Grandmother used to tell me and Lotti, "Never mess with older men, dey steals ya youth and gives ya all dey problems." Well...while I was growing older and still stuck on the booze that Richard introduced me to, he was aging like fine wine. He was the type of man who evolved with the times. Richard didn't want to face the passing of the years, so he stayed relevant by keeping up with the culture. He loved his jazz music. In that category, he did not sway. It didn't matter, though, the young ladies still flocked over him, and the older ones knew better but did it anyway. He was a smooth Daddy-O. The purist in me rejected new things like a cassette player trying to play an 8-track. It didn't work for me. Richard welcomed the '70s wearing bell-bottoms, platforms, and a wavy black flowing 'fro. He was always groovy, and I couldn't keep up. I'm classic to a fault...but a diva for sure.

I'd like to say that I stopped drinking after Bellevue Hospital. I didn't. All they did was give me more drugs but nothing for the interior pain. They had me taking cocktails of medications that mellowed my nerves, yet only a real cocktail could mellow my soul. When I wasn't drinking, I was placid. A visitor in my own body watching as a shell of a woman let life slip by, breathing but not alive. So, I drank to win back what was mine, and everyone knows you can't mix alcohol with medicine. When I wanted to drink, I laid off the meds and drank in spurts, and let me tell you, that didn't help with my depression or paranoia. I would stay dry for weeks, then go on drinking binges. Mainly due to Richard. Sleeping on a block of ice would have been warmer than our bed.

I didn't know where Richard was or who he was with half the time —both mentally and physically. He closed me out...now that I think about it, I guess I closed him out too. When we made love, I pretended he was Tiny and kept my mouth closed because I feared I'd scream Tiny's name. I missed him incredibly. It was a hollow feeling, like someone missing an amputated body part might feel. You grow to live without it, but the imbalance is always there. I still feel like that from time to time. But Richard ignoring me felt foreign. I saw how the waitress at the local diner looked at him and made sure his plate was piled high with home fries. My eggs were runny. The woman who bought her newspaper at the corner store at eight every morning just when he played his numbers lustfully stared at him. Now, I can't certainly say that Richard ever cheated on me except with his saxophone; he wore that thing out. It's like I said before about memories. I often wonder, are they accurate or just our opinions? Richard swore up and down that he was simply flirtatious. Anyway, at this point, I could barely stand myself...I was literally a shell of my former existence.

Whiney and untrusting. I became obsessed with gaining Richard's full attention. Tiny wouldn't write back. My letters were returned every time, and I was beginning to believe that maybe he was right about not waiting on him. So, I began nagging Richard about his whereabouts and not keeping a close eye on my girl, Poo. Who, as it would seem, showed up in the city already pregnant and making new friends. I was alone, and I hated being alone. One good thing I can say about the institution is that it forced me to know myself. To travel within my depths and pinpoint the scary areas.

Eventually, I took a job at Jo's old beauty salon that her sister ran. I didn't need the money; it was something to do. Our brownstone was finally fully furnished and orderly. There was nothing left for me to do there. I must admit, I loved the smell of freshly vacuumed floors, Pledge polished furniture, and bleached tiles—but how much cleaning could one do? I'll tell you what I did, I set a trap. Every morning I vacuumed my way out of the door. Leaving neat lines across the plush, fully carpeted floors so that I could tell if anyone was in my house. The beds were made a certain way and adorned with decorative pillows, always situated in a specific fashion. Crazy, right? I didn't think so. When you set a trap, you catch a rat. One night I came home to the subtle hint of cheap perfume lingering in the air and footprints on my floors. I called Richard at the supper club.

"Hey, lov-ah," I said, softening him up as I ran up the stairs to our bedroom.

"What's up, pussycat, you coming down tonight?"

"I don't know, I might." I slowly turned the knob to the bedroom door while simultaneously doing breathing exercises before pushing it open.

"If you do, bring my black and silver bow tie—this thing I got on is tired and giving me the blues." I didn't answer him; one of my gotdamn pillows was misplaced. "Mary, you there?"

"You ain't been home today? Why didn't you get another one?" I walked over to the bed and started sniffing around. "I'm tired; I might stay in tonight."

"Come on, dark and lovely, bring it for me. I ain't been home since leaving out this morning—Hey, Frank! You lookin' clean, bro! Yeah, blood! Don't get no stank on ya!" He laughed, interrupting our conversation to engage with someone else while my top was boiling over. Richard had fed me enough lies to fill a hog trough.

I was born at night, not last night. I hung up the phone and caught a cab down to Bayou House of Blues.

Feeling big and bold, I barged into Richard's office. He was sitting alone enjoying Jo's home-wrecking peach cobbler with a cup of tea while reading the paper.

He looked up at me perplexed and said, "You bring my bow tie?" He was right; the one he had on was tired, and so was he.

Growing sick of him and his drama, I marched over and literally spilled the tea into his lap. As he danced and screamed around the room, I used the nearest and bluntest object to beat the crap out of him. It took three guys to hold me down. I flew into a fit of rage, hurting Richard, me, and anyone else who got in the way.

"You, no-good, low-life, bastard! Don't you EVER let me catch you with no two-bit ho in my house ever again, you hear me! You hear me, Richard! Do it again, and I'll meet ya soul in hell! You better straighten up and fly right!"

Jo was always telling me, "Why don't you get more involved. It ain't good to be sitting around depending on no man—go back to school, find a hobby." She was right, but I mostly avoided people and situations back then because my temper went from zero to prison in seconds. That night, I gave Richard a second-degree burn on his groin area, and he wore a gold cap over a chipped tooth. But he stayed with me, and I never had to warn him about no women again. All I had to do was give him a murderous glance.

"Being crazy ain't all bad." I laughed.

If I had to say that Lotti's potion worked at all, I'd say it worked because Richard never left me. He couldn't. Instead, he introduced me to the waitress at the diner.

"Candace, this is my wife, Mary," he said, stuffing home fries in his mouth. "Her eggs are runny; can you fix that please, sweetheart?" I was proud, but I refused to eat those eggs that Candace brought back.

At the corner store, he said, "Excuse me, Miss. I see you every morning. My name is Richard." He extended his hand, and she took it, licking her lips and revealing the fork in her tongue like an ol' snake. "You see that lady sitting in the car? That's my wife, Mary...you got business with us?" That made me proud too, but nothing like going down to the courthouse and officially becoming Mrs. Owens. We had a quiet, private ceremony in front of the justice of the peace, with Fatso and Jo as witnesses.

And that's what Poo should have done with that no good, low life of hers to get him to act right. Beat him.

KICKIN' THE GONG AROUND

Nine months after moving into the city, Poo gave birth to a baby boy. She named him after his big-headed daddy, Minton Silas Williams, Junior. I nicknamed him Sy, the golden child because I didn't want anyone calling him junior. I didn't want them calling him Minton after his bum father, either. He was a perfect baby and deserved his own name, so Sy it was, short for Silas. The golden child thing was just something I called him. Not only was his skin the perfect shade of a golden sun ray, but he was the first male child born to the Auguste family since Diddy. Now, Diddy did have many outside kids, but we never knew anything about them. Sy was the golden child and secretly my favorite after Poo. Lawd, he was the chubbiest, cuddliest baby you ever wanna meet. Richard didn't realize what he missed with his kids until his heart melted over his grandson. Sy wrapped his tiny hand around Richard's finger as if to say, 'you belong to me', and it was over. We both instantly fell in love and put our heavy drinking aside. We had to be clear-minded enough to protect our grandson. Richard went out and bought that child an entire nursery set for the room closest to ours on the second floor—complete with airplanes, choo-choo trains, and toy soldiers. Poo didn't take to Sy like that. Shortly after giving birth, the itch of discontentment seized her once again. She felt robbed of her youth, and finding time to hang out in nightclubs meant more to her than being a mother.

Minton's business was just getting off the ground, so he was never home. He came to the city with a purpose and was fulfilling his dream. Poo, on the other hand, having not allowed herself the time to heal from the pain she left back in Louisiana, found the comfort she was looking for in the new and big city. She discovered alcohol, cocaine, and the arms of another woman. I don't know where that child picked up that notion, but it wasn't the first time. Lotti had mentioned she'd been with one of them Fontaine girls. That's what got her raped in the first place. I told Poo; I said to her, "You playing with fire, beb." But Poo wouldn't stop the drugs and seeing that woman. Dealing with Poo gave me the opportunity to see myself from the outside. It hurt watching her endure the same downward spiral. I didn't know how to reach her. It didn't dawn on me that she was suffering from depression, but she was. She desperately was trying to soothe her past.

It was going on three years when Minton finally connected the dots about Poo and the other woman. Richard and I were restoring our stormy relationship and being parents to our grandson when Poo called hollering on the phone. Minton caught her in bed with that ol' nasty gal.

"Tante Ma, he nearly choked the life out of me!" she screamed, just crying. Instead of killing her, Minton punched a hole in the wall and broke every bone in his own hand.

"Girl, I done told you! Ya sin will find you out. There's three things belonging to a man ya never mess with: one is his money, two is his pride, and three is his woman. Lawd helps the woman who messes with his money and steals his pride." I begged Poo to leave their apartment and come stay with Richard and me until things blew over. She was stiff-necked like her mama. She refused.

"I can't...I realized today that I really love him. I messed up fooling around with Terry. I don't even know why I did it. I guess it was because she understands me. She's warm, kind—"

"Well, damn, Poo...most women are. You best pack and get o'va here before that man gets home from the hospital. I told you he was bad news!" By then, Richard had heard my conversation and was getting upset, yelling in the background. He liked Minton, but he and Poo were building a relationship too. "Wait now, Richard," I said, trying to get him to calm down. He had put Sy in his playpen and was getting ready to leave. Richard didn't do any fighting; he was too pretty for that; he knew guys who broke body parts.

"Please, Tante Ma, don't let him come over here. I'll be okay. I can't lose my man. I've known Senior forever." Senior, that's what they started calling Minton after Sy was born. "And I didn't come all the way to New York City to lose my best friend."

We stayed on the phone until Poo heard his key turning in the lock.

"Tante Ma, I gotta go—he's back."

"Poo, lawd, chile Lotti, gone kill me if anything happens to you." Poo didn't respond. "Puah Marie?"

They made up that night, and nine months later, Elizabeth Gomer Williams was born. It was Halloween night, 1974. We all thought it was a joke when Poo's water broke in the middle of the dance floor at the bar's costume party. She was dressed like a pumpkin, and Minton was Peter, Peter the Pumpkin Eater.

Martita's mouth was full of laughter, and it was good to hear it again.

Poo and Minton considered the new baby a fresh start. Neither of them dealt with the underlying issues. Poo became submissive while Minton became distant. He threw himself back into work, opening a second cleaning business. Overcompensating from having his self-esteem bruised, he also threw himself into the arms of every attractive woman willing to mend his ego. Poo was trying to be a good partner and mother. She had stopped kicking that old gong around. But Minton picked up where she left off. He fell into drugs real bad. Poo blamed herself. She said she chased him out of love and made him feel like less of a man. The only way she knew to get him back was to join him in the nightlife they both enjoyed. Minton showed no opposition, it made him happy to dance with her in his arms and to drink until they stumbled home.

Disco music was in, and they both were pretty good dancers. Poo tried to get me into that boogie-woogie-woogie, but as I said, I'm classic. I preferred dressing to the nines: full gowns, satin gloves, a fox stole around my shoulders, and my neck and wrist full of diamonds or pearls. I shocked them all when I cut my beautiful long hair into a curly afro; it was falling out anyhow. I showed it off while doing the Tighten-up at one of Minton's red light parties. No one but Richard knew I could dance like that. Anyway, Poo started drinking and carrying on again. Our new grandbaby, Go-Go, got her own private room at casa de grandparents too. Poo swore that she left the coke alone and was only smoking grass. She said Minton got high enough for both of them. Somebody had to stay on the ground in that house.

IT DON'T MEAN A THING

"Listen, baby girl." I wrapped my arms around Martita's shoulders and drew her close. "Life is full of changes...and Lord knows we all make mistakes. What I don't want to happen is for you to be living out there feeling bad about your past and the things you can no longer change. Don't let the enemy steal your joy. You see where he got me, right?" Martita turned and wrapped her arms around my waist. We must have looked a hot mess because I was short and she was tall, but it didn't matter. We belonged to each other.

"Did Poo stay clean?" She asked, scooting back so she could put her head on my shoulder.

I sighed, "Things got worse before they got better...but it was when that no good man left that she started to grow again."

"He wasn't all that bad," Martita said, having seen worse. "He owned a business, took care of her. He didn't beat her...did he?"

"Oh, yeah, times definitely changed."

MINTON RECLAIMED HIS LOVE FOR POO BUT NOT WITHOUT repercussions. Whenever he felt suspicious, he grew jealous and angry with rage. Now, I never caught him hitting on my niece, and Poo never would fess up to any of my accusations, but I know about rage. I made my standpoint with Minton clear.

"You touch my niece, and I got a bullet with your name written on it." By then, I had traded the pretty little Saturday night special that Tiny gave me for a nickel-finished .44 Magnum I carried in my purse. Richard thought going to the shooting range would help with my aggression. NOT.

The first time Minton hit Poo, I found out by the kids. Little Sy was sensitive about his mama. He was around four years old but clearly upset because "Poo was bad and Senior hit her." I couldn't prove his claim or do diddly-squat about it.

They all laughed at me like I was crazy even though I saw the peace offering Poo wore around her neck. Every time they got into a fight Minton bought her something new. A gold herringbone neck-lace. A fur coat. Diamond earrings. The Grandmother used to say, "Don't mess with no woman o'va her man. Dey tells dey mess and makes ya mad as hell, den dey carry on lak nuttin, whiles you can't stand him. Whatever happens between a man and a woman is 'tween dat man and dat woman."

Every time I saw Poo with something new, I said, "Humph! What you do this time?" That made her mad.

The first time Minton hit Sy for mouthing off while defending his mama, they ended up in Disney World to get away from me. I shot after him in a blind rage. They took the kids down there and brain-washed them into believing nothing was going on and everything was good. But a drug-induced beast slowly grew within Minton, robbing him of himself. Soon he couldn't afford any peace offerings. He lost everything trying to pay for dope. Poo even lost the nursing job she had all those years because she was stealing meds for him to sell or use, I don't know. My bullet wasn't needed any longer; Minton was his own worst enemy.

You young folks are different from us growing up, I mean, sure, we had our vices, but it seems like young folks are too fast to get involved with drugs. Folks in my days were ignorant and uneducated about everything. For Pete's sake, pregnant women were smoking and drinking. We were told things like, get ya'self some giggle smokes. Light up and get real tall. You kids should know better with all your schooling and television. Both Poo and Minton were well educated. I don't know; it's a sad thing.

The last I seen of Poo and the kids, she was living with me and Richard trying to get her life back in order...and was doing well. She had a job working as a sleepover nurse downtown. Minton disappeared. He was a full-blown druggie by then. The kids were doing well, and Poo was seeing a nice gentleman—a steady Eddie is what we called the good guys. Speaking of good guys, as bad a father as Richard was, is how good a grandfather he became. He loved those kids. I guess knowing it wasn't his sole responsibility to care for them freed him to love them unconditionally. Although they were our responsibility for a good while there.

MARTITA WAS SHIFTING IN HER SEAT LIKE SHE COULDN'T GET comfortable. She was obviously not listening anymore.

"You tired? You ready to call it a night?" They were cleaning the cafeteria, so we moved into the Dayroom. Nurse Lindt worked hard to make the holiday special for everyone. We were given blankets to wrap ourselves in while enjoying a fake fire burning in the fireplace and drinking hot apple cider with bland pumpkin pie.

"I have something to tell you. Something I've never told anyone before," Martita said, crying instantly. Her face and eyes swelled up and turned red. "Remember when I told you about the man coming through the window and raping me?"

"Yeah." I stood to get her some napkins from the center of the table.

"Well, he did that more than once...or twice." She blew her nose. "He did it a lot." She looked me in the eyes with a grave expression, searching my face for a reaction. "My parents sold me for drugs. He raped me often, in the same room we all slept in, and they never moved."

"Damn," I uttered, holding and shaking my head. Martita's lips were trembling as she tried to keep it together. I knew then I had to be strong for her. I prayed inwardly for her protection while we were apart.

"Baby girl, you ain't in that." I stood again so her heavy head could rest against my stomach. "What happened to you is jacked-up for real...but you ain't in it. It happened to you, but it's not you. You know that, right?" She nodded, soaking my shirt with her tears. "It's like...what I see is a beautiful, kind, and gentle woman right here in front of me...but she's living in the past." Martita lifted her head and fixed her wet eyes on my mouth as I spoke. "Tita, you're hurt, you're scared...as you should be, but you are not there in that room anymore. You gotta move forward."

"I know, but what am I going to do when I get out of here...when I don't have you or the nurses and doctors. I'm scared."

"Poppycock!" I pulled her away; she was getting too comfortable leaning on me. I had already spoiled one girl. Martita needed to be strong. "You're going to be the woman that I know you are. Listen," I grabbed her arms sternly. "Martita, Martita, you're worried and upset about too many things when in actuality only a few even matter—or indeed only one, God. It's like what Nurse Lindt said the other day about looking for His blessings. We have to stop focusing on negative things and be more intentional about noticing His blessings. I know you know what I mean. Remember what you told me about your brother nearly dying, and God practically raising him from the dead? You've already seen His glory." She nodded again; I was good at giving advice but not taking it for myself. "God can do that for you! When you get a bad thought, think of something good that happened. I'm focusing on getting out of here. That makes my day...imagining myself living on the outside. Hell, I don't know what I'm going to do either. But my past has taught me this—those kinds of thoughts can be consuming. It's okay to live day by day, especially for people like us!" I patted her on the cheek, then tried to get that annoying bang from out of her face. "What about the exit plan you're working on with your social worker?"

Martita sucked her teeth. "I know, I know! I just wish you were coming with me." She turned away from me and to the table, pulling the blanket around her face. "My sister has her own life at the firm she's interning with. Lazarus is in college...and you're right; there was a time when no one thought he would speak or function again. But he made it." She turned to me. I was standing over her patting her back. "I nursed and prayed to bring my brother back to health. Now everybody has moved on and forgotten about me. I just don't know where I belong."

"Like I said, too many worries. One day at a time, my friend." I sat down and took her hand. "Listen if things don't work out between Sal and me—"

"What do you mean? He's a great guy; it'll work out."

"Yeah, but how will it look...an old lady living with a fine young man like that. Folks will talk...and he gotta get himself a life too."

Martita removed the blanket from her face and looked at me with a serious expression. "You wanna trade places?"

We both laughed.

"No, but all jokes aside, I don't know...I may want to build a home down south and rock on one of those porches Tiny used to talk about. I might need someone to look after me." Martita brightened up.

"Well, I hope you hate living with Sal."

We both laughed again, feeling new life in the air, rising like the sun.

PART VII
GUILT

"What we give our attention to – stays with us. What we let go of – will let go of us..."
- Cat Forsley

THEME FOR ERNIE

I was thrilled to see Martita leaving the hospital. She looked so pitiful, signing the release forms with her sister and brother standing over her. If only she could see how much she was loved. I got a little jealous, admiring their hugs and kisses. Although I had Sal, and Lord knows I was grateful for him, I missed my family. Talking about them in the past tense was easier than thinking of their present status. That was the hard part. Not because I didn't know where they were but because I was afraid of how they were doing. To be honest, I tried not to think of their whereabouts at all. Trouble followed our family. Wherever they were. It was bound to be unfortunate, and it made me feel like I failed them.

The next couple of weeks were challenging. I tried to stay focused by reading my bible while enjoying Sal's notes. I called him every day as he suggested, but he was never home. Martita and I spoke regularly. It seemed like she sat by the phone waiting on my calling hours; she always picked up. She told me she was taking secretarial classes, and it was going well, but she was bored. I didn't want to say anything, but I didn't think those classes were suitable for her. She was more suited for a counselor or caseworker or something because of her huge heart.

My meetings with Dr. Davis were going well. We had already started an exit plan with Ms. Simmons, my caseworker. Dr. Davis said he felt I was holding back. He suggested that I continue with the therapy sessions and asked if I would consider speaking at a group session. I hated the group sessions, but I told him I would think about it.

When Martita left, random people started approaching me, attempting to become my new BFF, as if the Lucy and Ethel duo had an opening or something. Of course, no one could take Martita's place. I figured since talking helped me and her so much, maybe I could be a blessing elsewhere or someone a blessing to me. I tried opening up to other people. Remember I said my temper went from zero to prison in seconds? Well, it got better. I sat patiently watching Ms. Rossellini stroke that damn silver toaster like it was a real dog or cat. It was hard to take her seriously, but I listened as she told stories about her late husband anyway.

"Fred had a mole on his back shaped like Elvis...the hair and every-thing. I swear!" She laughed, holding her right hand over her heart and the other in the air. "We entered a picture of it to Enquiring Minds, but it was rejected. A woman with a mole shaped like Dolly Parton's silhouette won that year."

Lawd, have mercy.

Then, there was Eddie, the perv; he was a nasty old thing, but he was scared of me. His stories started out normal but always ended with him sticking his dried-up ding-dong into someone or some-thing. He definitely had a problem. He and Mrs. Rossellini fought for my attention. So, I hid from them both, reading my bible. Sue took time with me. She made me feel special.

"How's my girl doing?" She fanned an apron around my neck. My afro had grown three times its original length and was full of thick bouncy salt and pepper curls.

"Awrite, how you?" I laid my head back into the basin.

"Okay, I guess." She immediately wet my hair and started lathering it up. Sue was a true beautician, as soon as you sat in her chair she began yapping and telling her personal business. "My husband recently retired...needless to say, it's been challenging."

"Oh, my." I started to reply that I could imagine, but I couldn't. I remembered when all I wanted was for Richard to spend his every moment with me. "Enjoy the time while you can," I said instead.

"Yeah, that's what I keep telling myself." We laughed.

"You know they say that emotional infidelity is as bad as physical infidelity." I heard that from Sally Jessy years ago, and it stuck. I wasn't one hundred percent sure of its meaning. Still, it registered, so I committed it to memory.

"So true." She paused, taking it in for a second. It was one of those seeping messages. "It's just that he's so needy. You know he wants me to retire, right?"

I opened my eyes and dotted them her way. "Oh, you can't do that! You bring so much light into this place."

She smiled, rinsing my hair. "It's my ministry, and I love it. To be honest, Mary; my husband was a district attorney. We don't really need my salary. I do this because it's where my heart lies."

"I can tell, and you should continue. I'm hoping to find my passion."

"Oh, you definitely have. We all love your stories. Just being around you is therapy. You should consider visiting institutions and speaking to inmates and patients once you're out of here." I smiled, thinking of the group sessions that I hated. My stories were personal and told intimately. "Henry just wants to spend more time with me, that's all. The kids are all grown—it's just us, now." Sue went on, rambling. I was thinking about Richard; after Poo got herself somewhat together, we saw less and less of her and the kids. We had to adjust to each other once again.

"You and your man gotta find something you enjoy doing together. Whatever you do, don't let him go off into his corner doing his thing and you off into yours...I mean, it's good, for a spell but not all the time."

"For sure, is that what happened with you and Richard?" I closed my eyes, thinking back.

"Yeah, we went down that road too."

RICHARD STARTED WORKING LATE AT THE SUPPER CLUB AND BAR, AGAIN. When he wasn't working, he was locked up in the music room at the brownstone, blowing his sax. That man cared more about that thing than me, and I grew jealous. Every Saturday morning, he bathed and polished it like it was his woman. Slowly up and down. In tender round circles. He was supposed to be massaging me like that. Baa-daa-baa-baaa waa waa waa, was all I heard. That same unfinished focused note he'd been working on for years. Over and over again. His groove was consistent; he stayed in the pocket, but he couldn't finish the song.

"Richard, can you take the garbage out?"

Baa-daa-baa-baaa waa waa waa...

"Rich, which dress? This one or that one?"

Baa-daa-baa-baaa waa waa waa...

"Honey, what you feel like for dinner?"

Baa-daa-baa-baaa waa waa waa...

"How bout a little something, something tonight?"

Baa-daa-baa-baaa waa waa waa...

I started calling that thing the other woman. Selmar was her name. By now, you should know how jealous I get. I had my hand wrapped around Selmar's slender polished neck many times to toss her down the garbage shoot. As crazy as I am, even I knew that would be Richard's breaking point. The point of no return. I guess he was acting that way because the kids were gone and he had stopped drinking; he needed something to fill in the gap. He knew he was a dead man if he looked at another woman sideways, so the music had to do.

That was all before our Rahab; that child was a blessing to the family. Her memory instantly drew sadness to my face.

"YOU OKAY, MARY?" SUE WAS BLOWING OUT MY HAIR WITH A ROUND barrel brush, making the curls fold under.

"Yeah, I'm okay. It's just that certain people are harder to talk about than others."

THAT SAME TUNE SCRATCHED AT RICHARD'S HEAD FOR YEARS. SAME tune, different combinations. Same tune, different melodies. Same tune, different instrument. He tried it all, and it scratched, and scratched, and scratched at his head. He kept playing and writing even when they said jazz was dead. After twenty years, he finally got the song out, and he and the band played it for my fiftieth birthday at the supper club. A big television executive was in the audience that night. Richard's tune was picked up as the theme song for a fall lineup show. The show did really well.

"IF YOU EVER CATCH THE ERNIE BRIGHTON SHOW IN SYNDICATION, that's my Richard's song. He was so proud of that thing."

"I remember that show! That was your husband's music?"

"Yup, the opening credits read: composed by Richard W. Owens. He poured his heart into that one—"

"That's it!" Sue yelled, cutting me off, staring at me through the mirror with her hands placed on her thick hips. "You know what, my husband is a jazz buff, and lately he's been playing this new song, and I always feel like I've heard it before. The Ernie Brighton Show—that's it!" She shook her head and went back to curling my hair. "Wow, wait till I tell Henry that you helped me figure it out. You know how it is when you get something stuck in your head. Anyway, we love the remake."

"Remake?" I stared at her through the mirror. "There can't be a remake." *The hell you say.* I sat up straight, getting agitated.

"Sure, it is. It plays in rotation on the jazz station every day, I swear."

"Well, I'm sure that my husband didn't authorize a remake."

"If he didn't, he sure does have a case—because I know that's the theme song from that comedy hour show you're talking about."

"Sue, you do know that Richard is dead, right?" It closed my throat to say it out loud. I started coughing. Sue stopped doing my hair and fetched me a Dixie cup of water from the cooler.

"I'm sorry for your loss, sweetheart. I didn't know. You speak of him so vividly...I just assumed." She patted my back. I could tell she was remorseful. Her eyes were somewhere else. "You know what, you're probably due royalties." She reloaded my cup of water, then started rubbing my back. I was still coughing. "I'll have to ask Henry about that tonight." Her gaze was still distant. "Hey, maybe that's something he and I can do together...investigate for you."

I wiped my eyes and cleared my throat. I was trying not to get angry thinking about someone stealing that damned song that Richard worked on for twenty years. *This has got to be a test of my nerves, Lord?*

"Thank you, Sue; I think that's a great idea." I decided to answer; after all, I hadn't even heard the song. *It might not be his.* Richard and our memories were in the past. I missed his friendship and companionship, but I was alive and had to start acting that way. I cleared my throat a few more times.

"Are you sure you're okay?" Sue examined my face.

"Yes, I am. Thanks for everything you do, Sue." She smiled.

"I'll bring the CD in tomorrow so you can hear it."

"What's a CD?"

Sue paused and stared at me for a while, then, she answered, figuring my questioning was understandable. I'd been in a coma-like state for the past ten years. "It's a compact disc. The latest fad." She answered, drawing a circle in the air. "Think of it as a 45 and 8-track having a baby."

"Hmm," I responded, trying to imagine the combination. Sue spun me around to the mirror. My curls were blown out and silky. I shook my head to see the bounce and body movement. "Ooh, Diane, chile!" I said, mimicking an old hair salon commercial. "This is really me!" We laughed. "I hate to waste it on this place."

WHAT YOU WOULDN'T DO FOR LOVE

It's funny how someone playing in your hair can make you sleepy. After getting my doo done and getting roused up, I figured I'd go lay down and sleep the frustration off.

"Tante Mags!" Sal yelled from across the room. I almost did a backflip into the Dayroom. Lawd, I needed strong arms wrapped around me in the worst way.

"Boy, I'mma get you!" I issued, walking over. He was sitting patiently at a table near the big window but stood when he saw me coming. "What you doing here?" We embraced tightly, and I planted my face into his chest. He squeezed me tighter. Sal was an excellent hugger. I could physically feel the sadness leaving my body.

"I had to come see you, I hope you don't mind, I—"

"Are you kidding! You know I love your visits, especially now that Tita isn't here."

"I know," he pulled out a chair for me. "It's just that I told you I wouldn't be here for a while, so—"

"Don't een worry 'bout that, beb," I said, searching for his bright smile. "What's wrong? You look different. Where's that smile—something got you down? You ain't leaving me, are you?" Instantly Martita's same fears crowded my spirit, and my heart started racing. I sat in the seat Sal pulled out.

"I'm fine, Tante Mags...your hair looks nice," he said, attempting to smile. A half-smile.

"Thanks." I could tell something was off. *Maybe he found out something about my family.* I quickly looked out the window to cast off any negative thoughts. Everything was covered in crisp white snow, and it reminded me of the seclusion room. I didn't want to think of that place, so I redirected my attention to Sal's colorful Coogi sweater. He was dressed differently, stylish—but like a gangster. Everything was expensive, jewelry and all. He took and squeezed my hands, and I looked up at him, exhaling. I hadn't realized I wasn't breathing.

"I'm sorry about my appearance," he said, noticing me eyeballing him. "I'm coming straight from work." I nodded, imagining all sorts of things. "Listen, I had to come see you today. You know that case I'm working on? I nodded again, praying he wasn't being relocated. "Well, not only is it top secret...it's also very dangerous." I squeezed his hand, now worried. He patted mine. "I woke up this morning thinking about you and all your stories, and...I couldn't help but wonder about Rah too." He raked his smooth black hair out of his face; it was loose from its usual sleek ponytail and falling into his eyes. I wasn't a fan of that style either. He had too much hair for a man. "I know I promised that I would be here for you, listen to your stories, and keep my own agendas on the back wall...but...real talk, no lie..." His eyes lowered to the table. "Tonight, I could very well be walking straight into my demise, and I feel like if I don't make it out of this mission, I'd like to have heard or known something more about Rah. I don't know..." He looked off into the distance, and I felt so bad for him. His heart was chained. Mine stopped racing and turned toward his emotions.

"I understand, beb. Really, I do...but now I'm worried about you. You're gonna be okay, right?"

He brought his attention back to me. I could see the anguish on his face. "Tante Mags, I wish I could explain—"

"Shhh," I patted and soothed his hand. I understood; he was an undercover cop. "No need to explain." I looked into his wide dark brown eyes and tucked my own fears inside. Dr. Davis was right; I was holding back. I released Sal's hands and sat back in my chair, silent for a change and gazing out the window at the snow covering every inch of the lawn. It was an appropriate backdrop for the memories that he wanted me to recall. "I been thinking and talking a lot about Richard and Tiny lately...well, to be frank, I never really stop thinking about Tiny. I'm always wondering if he made it out. Wondering if he's looking for me." I cleared my throat. Thoughts of him brought tears. "So, I get it. When you love someone, it's hard to let them go. Dr. Davis said I'm holding back." I looked over at Sal and took the napkin he offered for my eyes.

"YOU, holding back?" We chuckled.

"Yeah, right...but to be honest, I think I know what he's talking about." I looked back out the window; a blackbird had caught my eye. He landed in the middle of the lawn and tugged on something he found from under the snowpack. *How appropriate.* Diddy used to call me Blackbird. I used to think it was because I was so dark. Looking at that bird, I thought; *perhaps he thought I was resourceful.* I focused back on Sal. He was waiting patiently to hear about Rah. "Richard and Rah, now those are two names I don't like to use in the same sentence." Sal contoured his face in confusion. The word 'why' hung above his head like smog, but he was being respectful of me and didn't ask any questions. I propped my hands underneath my breast and got comfortable. It was going to take some explaining. "I've been avoiding talking about Richard and Rah together because I'm afraid you'll think of me differently."

"Never."

I smiled; Sal was sweet. "Before you came, I hid everyone in the back of my mind. I didn't want to think about the circumstances that led me here, nor the consequences that everyone, especially Rah, are possibly dealing with." I breathed deeply, thinking of a way to tell the story. Starting with Richard always helped. He was a huge part, anyway. "Well, if it wasn't for Richard, there would be no Rah...so I guess him and Lotti hooking up wasn't so bad after all, huh?" Sal agreed, making himself comfortable too. "Lotti and I stopped talking because of Richard...but if it wasn't for him, then you and I wouldn't be sitting here talking either."

"Yes, ma'am."

"MARY, I HAVE SOME BAD NEWS," RICHARD SAID WITH A SUNNY disposition, trying to brighten the dark news of Lotti's death.

Remember that Memorex commercial? That's what I thought of when he told me about my sister's passing. Is this live...or a dream? All I could do was sulk.

We're born into this world with a set of people, usually our parents, and siblings. Maybe grandparents, aunts, uncles, and cousins. Then when suddenly, your people are all gone, and you're the last man standing, everything feels surreal. It's a hollow feeling. For a person like me—bipolar, along with loneliness, comes fear. You get caught up in the sticky web of worrying if you're next in line, yet oddly enough, you don't mind dying either. At one time, Lotti and I felt like one person. When she died, a piece of me died too.

Sy and Go-Go, and eventually Rah, filled that pain. The family that Lotti and Richard made became my new people. If it wasn't for them babies, I don't know where I would be—probably in here earlier. Children have a way of replacing the lost. They give you a reason to live. But for a while, I hunkered down in sadness. Nary a day passed that I didn't mourn.

Sal covered his mouth and held his head downward. I wasn't aware of all that he went through during that time.

Poo and I hopped on the next thing smokin' and headed for Louisiana. We were the blind leading the blind. At the time, Poo was doing well. She still held her job nursing, and Minton, that's her man —a no good so and so, was still operating both cleaners. They had not so long ago bought a house in the South Bronx, on Charlotte Street of all places, when we got the news about Lotti. Poo and I fell apart, but I had to be strong for her.

Poo was living another life as if she were under the witness protection program or something. She physically and mentally abandoned her firstborn and was assuming a false identity like Rah never happened. Minton knew about the child; he could care less. Erasing Rah from his memory was easy. Besides Minton, Richard, and I, no one else knew Poo had an older child. Not her children. Not her friends. No one knew, and Poo grew comfortable living that twelve year lie. Until my beloved sister had a heart attack and died. I'll admit it, I grew comfortable with the lie. I had never met Rah; we only spoke when I called during Christmas, just as I did when Poo was little. I sent money every month—that didn't change. That was the extent of our relationship. So, when Poo and I boarded that plane to Louisiana, we carried more than luggage with us.

"Is that why y'all were acting all snooty—citified and special?" Sal asked, remembering the first time we met. "Y'all were acting like you were trying to erase all of Big Mama Lotti's memories."

I grunted, remembering how Poo swept through the bayou selling and taking things that belonged to Lotti and Rah." I wasn't that bad, was I?"

Sal sat up, "Not you so much, but Ms. Poo, she was a piece of work. She barely let me and Rah get a proper goodbye."

"Yeah, she did act up, didn't she? I stood by and let her do it too. It was her way of cleaning and clearing away the past."

It's like I said, neither of us had been back to Louisiana in years...and maybe we had more than our share of cocktails on the plane ride over. We needed the crutch to help encounter the past. I was hiding from demons while Poo was hiding from her own child, putting on airs like her mama used to do, worrying about what other folks would say. At the end of the day, I guess Rah reminded Poo too much of being raped.

"Ooh..." Sal, moaned, instantly growing sad. "Poor, Rah. No wonder I felt the need to want her so badly."

"I'm so glad she had a friend like you. Lawd knows she needed one. I hate to sound like I'm covering up for Poo. She was spoiled. She had a hard time thinking of anyone else but herself. Until you and Rah stood in front of us and your parents at Lotti's repast and you announced, on Rah's behalf, about that old nasty-azz doctor fondling her." Just recalling it made me mad. Sal shifted in his seat as well, groaning in his recollect of discontentment.

Thank God, Poo's motherly instincts kicked in. She showed up for Rah one hundred percent. I lost it, fed up with whatever curse that was lingering over the women in our family. I wanted to make Dr. Chester pay for hurting all of us.

I hadn't gotten wasted in a good while, but I got plastered on corn liquor that night. I sat in a hole-in-the-wall and let old hellhounds convince me to take a life.

"do it for charlotte," they told me. *"she fought your battles,"* they incited.

The drunkards at the bar answered all of my questions about Dr. Chester. They spoke of his many accolades and the whereabouts of the fancy mansion where he lived. By the time I finished drinking, I wanted more than anything to end Dr. Chester's existence. Bent on revenge, I ventured out to find him that night, seeking to deal him the hand he dealt Rah. I wanted him to die in the misery of losing hope and the torment of having no power. Drunk and staggering myself, I walked the entire way through the darkened woods adjacent to his estate, energized by revenge and talking to myself. I crouched behind the spice bushes bordering the good doctor's backyard. My heart was racing as I slipped a razor blade underneath my tongue. I tried to straighten my back, but my fifty-one years of life suddenly became apparent.

"I'll do it hunched over," I remember whispering, peeking around a bush.

The house seemed quiet. I noticed an inviting fire gleaming through a window from a fireplace in one of the upstairs rooms, and I imagined how cozy he must have been. I grew angrier. My only satisfaction was going over the plan I conjured up with my demons. I figured I'd make my entrance through the basement door. Learning he had a night maid from the fellas in the bar, I hoped our paths didn't cross. I intended on taking only one life. My detailed plan required slipping into Dr. Chester's room and straddling him in his sleep. I'd cover his mouth and nose until his face turned purple and his one eye bulged. Right before dying, I'd push his forehead back, revealing his neck, then spit the razor out like a snake and slice him across the windpipe. Laughing, I'd watch him gurgle and drown in his own blood.

"CRAZY, RIGHT?" I ASKED SAL, FEELING THE NEED TO MAKE SURE I hadn't frightened him. He made a winding sound widening his eyes. "Of course, you know what happened next." I sat up.

BEFORE TAKING THAT DEEP STEP INTO INSANITY, I SMELLED SMOKE. I remember looking up at the window where the cozy fire was but noticed no difference. I peeked from my hiding place and saw a blaze of fire coming from the front of the house. It lit the darkened sky. The next thing I knew, I saw Salmone Abrams, the preacher's kid, running across the yard toward the hedges.

Sal and I laughed.

"I MEAN, MY PLAN WASN'T AS ELABORATE AS YOURS; I WAS ONLY fourteen, but I remember wanting Dr. Chester to feel Rah's pain, probably just as much as you did." Sal recalled reclining in his seat and putting his feet up. "I know one thing; I'm glad you were there that night. You scared the crap out of me, snatching me through the bushes like that. Who knows what could have happened if you weren't there, though." We continued to laugh. "I knew I was in trouble."

"Shoot, you the one who saved my life. I think that's why I feel so connected to you now." He nodded, agreeing.

"Me too. Man, we took off into those woods, though, didn't we!" Sal laughed.

"I just knew you burned that man's house down."

"Yeah, and you were mad when you found out I didn't!" We had tears in our eyes from laughing. It felt good to finally laugh over such a tragedy.

"You know that's the only secret I've ever kept from my parents."

"Well, I told you you didn't have to tell." I shook my head. "Lawd, the child set the man's rose garden on fire." The thought conjured up more laughter. "I thought you killed the man while he slept under that cozy fire, but you burned his garden down."

"That's all I could do. Dr. Chester loved that stinking rose garden. He used to frighten Rah out there in that maze. I wanted to take something away from him like he took from her." Our hearts grew heavy again at the mention of her name. I drew Sal in and hugged him tightly.

"You don't ever have to tell, ya hear? And I'll take it to the grave." He smiled. It was our secret.

"You know, after that miserable coward killed himself, a few women came out with their stories on how he used to abuse them as children."

"Damn shame," I said. "I hate to say it, but I'm glad he killed himself."

UNFORGETTABLE

"I'm sorry we snatched and dragged Rah out to the city like that...I sure wish we hadn't."

"You do?" Sal leaned back with a boyish smile on his face, getting comfortable again.

"Absolutely, she was better off where she was. Living in New York, or should I say, living with us in New York was too much on her. Poo had that abusive junkie at home and she brought Rah right into the middle of all that—"

One of the orderlies interrupted offering coffee. "Thank you," I said, taking a cup and immediately sipping off the top. I liked it black, no sugar, no cream. She offered Sal one.

"No, thank you." He smiled, waving his hand and raking his long hair to the side. It had a lot of body and luster. Like the old-timers used to say, had he been a girl, he'd been bald.

"I did all I could do for Rah." I continued, holding the hot coffee to my mouth and blowing. "I bent over backwards for her just as I did the other kids. It's funny, but as much as Richard loved Sy and Go-Go, Rah quickly became his favorite."

THE MEMORIES WERE AS FRESH IN MY MIND AS YESTERDAY. RICHARD used to say that Rah was the only one who looked like him. I didn't think she looked anything like him—besides the deep dimples and complexion. Her sharp features favored our side. Then again, Rah had her own looks, with that brownish blonde hair and those eyes that switched up on you. Sometimes they looked green and other times blue. Richard said his mother looked that way. Now that I think back, I believe we were all missing someone and found them in Rah when we should have loved her for herself. That child had a light around her. Lotti told me she was cursed, but I felt a blessedness in her presence. She had a lot of sadness, but still a light.

I could sense the questions hanging over Sal's head again, but I continued. Lotti's voodoo notions were poppycock anyway.

When I met Rah, something in me told me that she would change this family. Her smile could brighten an entire room...and the way she danced...shoot, I thought I was the dancer of the family. Rah could outdance me any day. Poo used to wake her up and call her out to dance at those red-light parties Minton threw. Poor thang. Rah did so much for her momma. She wanted to fit in so badly. I went on rambling, trying to avoid the inevitable.

In Poo's own way, she loved her. She loved all her kids. She hated herself. I just wish she didn't let Minton mistreat them. He was a nasty druggie. He would do for the other kids and purposely leave Rah out. He yelled at her. She was always on pins and needles around him, and I pray for God he never touched her. I saw how Sy used to protect her...but no one would tell me the truth, not even Rah.

Sal and I both teared up.

I was glad when Poo and the kids came to live with us. Richard's health was declining. He suffered two strokes at the beginning of that year, followed by bouts of dementia. The funny thing about drinking is when it's held you together for so long, and then you stop, your body kind of falls apart—it's almost like the booze was preserving you somehow. That's how it was for Richard; he fell apart. Me on the other hand, I was doing fine for a while. I was taking my meds regularly and helping Poo with her mess. When Richard got sick, I turned to booze again. I couldn't seem to get the monkey off my back. I went straight into an alcoholic tailspin. Until I realized that Richard couldn't do without me. He had started falling and forgetting things. The thought of losing him propelled me into fighting for him. I didn't want to be the last man standing. Now look at me; I feel like I'm the last man standing. I knew God wasn't done with me yet.

The kids brought life back into the house. Go-Go, with her fresh behind little self, brought laughter; she kept us all going. Rah and Sy, the Irish twins, were teenagers and doing teenage things. They hung out with friends, went to parties, and wanted the latest clothes and stuff. Whereas I used to keep 'em fresh, as Sy called it; I couldn't, anymore. Richard needed me, physically, mentally, and financially. I sold everything but the neighborhood bar to pay for round-the-clock care. Richard was an infuriating man in his day, but he was mine, and he looked after me when I had champagne taste and beer pockets. Caring for him was a no-brainer. I would rather live in one of those holes-in-the-wall we first lived in than watch Richard suffer without proper care. So, my money was tied up, and it forced Poo to become a woman. She moped around for a while, feeling sorry for herself and searching for Minton—who just sort of disappeared. We were all convinced he overdosed and died somewhere without family to claim him. That's how bad his drug problem became. Eventually, Poo got a job, and she was seeing an older guy who was really good for her. Unfortunately, just like that, everything changed for the worst.

It was Christmas Eve, 1984; I remember it fell on a Monday that year. That morning the brownstone wasn't as active as usual during school and work hours. The kids had slept in, and Poo was coming in from work. It was around seven-thirty, and she had an arm full of gifts she took off layaway. I remember her gentleman friend, the cabbie...Jenkins was his last name.

Sal popped up and took out a small pen and pad set from his pocket and jotted down Jenkins, NYC cabbie.

He came into the house, helping Poo with the packages. That was the first time we actually met. I offered him some of the breakfast I was preparing for Richard, who sat at the table with his nurse aide, assorting nuts, bolts, and screws. That's how we kept him busy. The dementia had his mind slipping. He couldn't remember anyone but me. Although every morning, when Poo came into the kitchen to have coffee and toast with us before heading to bed, she worked overnight, he lit up. That morning, Richard, feeling frisky, coyly smiled and pulled Poo down into his lap; he was strong. The nurse tried to discourage him from doing those things, but Poo said it was okay. She played along, kissing her father's forehead and smoothing back his silver hair.

"I'll give you a dollar to make it holla," Richard said, and we all busted out laughing.

"You're not my type, Daddy-O," Poo answered, trying to stand, but he held her firmly around the waist, kissing her neck.

"Why not, beautiful, my money spends."

Poo patted his hands, leaned back, and pecked his cheek. "I usually go for men who aren't my father." She winked over at Jenkins, who had declined my invitation for breakfast and was waiting patiently for his goodbye kiss. Poo stood, and Richard looked so sad and confused after that. He went back to assorting nuts and bolts as Poo said her goodbyes to Jenkins at the door.

I remember giving the nurse aide the rest of the day for the holiday. Richard and I laid in our room and wrapped gifts for Poo while listening to music. He was in a good mood. The kids were up and running around. The brownstone was clean, decorated with Christmas cheer, and smelled of fresh glazed ham, collards, potato salad, and cornbread. I made an early dinner so that Poo could carry some with her to work, but she forgot it sitting on the kitchen table. I wish I could forget that night like that; just leave it sitting somewhere.

Rah and her narrow behind boyfriend had just left for a party. His name was Jayson, Jayson Simmons. The hazel-eyed Casanova is what I called him. Sal wrote that down too. They thought I didn't know what was going on in their bedrooms, Mhmm, but I knew everything. I was just tied up with Richard. Poo trusted the kids to tend to themselves and their little sister, Go-Go, who was grown enough to run the house her damn self. That night, Sy was home caring for Go, who wasn't feeling well. I don't know how they worked that out, but I had made up my mind to take Richard to the bar's Christmas party like we used to on Christmas Eve. I felt guilty about leaving Sy and Go-Go, but she was heavily medicated, and Sy had his WHT and Genesis. They were fine.

I dyed Richard's hair, got him out of that monogrammed satin robe and pajama set he always wore, and dressed him in his old hosting tuxedo. The cream jacket, black cummerbund, white tuxedo shirt with black buttons, and gold cufflinks. He looked sharp as a tack even though his frail body swam in the suit. I dolled up too, as best as I could with him forgetting things every twenty minutes. However, as I said, Richard was particularly satisfied that day and better than usual, which was good. I figured a night of dancing amongst old friends might do him well or me some good. He had already started acting like his old self in the tuxedo. He even asked for a cigarette, and I gave it to him. He was hugging me around my waist while I combed my hair in the mirror, nuzzling my neck. He said my eyes twinkled like the stars. Richard could talk like that sometimes. It made me feel young and beautiful. We had a stack of old records playing on the autochanger. I guess we were both feeling nostalgic because Richard whisked me around and kissed me like he remembered who we were long ago. Then, he began to remove my robe.

I looked up at Sal. "It's about to get real...but I have to tell it just as it was, okay." He nodded with his chin perched in his hand.

Richard being forward wasn't a shock; he was frisky during his illness too, but that time felt real.

Shocked, I chuckled and said, "What you doing?"

"I'm fixin' to make love to my wife," he answered with an unexpected authority that brought me back to his younger years. He made me put down the hairbrush and twirled me around.

We waltzed to "Unforgettable" by Nat King Cole and kissed tenderly. After all my hard work getting Richard dressed, he undressed. That night, my husband, who was diagnosed with a mind-altering disease almost a year to that date, made love to me. Not sex. This was sweet. It made me cry. He gazed over my body like it was his first time. I didn't expect much. I figured he'd forget what he was doing, and I'd end up in the bathroom with my gadget. But I was satisfied with being with him. Now, when he was done, that's another story; he went back into anxious confusion, but for eight minutes or so, I had my Richard back.

"Excuse me, miss. Have I missed my flight? I'm heading to New York to see my lady tonight," he asked, and I smiled, getting up and putting on my robe.

"No sir, your flight is running on time. We'll be departing in thirty minutes, so why don't you get dressed so you'll be ready." Richard looked down at himself and laughed.

"Yes, I will be needing my clothes."

"What's your lady's name?" I asked, helping him button his shirt. He always said, a river flower from Baton Rouge, Miss Mary Mags. I was the only person he remembered, which was sweet, but this time he said, Puah Marie.

I didn't think anything of it then. I actually thought it was a good sign that Richard remembered someone other than me. He didn't even remember Fatso when he came to visit, and he knew him longer. Fatso and Jo had moved to Maryland. Jo's grandmother fell ill. Ms. Ramsey was ninety-six years old, bless her heart. They went down there to care for her and stayed. Last I heard, they started a church and outreach ministry called Fishers of Men.

Sal wrote that down too.

When they left New York, Richard knew who they were. He offered well wishes and had me send a large floral arrangement to their home, but Ms. Ramsey lived. When Fatso and Jo returned to visit, he didn't know who they were anymore.

MERCY, MERCY, MERCY

T hat night Richard and I got into our 1984 white-on-white Cadillac Fleetwood Brougham, and I drove for the first time in fifteen years. I went straight to the bar, seven blocks down and around the corner. Everyone was glad to see Richard. As soon as he stepped foot into the place there was an explosion of cheer, and he came back to himself. I didn't even have to lead him to our table; he already knew the way. Lew had it roped off with a welcome back sign and balloons. Richard was so proud. He pulled out my chair, unfastened his jacket with one hand, flared the tails, and sat, crossing his long legs. You can't take away cool from a person. He asked for another cigarette. Mostly he held them in his mouth while enjoying the jazz music. I sat close by him with my arm thrown around his narrow shoulders as he tapped a beat out on my knee. My husband's eyes sparkled that night. He didn't remember the faces, but he remembered the good times and enjoyed himself without confusion.

Around midnight, Lew poured Richard a glass of champagne, and I let him have it. Relaxed, I had a few drinks myself. We danced, laughed, and I even sang. Before I knew it, I looked up, and Richard was gone. Panicked, I stopped the music and sobered up real fast. Lew and I looked everywhere for him. We all ran out and up and down the block. When I was about to have a meltdown, my spirit said, *"Go home."*

I got back in the car and tore up those seven blocks around the corner. When I reached the brownstone, the front door was standing open. I called Richard's name, but there was no response. Instantly, I started sweating. I don't know why. Maybe it was a hot flash, or possibly the mixture of alcohol with my meds. Perhaps it was the gut feeling I had at the bottom of my stomach wrenching me apart. I slipped out my .44 Magnum from my purse and thought of The Grandmother thumping her rifle on the wooden floor of that old shack years ago. She was ready to kill the one she loved for a greater love; that of a child. Somehow, I knew Rah was home from her party. She should have been. It was two or three in the morning. I walked past our bedroom on the second floor and even checked the bathroom, no Richard. I continued up the stairs to Rah's room on the third floor. The door was ajar, and the flickering of an antique bedside Fenton lamp I bought was casting rose-colored lighting through the crack and into the darkened hall. I quietly pushed open the door, rebuking the voice telling me to prepare myself.

The memory was so vivid; I had to hold on to the table. Sal's eyes grew wide, and his hands clasped at his mouth.

The fatality of my sanity was never more than an eye flutter away. My fears lurked just beyond the surface, ready to drown me at any moment. Do I know insanity? Yes, I do, and I wish I never knew such twisted pain. It's the type of pain that cracks you open and leaves you exposed. I held a gun to Richard's temple. I had to; he had our grandbaby bent over the bed in front of him, and she was crying.

———

TEARS STARTED ROLLING FROM MY EYES LIKE A RIVER. MY LIPS trembled, and Sal grabbed my hands.

"It's okay, Tante Mags. I'm here," he said with his tears and nose running. He knew what I had to say, and it hurt him just as much as it hurt me, but he braced himself like a man.

THE SIGHT OF RICHARD AND RAH TOGETHER WEAKENED MY VISION. AN enormous space cracked inside of me, threatening to swallow my existence. For the sake of my sanity, my mind quickly rejected what my heart had already related. I swallowed hard and racked my .44 with a swift steady force, releasing a bullet into the chamber. The click echoed through the silence of the room. Hearing it, Richard quickly opened his eyes. Then he felt the steel tap against his temple.

"Mary!" he yelled, coming to himself. "What you doing, crazy woman? I done told you about pulling guns on me," he stated, cutting his eyes toward me, nervous.

"And I done told you about messing with my girls," I gestured down toward our paralyzed granddaughter.

Alarmed and confused, Richard slowly backed away, pulling himself from Rah. Breathing slowly, he held his arms up in surrender, acting confused once again.

"I can't explain," he cried. "What's happening, Mags?"

"I don't wanna hear that crap!" I violently shook my head, grinding my teeth. "I can't forgive you this time. This is blood!" I pushed the gun harder against the side of his head. "Our blood! You, bastard!"

"What did I do? Please don't shoot." Richard cut his eye toward the shaking gun laid against his temple and then at Rah on the bed.

I guess Rah became aware that her grandfather was in and out of his deranged state because she pushed herself up and slowly turned around. Her eyes were dead, and so was Richard to me.

"No!" he yelled, as though seeing her for the first time and realizing his actions. "My baby," he cried from his pit. "The only one who looks like me."

Suddenly, and with a swiftness that caught me off guard, he removed the revolver from my hand and shot himself in the head. Freeing himself from whatever was happening to his mind.

"Aba, daba, daba, daba, daba, daba, dab,"

Said the Chimpie to the Monk.

"Baba, daba, daba, daba, daba, daba, dab..."

Rah began to repeat the lyrics to her favorite childhood song to occupy her mind. All I heard were demons.

"now, look what you did."

Blood was splattered everywhere, just like in the old shack when Mr. Lackey shot Diddy. I wanted to scream, but my voice hid inside of me.

"I don't understand." I heard Rah whisper, and I wanted to comfort her, but...

"what kind of grandmother are you? look what you did."

I fell to my knees near Richard's defaced body and sobbed. At that moment, I passively resigned myself to death and destruction. My fluttering emotions switched from grief-stricken to suicidal. As I reached for the revolver dropped inches from Richard's corpse Sy barged into the room. I guess he had heard the shot. Somehow, he sensed my attempted plot and quickly kicked the gun across the floor. With every fiber of my being, I wanted to end my life. So, I scrambled to retrieve it, but Sy tackled me, and we fought.

"Rah, call the cops!" He yelled several times, but she stood immobilized with blood sprinkled on her face and gown, mumbling that schoolyard chant.

I snapped, and I swear I separated from my body and started growling like an old junkyard dog.

"what kind of grandmother are you? look what you did."

If it wasn't for Rah's friend, Lydia, we called her Le-Le, showing up when she did, I could have taken Sy and ended my life; he was afraid of harming me. Le-Le, who met up with Rah at the party earlier and was spending the night, picked up a desk chair and started acting like a lion tamer. Unintimidated, she twirled the chair and shouted unknown words in Spanish, holding me back. While Rah calmly walked over to the smoking pistol, picked it up, and tossed it out of her bedroom window.

I went off, releasing the fury of the renegade of demons collected inside of me. I began snarling and growling. I lunged after the kids, scratching and biting as they escaped the room and held the door shut until the police came.

It took three officers to harness me down in the ambulance that night. All of Strivers' Row came out that early Christmas morning to witness the fall of the Owens' dynasty. I was immediately placed in an asylum and was unable to attend the funeral of the man who captured my heart on a tatty road in Baton Rouge. There were no goodbyes, no flowers. No hugs or condolences. Only ten years of darkness. Ten years of helpless silence! Ten years of loneliness and seclusion!

"I welched on God, and He abandoned me!" I cried uncontrollably.

TEDDY RUXPIN

Nurse Lindt ran over to assist, but Sal though emotional himself, was already holding me up. His body was solid and firm; his strength commanded my attention.

"Stop it," he issued sternly, not wanting to lose me again to another tangent. He grabbed my arms. The news about Rah gravely hurt him, and I didn't know if he wanted anything to do with me after learning how I let her down. My family didn't forgive me. "Stop it, Tante Mags. Stop it this instant."

Breathing heavily, I attempted to control myself. I could hear nurse Lindt ordering a sedative. So, I placed my hands over my eyes, focusing on my breathing. "Please, God," I whispered. More than anything, I wanted my freedom from that place. I didn't want to go backward. Recalling the incident brought forth too many sudden emotions. But just like that, a warming presence passed, washing over me, and my ears heard the whisper of a quiet voice.

"Mary! I'm still here...I never left you." I wiped the tears rolling from my eyes, and after a few breathless minutes, I spoke, whimpering, "I'm okay."

Nurse Lindt waved away the orderly, bringing the sedation needle; instead, she allowed Sal to continue holding me in his arms. We sat in silence for a few more minutes. I knew he was upset; it was a lot to unpack. I decided there in his arms that I wanted to reclaim my life. Everything inside of me shifted. My skin tingled with electricity, and my arm hairs stood on end. The news of what happened that night hurt Sal but recalling the story was a breakthrough for me. I had tucked that memory away for so long and held guilt and shame behind it that it grew into bondage. At that moment, I knew I had to let go if I intended to live and recover. I was finally willing to allow Dr. Davis to help. He wasn't like those other worthless quacks. He cared, and I was eager to believe and obey rather than understand everything.

Lifting my head off Sal's shoulder, I looked into his kind eyes and then up at Nurse Lindt, who had planted herself in front of me. There was no change in their expression of care.

"What?" I asked sarcastically. "The first time I open up and you all ready to sedate me? I thought Dr. Davis said crying was good for the soul." My light chuckle evoked laughter.

"Are you okay, sweetie?" Nurse Lindt asked, squatting between Sal and me, as she checked my blood pressure. Sal placed his chin on top of my head. I could tell by his heaving chest that he was still emotional.

"I'm letting go of old demons so I can start fresh," I reassured them.

Nurse Lindt smiled and patted my hand. "There you go," she said, removing the sphygmomanometer from my arm. Maybe we should wrap this visit up for the day." Sal turned toward her, pulling himself together and clearing his throat.

"I'm sorry," he said, "it's my fault. I incited the—"

"Don't you dare!" I interrupted. "It's time I release the past. You encouraged me." Sal smiled.

"How about fifteen more minutes, Nurse Lindt?" he asked.

"Okay, fifteen minutes." She responded, documenting in her chart before leaving.

"I'm sorry, Sal." I patted his hand as he let out a long sigh. "I blame myself for what happened to Rah. I should have never taken—"

"No, don't do that, Tante Mags." He squeezed my hand. "At this point, all we can do is pray. Pray that Rah is in a better headspace than we are right now. Sometimes taking the blame can turn into selfish motives. You know what I'm sayin'? You're removing whatever pain Rah...and even Richard were going through and feeling sorry for yourself. It's okay to deal with pain. Feel it. Our weaknesses were designed to open us up to God's power. He knows every tear exposed to your pillow."

I started crying again, this time exhaling and staring off into the corridor, counting square shapes. Sal was right. I made it through the recalling of that night that closed the doors on my sanity; it took ten years to open them again, but I made it through.

"Sal, I'm ready to live again. I want to find my family and live again." I sat up erect in my seat. "This old gray mare ain't what she used to be, but she damn sure got some kick left to her." Sal smiled and kissed my cheek.

"That's what I want to hear." He stood and went to pick up the Big Brown Bag from Bloomingdale's that he had behind the table and sat it in front of me.

"What's this?"

"Open it." He sat down.

I could see a furry arm peeking out. "I was wondering where my stuffed animal was." He smiled again, this time with the same enchantment that initially drew me close to him.

"You know, Tante Mags? I'm glad I came today. I don't like what I heard, but I'm encouraged. I can feel in my spirit that everything's going to work out with my case, and then I'll be back to bring you home with me. God led me to this. He's going to lead me through it. We'll find Rah and the rest of your family together." I smiled, pulling a beige bear from the bag. "Until then, I need you to be safe and continue opening up to your doctors." He reached over and rubbed the head of the bear I removed from the bag. "This guy is special. Always keep him by your side. I worry about you not having any company." The bear wasn't as cute as the others. It looked like one of those Teddy Ruxpin bears that Go-Go used to cry over. Sal pressed the ear, and it said in his voice, *"I'm always here with you."*

"Aww, I love it!" I hugged the bear; it wasn't so ugly after all. "Thank you." I bent over and kissed Sal's cheek. "This is perfect." I pressed the bear's ear myself.

"You're one in a million, Tante Mags," it said, and I hugged it again, gushing over it this time. Sal was beaming. He was such a thoughtful person.

"Make sure you carry it everywhere you go. I have about fifteen pre-recorded messages on there. They raised the dickens, trying to keep me from bringing it in here." I slanted my eyes, starting to get upset. "But Nurse Lindt approved it. I told her I might be away for a while." Hearing that made me sad.

"Sal, I got something to tell ya that I've been holding back on."

"Something else!" he responded sarcastically and smiled.

"Well, see, I've kinda been handling it myself because I didn't want you to get upset and worry." He took my hand and leaned over close to my face.

"Is it about the complaint order you filed?" I looked shocked, but I did sign Power of Attorney forms, amongst some other documents, allowing him to become my guardian and caregiver. "I already know, Tante Mags." He continued whispering. "I was waiting for you to feel comfortable enough to talk about it. That's why I got this bear." He smiled coyly and raised an eyebrow.

"Boy, you something else." I tapped his arm.

"Five minutes," an orderly announced, walking by.

"Okay, listen," Sal responded, sitting erect. "I'ma be back...the enemy was trying to get at me. He had me anxious about this assignment, but as I said, I can feel it in my spirit that everything's gonna be okay."

I was still worried for him but trying not to show it. That beeping device he wore was lighting up throughout our visit, and every time he looked at it, he frowned. I hugged my teddy bear tighter.

"Now, that's what I wanna see," Sal said, observing how I took to the doll. "Give him all your anxieties—just don't be like that lady over there." He motioned toward Mrs. Rossellini with her lap dog toaster, and we both burst into laughter. "Maybe just keep him in the room with you."

"Yeah, that might be a good idea." I put the bear back in the bag and stood with Sal, who was preparing to leave. "Sal, I just love you so," I took his hand and held it to my chest. "...and I know you're going to be okay. I'm looking forward to getting out of here and starting over." We hugged and he held me longer than I expected.

"I love you too, Tante Mags." He released me, giving me one of his hundred-watt smiles. I think I blushed. *Good Lord, I hope we find Rah. He is God's match for her.*

"Hey," Sal lifted my chin. "Earlier, you said you welched on God, and He abandoned you. I feel I need to tell you that that couldn't be further from the truth. God is here with you...even when it feels like He's not. Don't let the impact of the world shatter your thinking. The hiddenness of God isn't His abandonment. And even if that were true, the Word says, blessed are those that God corrects. So do not despise the discipline of The Almighty. For though He wounds, He also bandages."

My eyes welled up as I nodded, trying to keep from crying. I felt that warming presence again.

"Can I pray?" Sal asked, taking both of my hands with his head already held downward. I lowered my head, and the tears escaped. The last man that prayed for me was Fatso. Sal sighed deeply and closed his eyes.

"Father in heaven..." he lightly swung my arms. "Please help us to believe that you are always working in the background, doing far more and much better than we know or understand." I couldn't keep the tears from rolling. Immediately, I knew that the posture of Sal's heart was inclined unto the Lord. As his soul soared in communication with his Father, he expressed everything I felt and couldn't relate. Lord knows I was trying to get to his level of faith, but that was the problem—I was trying. Sal's love filled the space between God and me, and brought me in closer.

PART VIII
CLEANSED

"A person often meets his destiny on the road he took to avoid it" - Jean de La Fontaine

CHEEK TO CHEEK

All I could do was sleep when Sal left. The aftermath of the emotions I put myself through came down like a ton of bricks. I retired early that evening and slept past dinner, only waking to relieve myself, identify, count, and take the nightly pills that Judy, the evening nurse, brought in. She asked if I wanted a sandwich or something, but I declined. I didn't budge for the rest of the evening, ignoring the other nurses when they came to check in.

That next day, I gobbled down breakfast like someone was taking it away, then sat quietly in a corner reading from my bible. I had come to an understanding, and an air of tranquility surrounded me. It was God's peace, and it had always been there hovering, but being stiff-necked, I worried too much and took matters into my own hands that His peace never had a place to land. He kept me anyway, and I was grateful. I was ready to make the necessary changes in my attitude, health, and overall well-being. I was only sixty-three years old, but I felt and looked one hundred and sixty-three. As far as I knew, I was the last of the Auguste clan; they had all died too young. Being the last man standing all of a sudden was an honor.

It didn't even bother me when Ms. Rossellini joined my table. I read out loud from the book of Hebrews, and she excused herself after having coffee.

"That's nice, sweetheart," she said in a shaky Italian accent. "Maybe we'll catch up for lunch. I didn't get the chance to tell you about Fred's uncle, Louie, the barber. He drove a mobile home straight into the Passaic River in '69—and lived to tell about it."

Now that's interesting. "I'll be looking forward to hearing that," I responded as Mrs. Rossellini rolled away in her wheelchair, intercepting Eddie from joining me.

"She's a drag today," she told him, waving me off. "Don't even bother." I couldn't help but laugh as they turned away to entertain one another.

She better watch out for Eddie. I chuckled while sipping my coffee. *Keep a sharp eye on that toaster; he'll stick something other than bread in there.*

"Mrs. Owens," an orderly called, tapping my shoulder and disturbing my thoughts. "You have an emergency call at the front desk." Straightaway, my legs turned to Jell-O; I couldn't stand. My first thought was *something happened to Sal.* "Who is it!" I asked, unable to move.

"Ahh..." She looked down at her notepad. "Mmm, a Mr. Abrams..." I panicked, and I don't know why I thought it was Sal's father, Pastor Josh. The orderly touched my shoulder again because I looked confused. "Your grandson." She clarified, and I stood immediately.

"Hey, beb!" I yelled in excitement before getting the phone to my mouth good. "You okay?" I could hear loud hippity-hop music playing.

"Turn that down." Sal issued to someone before answering. "Tante Mags, I'm excellent! Take this turn right here, bruh." He was obviously in a car with someone. "Yeah, Tante Mags, I'm sorry. I'm out with my partner; we're working."

"You scared me, boy! Did everything work out? You—"

"Yeah, yeah, it did, but listen, auntie...I found your family."

I swear the lights went out in my head for five seconds or more.

"Tante Mags, you there!"

"Say that again."

Sal chuckled. "I found Rah and 'em!" He yelled in excitement.

"Congratulations!" His partner shouted from the background over top of the music he was still listening to and singing.

"Well, actually, we found each other—accidentally," Sal added, "but, yeah—I know where they are."

"Sweet Jesus," I mumbled as a waterfall ran from my eyes.

"Should I make this turn?" his partner asked.

"Yeah, the turn at the light. Listen, I can't talk long. I just wanted you to know that I found them. They're okay, but..."

"What...what?" I cut him off because he hesitated. I knew they were in some kind of a mess; my spirit told me that long ago. "Tell me, Sal. I can take it."

"I can't tell you much because of the case I'm on, but Rah is mixed-up in it—What's up, ma?" I lost him again to another conversation. I could hear outdoor sounds.

"Ay, Papi, you lookin' good! You a ball'a? You got sumphin for me?" A woman asked then there was a muffling sound. Sal must have covered his receiver. The car door slammed. I could hear people talking loudly over horns honking, a dog barking, a car alarm going off, and the sounds of kids playing and laughing.

"Sal! You, there?"

The car door shut again, and the noise quieted down.

"Yeah, Tante Mags. I'm working, and I gotta go, but I can't believe we found them!" His laughter sounded like relief. "Rah is knee-deep in sum bullsh—I mean, she's really got herself in a bind." He was confusing his work language with speaking with me. "But she wants out, and I'm here to help. We're all coming to get you out of there soon." There was a loud thump or bang.

"Yo, hurry up!" I heard a male voice say.

"Chill! I'm coming...pfft. I gotta go, Tante Mags. I love you. You don't know how happy I am."

"Sal, I am too! You okay, though, right?" There was a lot of noise.

"I'm good. Don't worry, I got you—Yo! Get off my car! Pfft, this stupid—I Gotta go!" He hung up abruptly.

I held the cordless phone to my forehead for a second, imagining what was happening and praying in my spirit. When I looked up to hand the phone back, I thought I saw Nurse Mulligan disappear into a conference room from the corner of my eye.

"Is everything okay, Mrs. Owens?" The orderly asked from behind the nursing station, waiting for me to pass her the phone through the window.

"Oh, I'm sorry." I slid it to her, looking through the station for Nurse Lindt, my go-to person. She wasn't there. "Did Nurse Mulligan come in here today?" I heard myself ask in a panic.

"Who?" she responded.

"Nurse—"

"Mary!" Sue yelled from across the room, running toward me. She wasn't in her uniform; she was nicely dressed in a tweed skirt set and silk blouse. We hugged, and she started talking before catching her breath.

"I brought in the CD!" She fanned a square casing at me as she keyed herself into the nursing station. "I can't stay long. I forgot I'm off today. Hi, Nicole." She said all in one breath to the orderly who handed me the phone. "My husband's job is giving him a retirement party this afternoon." My mind was racing, I thought I saw Nurse Mulligan, but Sue was talking a mile a minute. "You okay, Mary?" she asked, placing the circular disc into an opening on the radio sitting on the countertop. "You're going to feel a lot better after hearing this. I promise." She didn't wait for me to respond; she was too excited. She slid the open CD case through the slot in the glass partition separating us. "Read what's underneath cut number seven." She said, forcing her chubby hand underneath the glass partition and pointing to the place she wanted me to read.

"Written and composed by Richard W. Owens." We read together. My jaw fell open seeing Richard's name in print with all the accolades.

"You got some royalty money waiting for you, baby!" Sue said, rolling her neck and twisting her mouth in excitement. "Henry said the band just won a Grammy with this song." She pushed the play button before I could respond, and more tears ran from my eyes. I was listening to Richard's baby. Sue ran out of the nursing station, took my hands, and started dancing. "Look at God." She whispered in my ear. I closed my eyes and smiled as I waltzed with her, forgetting about seeing Nurse Mulligan. It was only the devil trying to steal my joy anyway, and I was done with that.

THE SIDEWINDER

After Sue Left, I proceeded with my day—smiling. Nothing could go wrong. Sal had found my family, and the composition that Richard wrote years ago won a Grammy. The day floated by with high expectations and images of loved ones scrolling through my memory. I saw many people coming and going into the unit, but no Nurse Mulligan. I met with Dr. Davis and my social worker, Ms. Simmons, together that evening. We had a good discussion. They were still working on my release plan. They both agreed that my leaving the hospital wouldn't put others at risk. I didn't know what the hold-up was, but Dr. Davis' hesitation to answer my questions led me to believe that the institution was at fault. I imagined they were worried about me suing them and trying to come up with a solution to get rid of me without any consequences. Little did they know, I didn't care about no money. I only wanted my freedom back.

I had a hot shower that night after dinner and went to bed, anticipating a new day. I was trying not to be anxious but couldn't help getting excited. I wondered how everyone looked and how they had aged. The kids were all adults. *They probably won't recognize me.* Removing Teddy Ruxpin from his Bloomie's bag, I placed him at the foot of the bed in front of all the other stuffed animals and pressed his ear for a goodnight word.

"I can't wait until we're together!" he said.

"Me either," I answered out loud, patting its head and trying to reject the desire to press it again. I promised myself I'd listen to it once a day until Sal returned so I wouldn't run out of new messages so quickly.

"Knock, knock," Judy, the night nurse said, before entering the room. I had intentionally left the door open for her. She smiled and sat a small white paper cup containing my pills on the bedside tray for my examination. It was our nightly routine—because you know—fool me once, shame on you. Fool me twice; shame on me.

"How are you this evening?" she poured the pills onto a napkin.

"I'm good—ready for some sleep. I had another exciting day."

"I heard it through the grapevine," she revealed, still smiling. Judy was a doll, but you could smell her armpits from a mile away. Whatever country she was from, they didn't believe in deodorant.

I counted and identified the pills quickly to let her go. Five. One small yellow one. Two oblong white capsules. A tiny white dot pill and a beige-looking horse one cut in half. Judy and I said goodnight before she turned out the lights and closed the door because we both knew that the tiny white one was a mild sedative. We had no idea that another nurse, the one with the facial tic who used to help Dino hold me down as Nurse Mulligan doped me up, had tampered with one of the oblong white capsules.

"Judy," she called when they were in the hall. "Is that your patient running through the corridors?"

"Where?" Judy turned to look. That's when the shaky one, that's what I called her jittery behind, switched my pill cup.

The sensation of the medication hit me almost instantly. I remember thinking—*what the hell!* I knew something was off. The clock, caged in on the wall, loudly ticked, counting down the seconds of my life. I felt like I was tripping, floating, and wanting to do something to ground myself, but only being able to laugh. When you need someone, they're never there, and when you don't need them, they're always around. Before I knew it, I passed out.

Sometime during the night...or it could have been thirty minutes later, as usual, Judy came back to check on me. The shaky one, who I later found out was Nurse Mulligan's sister, burst into the room with news of another patient eloping.

"Go, go!" she yelled to Judy, turning the lights on. "I'll handle Mrs. Owens—she's sleeping anyway."

"Ugh! Just great. It's going to be one of those nights." Judy sounded, racing out of the room and into the chaotic hallway.

The shaky one stood over my bed hauntingly, staring down at me. She even looked like Nurse Mulligan. "I have a message from my sister." She pulled out one of those long needles.

I blinked, trying to keep the room steady.

"Find your bearings," a voice that sounded like The Grandmothers suggested. But all I could do was laugh. At least, I think I laughed, anyway.

"Don't worry, it'll all be over soon...and I'll make it look like a bad reaction." She tapped the needle with shaky fingers and a twitching face. "Have a nice trip, songbird!" she added, stretching out my arm but then hesitating. I wanted to scream.

Suddenly I heard a faint uttering. Grunts. Monkey noises. I looked over at Teddy Ruxpin, wanting to ask if it was him and wanting it to be him. I desperately stared into his glowing red eyes. Frightened, I flinched.

"Hold still!" the shaky one issued, breathing heavily and mumbling something under her breath about always having to clean up her sister's mess.

My days were numbered; my life was ending. *Lord, please,* was all I could think to pray. "Help," I was able to whisper.

"You're going to need help." She held the needle in her fist raised high above her head, deciding to stab me with it because her hands were shaking profusely.

"Monkey," I said in a louder voice, flinching again. This time, I saw one come out from behind the chair. "Monkey!" I said even louder, startling my attacker before she could administer the drug. Thank God the Monkeys were everywhere. They caused me to jump, knocking the needle out of her hands. I was having the same hallucination reaction from the overdosing that Nurse Mulligan used to give me. Before I knew it, I was jumping in the bed like a five-year-old trying to catch those monkeys by the tails because I didn't want Judy to come back and find them there. "Get out of here!" I yelled at them.

I wanna tell you more, but that's all I can remember. I woke up harnessed on a thin white mattress on the floor of a seclusion room. My arms and legs were wrapped tightly in four-point restraints as they forcibly medicated me some more. They left me in a locked room for hours as a guard watched through a small wire-glass window. Nurse Lindt and Sue weren't there that night. But He was.

AT LAST

There were no colors to count. Only white. No shapes to identify. Only squares. No sounds. Only mine. *What can I see? Nothing. What can I touch? Nothing.*

"This is some cruel shit!" I screamed and screamed at the locked door until I was hoarse.

I was trying not to acknowledge the gathering of voices in my head whispering against me...but their accusations were valid. *Was my birth an omen?*

"How much longer, Lord? Cursed is the day that I was born." I finally announced, staring up at the ceiling. My soul was in deep anguish.

"It would have been better had I died!" I screamed to God. "Mama would still be alive. Lotti would have both parents full of life and light had only I been strangled by the umbilical cord. They all would have cared for the Grandmother in her aging." I turned my vision to the padded wall nearest me. "Richard and I would have never met." There would be no meeting on that old dirt road. "He and the band would have continued playing local joints, enjoying their minimal success until old age." My lips trembled as my eyes teared. "Tiny would have found another successor for The Madame's business, one more obedient. There would be no supper club, no bar, no rat fink stool pigeon to burst into the room and conspire against him. No Poo..." I paused at the thought of deterring lives.

No Puah. No Silas. No Gomer. No Rahab. I couldn't imagine life without their light.

"No Salmone...no Martita." My speech was broken and weak. "Who am I? Who am I to question Your better judgment?" I shook my head, feeling tormented by my own thoughts. "I am no one...and You, You are the master of the universe. The creator of all things," I rationalized. The Grandmother used to say, never question the creator—His will is His will. "But why God? I don't understand. Why was I born to see all this trouble? Am I so wretched that you won't spare me? "Why have you forsaken me! Why do you hate me?" I cried out loud...or I could have been dreaming because suddenly there was darkness. Scared, I shouted, "Jesus! Jesus! I'm sorry for questioning you."

As I began to cry, the darkness trembled, but He was not in the darkness. After the darkness, coming from nowhere, a brisk wind blew, which made the hairs on my body suddenly stand on end, but He wasn't in the wind. And after the wind came a gentle whisper.

"Mary." When I heard it, my eyes grew wide with fear. *"Even an ox knows its owner, and a donkey recognizes it's master's care - but you refuse to know me."* I tightly closed my eyes, fearing I saw His presence and He came to take me away. *"I'm still here, Mary."* The subtle voice I heard all my life continued to speak over me. *"I'll free you when you free yourself to love me. I'll remove the stone."*

"How!" I cried, tired of trying to figure it all out on my own.

"Make Me the Lord of your life. My grace is sufficient for you, for My power is made perfect in weakness. Why do you look for the living among the dead? He is not here, He has risen!"

When I heard these things, I turned my head and wept, praying to Him for what seemed like hours. Because I saw Him with my own eyes, He revealed who He was throughout my life. He was the way maker in the tiny shack, the miracle worker in the car accident, the promise keeper throughout my darkness. He showed me the pointers in this world that were meant to lead me to Him: River John, Fatso,

Joanna, Mary, Martita, Susanna, Salmone, Rah. I saw when the stone was rolled back from the entrance of my heart. My Savior lived. I felt the shackles as they were physically released from my arms and feet.

"Mary Magdalene, from whom seven demons came out, Peace be with you! As the Father has sent me, I am sending you."

Feeling groggy, I opened my eyes to a strange hospital room. My heavy eyelids fluttered and closed again. *I'm alive,* I thought, forcing myself to reopen them. The light coming in from the glass-paneled door was blinding. I attempted to move my hand to rub my eyes, but it felt weighted down. Downcast, I knew I was still being harnessed and deemed my encounter was simply a dream. I turned my head slightly to cry into my pillow and found Sal sitting nearby asleep in a chair. He was the one holding my hand. My soul yelled, *"cry, girl, you've been saved,"* and I did. I wept so deeply it startled Sal from his sleep. He jumped up.

"Aww, Tante Mags," he uttered, with a smile brighter than that coming in from the fluorescent lighting in the hall. He kissed my forehead and whispered, "I told you I'd get you out of there." I tried to lift my other hand to embrace him, but it too was confined. I turned my head the other way to find out why, and my nose brushed against thick, soft curls that smelled like coconuts. A woman was curled up under my arm.

"Ms. Poo!" Sal called, slightly standing to rub her shoulder. "Tante Mags is up."

DON'T MOVE MY MOUNTAIN

You're probably wondering what happened. As I was told, Sue returned to work the next day and found me restrained. She immediately contacted Nurse Lindt, who was on vacation, but she took the next flight back to Long Island just for me. By this time, I was so fatigued that I didn't resist the care team as they removed me from the padded room. My strength was sapped as though in the height of the summer heat. I collapsed in Sue's arms.

"What did they do to you?" she cried, removing the hair plastered to my face from sweat. "I'm so sorry, Mary. I'm here now."

Sue refused to allow them to medicate me any further until Nurse Lindt arrived. She fought and put her job on the line on my behalf. She had no answers for my behavior but knew something must have gone wrong. The hospital was calling it a relapse. Sue prayed and rebuked them, convincing Dr. Davis to delay any decisions. He, too, wanted for my release.

When Nurse Lindt returned, the place was in complete disorder. There was an influx of agitated, psychotic, and manic patients all at once. Despite it all, Nurse Lindt demanded to see my charts from the previous day.

"There has to be some sort of foul play," she insisted to the board of directors. "Mrs. Owens has shown nothing but progress. I find it coincidental that this...amongst other strange occurrences, happened when Nurse Sue and myself were out. Gentlemen, taking Mrs. Owens' prior care into consideration, I strongly suggest we quickly investigate."

There was no need for their delayed response. Sal, Poo, Sy, and Rah all showed up demanding my release. Sue and Nurse Lindt sat them down and explained what happened. I was in a bad state. Worn out from groaning, I was dehydrated and depleted. I couldn't speak, only sleep.

"Nurse Lindt," Sal said. "I know this is against the hospital's regulations, and I'm sorry in advance for what I did, but I was worried about something like this happening in my absence. May I please have the stuffed animals that I gave my aunt," he asked.

No one knew that Teddy Ruxpin was wired with a nanny cam. The entire evening was recorded. Later, Nurse Mulligan, her sister, and Dino were arrested for the misconduct and abuse of mentally ill patients during their time at the facility—which was subsequently closed down.

They say that pain strengthens the mind. Well, I was back, babee! God's ways are always greater than our ways. What seems like the end of the world to us is the beginning of healing and restoration. I was released into Sal's care. That case he was working on was closed. The NYPD made over twenty arrests and recovered nearly a million dollars in uncut cocaine. Three died in the ordeal, but Sal managed to get my family out unharmed. After four and a half months of hearings, we were all finally allowed to move on. Sue and her husband, Henry, helped me to collect the royalties from Richard's composition, as well as compensation from a malpractice lawsuit they insisted on me pursuing. They also helped to recover whatever monies the IRS owed me after taking everything Richard, and I owned in fulfilling a tax evasion. I left New York City and, along with Sal, moved back to Louisiana with a pretty penny in the bank.

Sal and Rah rekindled their relationship and were immediately wed and with child. Rah started a successful beauty line, simply titled

Lotti, made with love from all the herbal potions passed down from The Grandmother. I was particularly proud of that endeavor. Sal transferred from the NYPD to the NOPD effortlessly and quickly became a sheriff. Although we all hated his profession, we respected his commitment to bringing forth law and order. After all, it did bring us all together. And speaking of bringing us all together, I was reunited with my beloved Tiny.

Not a day passed that he didn't remember his love for me. We picked up right where we left off—older but wiser. Fate brought us together. William 'Tiny' Daughtry was released from prison three years prior to my release from the mental institution, spending twenty-one years in prison for a murder he did not commit. Before we reconnected, he lived in a nursing home community in the Pelham section of the Bronx near his son. Here's where the story gets crazy-- er. Tiny's son, Jeremy, the cute little boy with the smooth chocolate skin and dark penetrating eyes, turned out to be mixed up in the affair that Sal was working undercover on. Jeremy grew up to be a big-time drug-lord and racketeer with the Jewish Mafia. Rahab and Gomer got caught up in his mess. They were fascinated by his looks, money, and charm.

Tiny and I married and built a home in Baton Rouge with a wrap-around porch viewing the entire property from every angle. Sturdy white wooden rockers were placed on all four sides of the house. When we weren't traveling, driving around the country instead of flying because my nerves were shot, we rocked in our chairs watching our grandson play in the yard. Sal and Rah's son, Boaz, was our world. We called him Shadow because he looked like and mimicked his dad. Lord, that child was a rough customer—all boy. He gave Tiny and me a run for our money, but he kept us young at heart. There were other grandkids, but Shadow and his cousin, Liam, Go-Go and Jeremy's baby, had special places in my and Tiny's hearts. Even though there was a lot of drama behind Liam's birth, he connected our family with Tiny's, and I found that amazing.

Now, you don't think that I forgot about my girl Martita, do you? She moved to Louisiana with us and became a social worker at the local mental health facility. I also volunteered to speak monthly at their group circles. Martita completely changed her entire life around. She lived with Tiny and me, and along with Rah and Sal, she cared for us in our old age. She never did marry, but she had fun dating. Her sister and brother, and their families, along with Poo, Sy, and Go-Go, and their families, came to visit every summer for our annual family cookout.

Life is funny; being born with no religion or hope growing up, I never spent an hour or day in church. Yet God still scooped me up off a clay dirt floor and showed me His love. I dug myself a hole, scooped it out, and fell into the pit I made, but God saw me. He saved me from myself. He's always been the source of my strength and the strength of my life. In return for my gratitude, I immediately presented myself as a child of God, giving light and hope to those in need. I don't want to sound like everything was hunky-dory or pretend that I didn't have bad days because I did. I was freed from my demons but battled with residues of depression. My stumbling block. The thorn in my flesh that kept me on my knees in prayer. Through prayer, therapy, medication, sunlight, exercise, and an overall health change, I grew to manage and control my emotions. It was a pain in the neck, and there were times I felt like giving up. Three times I pleaded with the Lord to take it away from me. Sometimes, it was just a matter of having your meds tweaked. Over the years, I built up a tolerance for them. In those times, I had to remember what I prayed for. I learned it was okay not to be okay all the time. I'm not broken; I'm bent and leaning on the Almighty.

Tiny, who was still gentle with me, along with the Lord, whom we both committed our lives to, saw me through the rough times. Most days were filled with joy because I had come to know and believe in our Savior. My belief was more than words written in a book. God was my father and friend. Like I said, I couldn't altogether ditch the meds, but I learned to live despite my downfalls. The mountain of depression was there, but God gave me wings to fly around them. I walked with the Lord for the remainder of my days. I felt like God brought me through for a reason, and I didn't want to miss my window to witness His grace and mercy.

Tiny and I used all the money we gained throughout the years, doing the wrong things to do something right. We built churches, just like Fatso and Jo did. I didn't need as many diamonds as I once thought. Giving back and teaching was much more gratifying. Yes, I became a teacher. After reading Sal's bible in its entirety every year, I became a Sunday school teacher. And Tiny, the most handsome silver fox deacon I've ever seen. Tiny and I spent our golden years glorifying God, traveling the country, and helping to care for Shadow until he was old enough to take care of himself. At least that's what he thought; he loved his Tante Maw-Maw and Papa Wil. They all did. We were the elders of the family, and I was finally proud of the title. Long life brings understanding. But needing me couldn't keep this blackbird from traveling home. At eighty-five years old, the day after my beloved was put to rest, I closed my eyes surrounded by those I loved most. Richard's song played softly in the background as I hummed out the melody. I knew all was well, and he, Lotti, Mama, The Grandmother, Tiny, Fatso, and Jo were waiting for me to join the band on the other side.

If I've learned anything, I know for sure that every day we're growing into new people, shedding old skin, and coming into ourselves. Spiritually, mentally and physically. Our situations are unique to us but not unique to God. My friend, you are not alone.

THE END

EPILOGUE

"The greatest test of courage on earth is to bear defeat without losing heart"
Robert Green Ingersoll

THE APOSTLE TO THE APOSTLES

Mary Magdalene, the one cleansed of seven demons. Could anything in her life ever make her feel more of an outcast? Most commentators agree that the seven demons were most likely the severity of her problems. The number seven symbolically refers to completeness. Likewise, the Gospel authors probably suggested that Mary was filled or overwhelmed with demons, thus highlighting the miraculous nature of Jesus' cure. In the first century, demon possession was widely associated with the cause of physical and psychological illness. The seven demons were a way of saying Mary's problems were severe. Jesus cast out the demons, and Mary's new mindset and faith in her healer changed the course of her life. Whatever the cause of her possession, Mary's cleansing was the catalyst that propelled her enrollment with the Jesus movement.

Luke 8:1–2
Soon afterward Jesus began a tour of the nearby towns and villages, preaching and announcing the Good News about the Kingdom of God. He took his twelve disciples with him, along with some women who had been cured of evil spirits and diseases. Among them were Mary Magdalene, from whom he had cast out seven demons; Joanna... Susanna; and many others

who were contributing from their own resources to support Jesus and his
disciples.

Mary Magdalene, sometimes called '**Mary of Magdala**' (meaning
that she came from a village on the shore of Galilee called Magdala),
was one of Jesus' followers. She also witnessed his crucifixion and its
aftermath. Mary, by far the most common Jewish name for females
during that time, was possibly called Magdalene to distinguish her
from the other women named Mary who followed Jesus. The fact that
she helped support his ministry out of her resources indicates that she
was probably relatively wealthy. The Gospels identified her as a key
witness to the empty tomb and most famously the first to see Jesus'
resurrection. Without Mary, Christianity might not exist.

Mark 16:9-10
*Now when he was **risen** early on the **first** day of the week, he appeared **first***
to Mary Magdalene, from whom he had cast out seven demons. She went and
told them that had been with him, as they mourned and wept.

Mary Magdalene was mentioned by name twelve times in the
Gospels, more than most apostles and more than any other woman in
the Gospels, other than Jesus' family. In some religious traditions,
Mary is called the 'apostle to the apostles' because she announced to
them what they, in turn, would announce to all the world - "*I have seen
the Lord!*" *Then, she gave them His message.* The definition of an apostle
in its most literal sense is "one who is sent off." Yet so little is known
about this mystery woman.

Why is the Mary Magdalene story vital to us today? Not only was
Mary a seven-time failure, the first witness of the risen Christ, and a
symbol that a divine being can move through both women and men
uninhibitedly, she teaches us today through her obedient servanthood
how faith works. How many years did Mary suffer from the afflicting
demons that plagued her life? Even a woman of her financial standing
couldn't afford the cleansing of her soul. With nothing left, Mary
decided to see the charismatic Nazarite whom she heard miraculous

things about. In her desperate search for freedom, Jesus' inspirational message spoke to her. Tormented, she took her chances and laid her problems at His feet. It possibly took only a touch, a word, or maybe even a glance by Him, but at that moment, Mary was cured. She then decided to believe in the young carpenter. Being a woman of honor and loyalty, Mary gave not only her money but her time, service, and plans to Jesus' cause. Finally reaching a teachable spirit, she stood and quietly yet faithfully served Him. Mary Magdalene learned that testing is challenging, but the result should be a deeper relationship with your Savior.

My Name is Mary Magdalene follows the life of a woman as each of her demons is identified through her long battle with depression and how faith changed her trajectory. For many years Mary Mags fought these demons even when the war wasn't hers. Depression is not the fault of the person suffering. It is a condition that can refine your faith; it is not a punishment.

<u>John 9:1-3</u>
As Jesus was walking along, He saw a man who had been blind from birth. "Rabbi," His disciples asked Him, "why was this man born blind? Was it because of his own sins or his parents' sins?"
"It was not because of his sins or his parents' sins," *Jesus answered.* ***"This happened so the power of God could be seen in him."***

This fictional Mary was cleansed of her demons and chose to know the joy of the Lord to totally denounce her condition. She learned to live and not focus or give power to the thorn in her flesh. God usually gets the glory when we are healed *BUT* are we willing to give Him the same praise when we aren't? Pain is not always punishment. As long as we are living human beings, we will be subject to pain. God is not uncaring; in fact, knowing Him is better than knowing all the answers. As *Ephesians 3:20-21* states, *He is able to do immeasurably more than all we ask or imagine, according to His power that is at work within us.*

234 | JC MILLER

There's a dangerous misconception that says depression is not real. The reality is that depression is as real as cancer or a common cold. It's an illness that impacts the brain's ability to function as it should. You'll have to trust me when I say that God is hurting more than you are over your pain. One day we all will understand; until then, will you trust Him while suffering? Trusting God is more than a feeling; it's a choice to have faith in what He says and who He is, even when rationalizing leads you to believe something otherwise. The Lord is saying, bring me your mind for rest and renewal. That's the lesson that Mary had to learn.

Clinical research proves that people living with depression or anxiety have an overactive amygdala. Which is like the brain's threat center. In prolonged states, this threat center disrupts the brain's ability to process thoughts and balance moods. The good news is that **You are not broken,** and acceptance does not equal spiritual failure. Mental illnesses, depression, and anxiety are not your identity; it is a condition affecting you. Redirect your focus. I know it's easier said than done. I heard it best said, "depression is not a 'works' fight; it's a 'focus' fight." The apostle Paul says, in *1 Timothy 6:13, "Take hold of (focus on) the eternal life to which you were called.* The quickest way to focus, or redirect your mind on God, is simply to whisper His name. *Help, Holy Spirit.*

I'm not going to sit here and try to preach or pretend to know the answers, acting like I know how it feels to suffer from these mental illnesses. I do not. During this season of COVID, I've experienced my share of fear and anxiety. PTSD is what The doctors call it. The thought of having to live in that perpetual state is frightening. I have learned from my personal ordeal to stay focused on the maker and not the outcome, the potter, and not the clay. It's easy to get oversaturated with the concerns of life and forget to look to and acknowledge the creator of life. I verbally had to tell myself to stop and focus. *To whom do you belong?* Every day became a stepping out on faith pledge. We have to believe that the Word of God is holding us up more than we are trying to hold Him! God's love has a way of unfolding and enfolding us at the same time.

Anyone with a major depressive disorder would benefit from combining medication with a healthy lifestyle and stress management. Depression symptoms sometimes respond best to a combined treatment approach. There are no genie in the bottle answers for depression and other mental illnesses; manifestations of every condition are specific to each individual. Not everyone responds to treatment in the same ways, and it might take some time to find the most effective approach. It's hard to motivate yourself to start living more healthily, and it is always easier to give up. Still, depressive episodes or other mental health conditions may not improve until you get the correct diagnosis and treatment. Your bad days may be more bearable if you look after your body and your mind.

If you or someone you know deals with depression, anxiety, or other mental health issues, please consider the resources below. Until next time, I leave you with this: when you're hanging on by a thread, make sure it's the thread from the hem of the Almighties garment.

Job 36:15
But to those who suffer He delivers in their suffering. He speaks to them in their affliction.

RESOURCES

If you or someone you know has been diagnosed with a mental illness, or has concerns about their mental health, there are many ways to get help. Each one of these resources are available for you to use. If you feel like you need to call – do it. Step out on faith. You are not alone.

(Paperback readers, scan the QR Code below to link to the following resources)

- **Call 911**

If you or someone you know needs immediate assistance, call 911 or go to the nearest emergency room.

- **National Suicide Prevention Lifeline**
- **Call 1-800-273-TALK (8255); En Español 1-888-628-9454**
- **Lifeline Chat**
- The Lifeline is a free, confidential crisis service that is available to everyone 24 hours a day, seven days a week. The Lifeline connects people to the nearest crisis center in

the Lifeline national network. These centers provide crisis counseling and mental health referrals.

- **Crisis Text Line**
- **Text "HELLO" to 741741**
- The Crisis Text Line is available 24-hours-a-day, seven-days-a-week throughout the U.S. The Crisis Text Line serves anyone, in any type of crisis, connecting them with a crisis counselor who can provide support and information.

- **Veterans Crisis Line**
- **Call 1-800-273-TALK (8255) and press 1 or text to 838255**
- **Veterans Crisis Chat**
- The Veterans Crisis Line is a free, confidential resource that connects veterans 24 hours a day, seven days a week with a trained responder. The service is available to all veterans, even if they are not registered with the VA or enrolled in VA healthcare.

- **Substance Abuse and Mental Health Services Administration**

Call 1-800-662-HELP (4357)

You can find mental health services in your area including referrals to local treatment facilities, support groups, and community-based organizations for individuals and family members facing mental and/or substance use disorders by using the Substance Abuse and Mental Health Services Administration National Help Line. The Help Line is a confidential, free information service that is available 24-hours-a-day, 365-days-a-year in English and Spanish.

- **Mental Health America**

You may also find referral assistance at a local Mental Health America office or crisis center. Mental Health America may also provide mental health care services and crisis centers.

- **A Prayer Hotline**

700 club prayer line: Call 1-800-700-7000. *Prayer is not asking. Prayer is putting oneself in the hands of God.*

- **Referrals**

If you or someone you know is in search of a mental health provider, there are several different routes you can use to obtain a referral to a provider.

1. A referral can come from someone you trust such as your relatives, friends, family doctor, or clergy.
2. Your local health department's Mental Health division or Community Mental Health Center provides free or low-cost treatment and services on a sliding scale. These services are state-funded and are obligated to first serve individuals who meet "priority population criteria" as defined by the state's Mental Health Department.
3. Your company's EAP can issue a referral to a provider. Contact your Human Resources office to get more information about your company's EAP.

Consider getting information for more than one provider and interview each of them before choosing the one that would best suit your needs. Your health insurance company can also provide a list of mental health care providers for you to choose from.

QR Code for RESOURCES

CHARACTER GLOSSARY

- **Mary Magdalene** - Traveled with Jesus as one of his followers. She is listed in Luke as being one of the women who provided for Jesus out of their resources. *Gospel of Matthew, Mark, Luke, and John*
- **Salmon** - Married to Rahab. Father of Boaz. Great-great-grandfather of King David. *1 Chronicles, Ruth, Matthew, and Luke*
- **Simon-Peter** - Passionate and loyal, Peter, also known as Simon Peter, Simeon, Simon, Cephas, or Peter the Apostle, was one of the Twelve Apostles of Jesus Christ, and one of the first leaders of the early Church. *New Testament*
- **Joanna** - Joanna as mentioned in the gospels was healed by Jesus and later supported him and his disciples in their travels. She is one of the women recorded in Luke as accompanying Jesus and the twelve and a witness to Jesus' resurrection. *Luke*
- **Susanna** - Susanna is one of the women associated with the ministry of Jesus of Nazareth. She is among the women listed in Luke as being one of the women who provided for Jesus out of their resources. *Luke*

- **Martha** - Martha, or Martha of Bethany, is the sister of Mary and Lazarus. The Woman they say was more practical than spiritual. Martha was witness to Jesus resurrecting her brother, Lazarus. *Luke, John*
- **Mary** - Mary or Mary of Bethany is the sister of Martha and Lazarus. Mary appears in connection to two incidents: the rising from the dead of her brother Lazarus and the anointing of Jesus. *John*
- **Lazarus** - Lazarus of Bethany, also known as Lazarus of the Four Days, is the subject of a prominent sign of Jesus in John, in which Jesus restores him to life four days after his death. *John*
- **Thomas** - Thomas was one of the twelve apostles of Jesus Christ. Thomas was also called Didymus which is the Greek equivalent of the Hebrew name Thomas, both meaning "twin." Scripture does not give us the name of Thomas's twin. Doubting Thomas is a reference to the Apostle because he refused to believe that the resurrected Christ had appeared to the ten other apostles until he could see and feel the wounds received by Jesus on the cross. *Matthew, Mark, Luke, John*
- **Matthew (Levi)** - Matthew the Apostle, also known as Levi, was, according to the New Testament, one of the twelve apostles of Jesus. As Jesus went on from there, he saw a man named Matthew sitting at the tax collector's booth. "Follow me," he told him, and Matthew got up and followed him." *Matthew, Mark, Luke, Acts*
- **Rahab** - A harlot in Jericho. Believed in the Lord. Hid the Hebrew spies and was saved when the walls of Jericho came tumbling down. Great-great-grandmother of King David. *Joshua, Matthew, Hebrews, James*
- **Puah** - One of two midwives who attended the births of the Hebrew women. They were ordered by Pharaoh to kill the baby boys but let the girls live. *Exodus 1*
- **Silas** - Leading member of the early Christian church.

Accompanied the Apostle Paul on his missionary journeys. *Acts, Thessalonians, 2nd Corinthians, 1st Peter*

- **Gomer** - The wife of the prophet Hosea, referred to her as a "promiscuous woman." *Book of Hosea*
- **Lydia** - First documented convert to Christianity in Europe. A seller of purple. *Acts*
- **Mary** - Mary of Clopas was one of the women present at the crucifixion of Jesus and bringing supplies for his funeral. We are not sure if *Mary of Clopas* was the daughter or wife of Clopas. *John*

CREOLE DICTIONARY

Laissez les bons temps rouler
[Lay say lay boh(n) toh(n) roo lay]
Let the good times roll

Lagniappe
[Lahn-yop]
Something extra

Pauvre ti bête
[Pove tee bet
Poor little thing

Ti (masculine)
[tee]
Junior

Tante
[Taunt or tanty]
Aunt

Cher
[SHA]
Term of endearment; my
sweet

Comme Ci, Comme ca
[COME-SE, COME SAH]
So-so…

Fais-do-do
[FAY-DOH-DOH]
A Cajun dance party

Gris gris:
[grē-grē]
Put a spell on them

Come see:
Come here

Ça c'est bon
[Sa say boh(n)]
That's good

Ça va
[Sa va]
How are you? or I'm well

C'est tout
[Say too]
That's all

komen ça va:
[ko.mã sa va]
How's it going?

Pass a good time

A phrase used by natives of New Orleans when they feel it's time to start having a good time

Making groceries

Buying groceries

Roder

[Row-day]

To run the roads and never stay home; wander

Couyon

[coo-yawn]

A foolish man

Li santi bon pou pale kreyòl

It feels good to have someone to speak Creole with

Çé bon, mo byin

[say boh(n), mo bin]

I'm good, thanks

Bonswa

[bonsoir]

Good evening

Bel' Kay

[Bell kay]

Beautiful home

Piti á piti'

[pit-zee ah pit-zee]

Little by little

LETTER TO READERS

Dear Reader,

Thank you for reading, **My Name is Mary Magdalene**. I would greatly appreciate it if you would share this book and review it on Amazon.

In return for your kindness, please subscribe to my website www. authorjcmiller.com and receive a free PDF version of my favorite cake recipes from my motivational cookbook, Finding God in The Kitchen: Christ and Cake. Thank you for your continued support.

—**JC Miller**

ALSO BY JC MILLER

The following sample passage is another eagerly anticipated spin-off of JC Miller's 'I AM RAHAB: A NOVEL' series, 'SOMETHING ABOUT RUTH'. Coming soon. Enjoy.

CHAPTER ONE

The defined, high-pitched night song of the cicadas never seemed that haunting before. Amid the quiet after the storm, the chirping was as noticeable as the sound of your own breath. It took on a deafening reminder to those crowded like sardines in the Superdome that the world around them continued. However, their lives would never be the same.

Naomi had lost her sense of timing, but she wasn't alone. Thousands lay staring at the opening in the metal roof, ripped apart by the raging winds, gazing at the stars and listening for anything that sounded familiar. They were afraid. The sounds of darkness crowded them in even more, and there wasn't room left for not another thing. They were used to the violent sounds coming from the inner-city wards, but most had never heard cicadas put on such a clatter or hadn't taken the time to listen.

Naomi and her small family of four had moved from the gathered arena area to the exhausted lobby exit two days ago. There they bumped into a family member who was free from the chaos; he promised to return and retrieve them. "It's just a matter of time," she kept repeating to her family, trying to keep them encouraged. The reality was the situation looked grim. They had lost everything but their lives and the clothes on their backs. The NOPD, FEMA, other organizations, and ordinary civilians were doing their best to free those entrapped in the stadium.

Before Katrina, the Superdome seemed like a safe place to shelter. It was now as dangerous as any back alley. It was a fight to survive the poor conditions thrust upon them. For Salmone to make it back through the madness to rescue them would take a miracle...

ABOUT THE AUTHOR

JC Miller lives in the scenic Pocono Mountains of Pennsylvania with her husband, children, and floppy-eared Bassador.

Raised by a single mother in the Bronx, JC pulls from early experiences to showcase the soul of urban survival through faith-based novels. She also dedicates much of her time uplifting women via her blog and creating content with partner and friend, *MR Spain,* through their publishing company, Jess, Mo' Books LLC.

On her days off, you can find JC whipping up her famous Red Velvet cake and listening to songs from her impressive vinyl record collection.

Website: www.authorjcmiller.com

Blog: www.authorjcmiller.com/blog

 facebook.com/Theycallmegomer

twitter.com/authorJCMiller

instagram.com/author_jc_miller

www.ingramcontent.com/pod-product-compliance
Lightning Source LLC
Chambersburg PA
CBHW070857250626
47159CB00003B/1099